If Tomorrow Never Comes

Elizabeth Lowe

If Tomorrow Never Comes

Copyright © 2012 by Elizabeth Lowe

ISBN 9781520352367

TO MY MOTHER
WITH LOVE

Her determination to survive over whelming odds
throughout her lifetime, her love and encouragement
made me the person I am today.

Foreword

If Tomorrow Never Comes
By
Elizabeth Lowe

In the Southside of Chicago, Jordan Montgomery survived for years as a street urchin her house a cardboard box her bed concrete. A life she chose, the only way of enduring each day considering the dreadfulness of her past that left her with no family at a very young age. In dire need, with no other means of support, she became a currier for a drug lord, unknowingly a decision that placed her life in eminent danger. On a collision course with Chicago's infamous DEA agent, both strong willed, intelligent, and heroic, a war ignites.

Known to be the best, Jake Morgan spent his career fighting drug lords, the past two year's one in particular, Scorpio. A cunning, ruthless warlord, who managed to strip Morgan of everything he owned, and the two people he dearly loved. After an unsuccessful raid brings him face to face with a currier who possess' the knowledge necessary to bring down Scorpio, revenge becomes his master. Nothing more than a worthless junkie, he considers the currier expendable. An unexpected meeting with Jordan Montgomery becomes a challenge of his lifetime.

Chapter 1

Apprehensive, Jordan held her breath while perusing her eerie surroundings. Born no dummy, she knew few stood a chance in this district. Surely, her past rendered her brain dead or she would turn around, now.

It was the middle of the night, the darkness like that of the northern seas. The heat bearing down hard seemed alive ready to devour whatever dared to penetrate it. Becoming desperate to suck in a breath, her lungs expanded to the max inhaling a rush of humid air as perspiration dripped madly down her forehead stinging her eyes and blurring her vision.

At this hour, there were no visible inhabitants human or otherwise. An area consisting of several blocks claimed years ago by drug lords who allowed no one but their own to cross the invisible boundaries a neighborhood of decaying buildings and boarded up houses in desperate need of demolition. Streetlights were non-existent, the bulbs perpetually shattered by thugs, the only light filtering through newspaper covered windows. Convinced only a lunatic would enter the south side of Chicago during the day, let alone at night, police had ceased protection. If anyone or anything loitering in this area attacked, Jordan knew her screams would go unanswered. No one would know what happened to her, no one would find her body, no one would care, and yet she felt safer outside than inside the building soon to be entered.

Suddenly penetrating the frightening quiet pressing in on her, a dog barking in the distance made her practically jump out of her skin. Stealing her emotions, she reminded herself that over the years there were numerous nights, just like this one, when apprehension lashed making her wish her task was over. Then she could return to her meager existence where she could disappear inside herself, the only place she felt safe. As if a flower carelessly pulled up by the roots and tossed aside, Jordan was alone in the world.

With broken glass crunching beneath her feet, slowly, cautiously, she traveled over cracked, and heaved sidewalks cluttered with debris. Holding her breath prevented inhaling the putrid air bursting with the stench of garbage as eyes on full alert flicked wildly from side to side. Briefly, she thought about the once thriving community, and its demise and how recently, several buildings had burned to the ground, ruins still smoldering inundating the air with the gagging smell of smoke. Just like her, Chicago surrendered a community of its own.

A few yards ahead, there was a two-story house sandwiched between others of similar style. Despite the inability to see the number, it had to be the one for there was only the barest glow of light escaping around the edges of carefully drawn shades. Stepping warily, despite her slight weight and trembling legs, she climbed the steps creaking and groaning due to years of deterioration. Trying to shore up what courage remained threatening to mutiny, she glanced over-head the porch roof, sagging and full of holes, appearing as though it would collapse any minute. Feeling unsteady, she quickly clutched the railing that almost gave way due to the lack of support. Regaining her balance just in time prevented falling between the cavities in the porch flooring exposing mud, and garbage beneath. Something moved possibly a rat scrounging for food, she thought. Like lightening shivers shot through her. She hated rats.

Collecting her scurrying emotions, Jordan knocked the secret code upon a graffiti covered door questioning the necessity considering an occupants piercing eyes peering through a small slit of a grungy window were scrutinizing her every move. A daunting length of time passed as she waited impatiently, sufficient time for her imagination to run wild. As if a bomb about to explode any second, anxiety gathering inside her grew in intensity pressing against her lungs. Intuition was telling her something or someone was behind her. Struggling to rein in scurrying emotions, spinning around, bravely prepared to face the demon closing in; she discovered nothing more than her own emptiness, and despair solidifying in her throat. A chill racing over her skin seeped bone-deep.

Interrupting the last second urge to run, an un-expected gasp escaped when the door swiftly squeaked open. Inhaling a deep breath hoping to slow her heartbeat to a steady thump, thump, thump, squaring her shoulders, and straightening her posture, with a demeanor that spoke of false bravery, she crossed the threshold of hell.

Squeezing her slender body through the partially opened door brought her to an abrupt halt against a giant of a man whose mid-night eyes were boring through her. Despite a cold sweat slicking her body, sour with the scent of fear, she glared back with undisguised contempt that immediately ended his perusal. In retaliation, he ripped from her hands a sizable brown paper package that she felt certain had been become glued to her skin.

Though experience should have cautioned her, she made the mistake of taking a step forward, an advance thwarted by a substantial black hand.

Regardless of layers of tattered, mix-matched clothing, she felt his thick nails biting into her soft flesh as his bulging eyes, framed by a wide face, radiated disdain, and disgust. Screaming inwardly, repulsion rising high, scalding her throat, awakening retching impulses, made her desperate to tear free. Obviously pleased with his intended intimidation, massive muscles turned the towering beast directing him toward a door across the room.

Using anger to burn away other emotions, Jordan swiped at the perspiration still dripping from her forehead, and smearing her camouflaged face. The bastard had nerve she steamed. No man ever touched her. No man ever would again. She made sure of that.

Restlessness grew steadily while she irritably awaited dismissal. Time well spent surveying her environment survival upper most on her mind. Typical of those seen nightly, the dimly lit room was barren except for a dilapidated table containing a scale, and various sized plastic pouches alongside mounds of white powder. Behind the table were four men, with piercing eyes, wearing surgical gloves, their clothing exposing scars on one or more body parts most likely inflicted by knives, chains or bullets. Long greasy hair dangled from scarves wrapped around each head, their, beards, and mustaches long neglected, teeth decayed. Clad in leather and denim purposely exposing numerous tattoos, despite their unnerving appearance, the thugs were no longer menacing. Neither God, nor the Devil himself frightened Jordan.

Perhaps though, as the door to an adjoining room swished open to allow the black man passage, then closed, the fragrance of expensive cologne wafting in the air awoke a smidgen of barely recognizable apprehension. It was apparent in Jordan's stiffening stance, and her irregular palpitations increasing her impatience to escape.

Behind the door an elegantly garbed, aristocratic looking man, whose presence dominated the room, now held the brown package.

Hastily tearing one end open, a freshly manicured, pinkie nail scooped the white gold. Raising the powder to his well-shaped lips, a snake like tongue darted for a taste. Obviously pleased, he sniffed the remainder up his nose. Within seconds, narrowing pale blue eyes turned to glass followed by a gratified smirk. Puffed up with self-righteous pride, running a restless hand through his hair, he glared at the black man, "Pay that bitch, and get her to hell out of here, her stench is making me ill," Scorpio shrieked. Obedient, and extremely well compensated, his bodyguard eagerly granted his masters wish.

Chapter 2

For the umpteenth time, Jake's trained eyes quickly scanned the assigned areas where his team held positions awaiting a signal. Men personally selected, and trained, who believed in him, and his goals, with whom he entrusted his life. An experienced squad, some single, some married, some with children that in return trusted him with theirs. With nothing left to lose, he would give his life to protect their families from experiencing the unbearable loss of a loved one, a loss Jake, understood, had not recovered from, and was convinced he never would.

Like the intricate workings of a clock, every-thing was on schedule and going as planned. After months of undercover investigation, and the complex planning of the raid, to his relief the moon, and stars were cooperating by hiding behind a thick blanket of clouds.

Under surveillance was a two-story house surrounded by others in the same deteriorated state. Buildings so close together, the pathways so littered with garbage he was confident his team would have sufficient cover. For the first time in years, Jake dared to hope the conditions were signs of good luck.

Glancing once again at the green glow from his watch informed him it was three A.M. It was now or never. A burly hair covered arm swiped at an abundance of sweat drenching his forehead. Whether it was the hot, humid evening or the fact that after two years he was finally closing in on Scorpio, he did not know, but one thing was certain everyone acquainted with Jake knew it was not due to fear. No one moved. No one breathed. All eyes were focused on Jake his, cap worn backwards, face smudged with camouflage, navy blue tee shirt proudly displaying bold yellow letter's DEA. The revolver in his hand his only trusted ally during fifteen years of service. Though considered by most a mean son of a bitch, Jake was the best of the best. A leader among men who, despite the odds had, successfully accomplished impossible assignments, organized more victorious raids, busted more drug rings, sent more men to prison than anyone in Chicago's history of drug enforcement. Over the years, he had proved himself worthy of admiration and respect, the reason why his commander allowed him to get away with breaking every rule in the book. It did not matter that, Jake had a rotten disposition, few friends, no wife, or family, or, that most thought him to be the Devil's advocate all too ready, and willing to comply. A straightforward honest man Jake never expected more than he was willing to give always taking the risks necessary to protect his team from danger. Brains and guts ruled him, the formula necessary to be a good DEA officer, the reason no one refused an assignment to his team. However impossible he was to work with, and to please, plain and simple, Jake never lost an officer.

Thick with anticipation was the summer air when Jake finally gave the signal that penetrated the barriers of hell. With precision, a pair of officer's crashed through two front windows. Two others kicked open the rear door. Flanked by a team member, Jake's body slammed into the front portal where without hesitation, firing two shots into the ceiling, he yelled, "DEA! Don't move. You're under arrest." One on one officer's tackled men greater in size foolish enough to attempt an escape. Despite the loudness of the shuffle, in the background Jake's voice could be heard shouting, "Stop or you're a dead man." In a blink, there was a bang, a streak of red, gray smoke puffing from a red-hot cylinder. Jake's precision shot had sprawled the stupid bastard on the floor, if he had listened; he would not be oozing blood from a hole in his heart.

Not in the least did the chaos hinder Jake's keen senses. Out of the corner of his eye, he saw a door-knob move. Having smelled his adversary's unmistakable fragrance engulfing the room, Jake was certain he had the yellow belly Scorpio trapped. Eyes glued on his men as they cuffed three captives lying on their stomachs secured by a foot between their shoulder blades, he eased backward toward the door.

"Try it, ass hole. Go ahead, make my day, and there will be a four inch hole in the back of your skull," a young man yelled while locking cuffs on a body of brawn, Billy's bravery never failing to bring a brief smirk to Jake's weather beaten face.

Assured his team's attention was on business, Jake felt confident no one would notice him open the door. At last, he would be alone in the dark with his enemy. Despite one hand gripping the doorknob, the other holding a gun cocked to fire, Jake hoped it would not be necessary. He wanted Scorpio alive. The bastard was going to pay for everything he had done, everything he had taken, oh, yes, pay indeed, he fumed, suffer the most agonizing torture known to man, he would see to it. Besides, he was not worried, not in the least; the maggot would not fight, would not break a nail or muss his hair, or wrinkle a ten thousand dollar suit. So positive was he, releasing the pressure on the trigger, Jake boldly entered a . . . closet!

It was pitch-black, the rank-smell so gagging he covered his nose and held his breath as his gaze plummeted to a huddled pile of rags. The dim light through the slight opening of the door exposed golden nugget eyes spread wide in defiance as if he were an intruder in its domain. Stomach retching from the rancid air, as if a skunk had released its defensive mechanism; coughing to clear his lungs, he jerked back quickly slamming the door to avoid the lethal odor. Oh, there was something in the closet all right but, to his exasperation, it was not Scorpio. Disappointment, frustration, and pure unadulterated anger, rushed his senses. With his body barricading the closet door, spinning around he angrily barked orders. "Check the other rooms, God Dammit. I'll check the closet," a command scattering his men like flies.

Mimicking Jake, Billy fired a warning shot into the ceiling before cautiously opening another door. Five DEA officers followed close behind.

With a strong whiff of cologne inundating their senses, eyes shifting from one to another, they huddled over an escape hatch in the floor. Aware of what awaited their announcement; ranting, swearing, smashing of everything in Jake's way, each wondered who would be stout hearted enough to make the report.

It would be Billy. From the first day of his assignment to the team, Jake favored the lad. It did not matter that Billy was the youngest; he was street smart, and one hell of a scraper, the only one, to date, brazen enough to go head to head with Jake. Surprisingly, when Billy informed his hero, uncharacteristically calm, Jake accepted the explanation, and then ordered the group to the precinct with their prisoners.

Scorpios' cunningness invaded Jake's mind. True, his enemy escaped this time, but thanks to the events of the evening, he felt closer than ever before. At last, he had the next best thing, a courier. How perfect, he mused, pride swelling his chest, to be the only one who knew the courier existed, trapped inside the closet. It took diminutive effort envisioning the many ingenious methods he would use to secure the information he craved. In the end, one way, or another, the cowardly swine would cooperate.

While glorious moments of revenge traveled the avenues of his mind Jake, lingered watching professionals cordon off the area, as the forensic crew bagged, and tagged evidence that left a fine, black residue clinging to everything, as the police photographers snapped pictures of the deceased before, during, and after, being zipped into black bags. A time when smoking one cigarette after another, supercharged mentally, and physically, Jake paced the crude dirt littered floor in front of the closet.

An hour later, with patience dwindled, angrily snuffing out a cigarette beneath his sneaker as if it was the enemy, he shouted, "Jesus Christ, how goddamn long is it going to take to sweep this place?" Familiar with Jake's hostile impatience, without acknowledgement, the crew hastily finished and left.

With another second of confinement, Jordan was certain she would suffocate. Staring into the void of blackness, like a candle burning up her mind, visions of horrible memories had saddled up, and were riding their stallions across her consciousness. The Closter phobic space stealing her breath made moving impossible. Anxiety had increased body temperature causing layered clothing to cling maddeningly and thirst to swell her tongue to the gagging point. Surely, she would pee her pants any minute, and had it not been for her proficiency at closing her mind to all sensations, all emotions, she would have.

Throughout her confinement, premonitions pertaining to the inhuman beast on the other side of the door gnawed at her insides. Somehow, she knew he would wait. Inevitably she would face the varmint like she had . . . Chill's running the length of her spine forced thin fingers to search for the knife safely tucked in the waistband of her baggy men's pants, and lock around the handle. Oh, she was not afraid, as a youngster, she had faced fear, faced pain, and endured. This man could do whatever he wanted, except touch her, if he dared, without the slightest feeling of remorse, she would plunge the sharp blade into his flesh, dissect his intestines, and rip his guts to shreds, having done it many times before in her subconscious she mastered the ability.

The banging shut of a door and the frightening quietness that followed built an invisible protective shield against the trembling toying with her. At last, the waiting was over; finally, she would meet the infamous fiend, the only person Scorpio feared. Couriers often spoke of the DEA agent with balls of steel, the demon incessantly escaping the wraith of Scorpio's thugs. What kind of person existed that could frighten a man of Scorpios' power? Before, she never bothered to put a face to the tales, now her imagination was in overdrive.

All at once, light flashed across her features followed by a gruff voice. "Get your ass out here."

Stubbornly, Jordan refused.

With a tone full of airy arrogance, "God dammit, you either get your ass out here or I will come in after you." The smell blasting Jake upon opening the door making him pray such measures would be the last resort.

Again, his prey balked at his bidding.

Lacking the virtue of patience, reaching in with one hand, he grabbed the body by the back of the collar. In response, teeth as sharp as razors sinking into layers of skin turned flesh rapidly crimson.

"You mother fucker," he wailed. Anger whipped into a rage, both hands clutching the shoulders of the form, forcefully hoisting the body, flung it into the room, and onto the floor. Amazed at how effortlessly he lifted the puny lump of shit, Jake stared at the sprawled out body of rags. Two sets of eyes, one of green the other of gold, telegraphing hatred dared the other to move.

Masterfully removing his handcuffs, Jake reached for Jordan's wrists, but never succeeded in securing them before thick-soled boots connecting with his shin propelled the handcuffs into the air. Hands grasping his leg, sputtering vulgar obscenities, he careened to the floor landing beside his captive.

Previous plans were now going to pay off, Jordan thought smugly as she swiftly crawled toward her escape route, an attempt thwarted by a hand snatching clumps of short-cropped hair. In response, reflexes rolled her toward her assailant, flailing fists connecting first with Jake's jaw, then his cheek, forehead, and lastly his nose. Even an idiot would have released the beast, but before the thought finally penetrated his thick skull, a body landed with a thump on his stomach forcing his intestines into his throat. With his defense mechanisms completely obliterated, his attacker's fingers wrenched his hair, and bashed an already throbbing head against the floor.

Though he was tired, very tired, and hurt in assorted places, all thanks to the creature on top of him, Jake could not help but admire the kid's spunk, a flickering thought quickly followed by the urge for revenge. The time was long overdue to show the swine who was boss. Out of breath, and energy, using a thrust fully intended to be painful, his fist connected with jawbone. Twin ice picks pierced Jordan's jaw before stars flickered briefly, and the shade of darkness lowered sending her with a thump to one side.

Chapter 3

Upon plucking the limp body from the floor, to his utter shock, Jake's hands accidentally grazed bountiful breasts, the incident giving him pause. Unbelievable as it seemed, beneath the dirt, grease, and horrid smell, was a female, of all things. Tonight when he believed he might be lucky, he should have known better.

He was living his worst nightmare. A woman was the least of his expectations, the discovery costing him a few seconds of control before returning to being damn ornery. Envisioning a female prisoner, seething ruptured into cussing, so much for his interrogation plans. Obviously, she was a real bitch, and he had known enough of that breed to last a lifetime. Well, she would pay for stealing his moment of glory, if it was the last thing he did, yes, indeed. Troubling him now, though sorely tempted a few times, Jake never struck a woman. Guilty feelings evaporating instantly when upon frisking her, he uncovered a knife typically carried by gang members. Now convinced she was dangerous, he vowed to find out her capabilities, and what crimes she had committed.

By the time, he tossed his prisoner onto the back seat of a weather-beaten, sixty-nine Mustang the sunrise had peaked over the horizon.

Hiding his hostage, becoming top priority, masked the dawns early light gradually exposing the immensity of the decade neighborhood.

Stolen glances in the rear view mirror were unsuccessful in determining her age due to the layers of filth. Besides age did not matter, he was too busy wondering why a female would allow herself to look so appalling. Possibly her face was scared, pock marked or disfigured, he rationalized. Not only was her hair an undecipherable color but also stuck out in sprigs here, and there, cut within a few inches of the scalp as if, with no thought at all, someone snipped it. She weighed no more than a hundred pounds for he easily slung her over his shoulder. Mulling her condition over in his mind, he concluded, she was nothing more than another punk junky making deliveries for daily fixes. Well, he thought self-righteously, she would talk, and soon when withdrawal kicked in.

The moment Jake arrived at his apartment, unable to cope with the horrid odor another second, he dumped the still unconscious body on the bathroom floor. Securing a chain around the sink leg, he attached handcuffs to her wrist. Appraising the close quarters, he concluded there was sufficient freedom to use the facilities, although the stench made him doubt she knew how.

Trying to end the nagging guilt plaguing him, he searched for sweat pants, a shirt, socks, a towel, and washcloth, and placed them on the toilet. Opening the medicine cabinet, retrieving a new toothbrush, and toothpaste, he placed them on the sink. Chest puffed with confidence, he was certain she would take the hint.

Entering the kitchen Jake went directly to the refrigerator to snatch a can of beer, his mind set firm that, before his interrogation began, his captive would remain in the bath-room until she, washed, brushed her teeth, and changed into clean clothing and Jake's mind, once made up, never wavered a fraction of an inch.

Awaking on a, hard, cold, tile floor, with every thought escaping her, Jordan was not sure what happened. Only two things registered a sore wrist, and the hammering pain in her jaw shooting to her head like a rocket. One moment she had no idea, and then she did. Madder than a wet hornet, she shouted her contempt, "You son of a bitch. I will cut your heart out, and eat it for supper." Using every heathen word known to humankind, and then some, her verbal attacks continued along with kicking the wall, screaming and spitting at the door. Though no answer came, she knew the male pig in the other room heard her.

Their encounter in the dim light did not reveal her kidnappers' appearance, except for height. The pain in her jaw attested to his strength. Besides, she did not care, he was a male, and that made him her enemy. Fuming flared consuming her thoughts, well, she would fix the bastard.

While making plans to get even, one-minute gruesome ways of torturing him peaked in her mind, the next, questions. What kind of person would treat another human like an animal? Did he think a DEA officer, with a badge made him superior, and invincible? A malicious smile tugged at Jordan's lips, inwardly, she chuckled. His brains were obviously located at the other end of his anatomy, the moron gave no thought to the plugs for the sink, and tub easily reached with her free hand.

Hearing water running, gratified his prisoner took the hint, an identical chuckle rumbled inside Jake's chest. Having been on the telephone for some time, learning the results of the interrogation of his captives, he did not notice water seeping from under the bathroom door. A puddle that was quickly growing larger by the second as it spread over the bare floor, and crept closer to his feet. A loud pounding on the door, and a woman's voice yelling something about water coming through her ceiling finally penetrated.

"Holly shit," Jake, bellowed, his cell phone careening to the floor. Charging the bathroom door, slamming his shoulder into it, flung it open with a crash. Water was overflowing from the sink, and bathtub. Slipping, and sliding on the tile floor made it necessary to grasp everything within reach to prevent falling flat on his face, a towel bar, barely clinging to the wall, broke free. In his haste to reach the knobs, and remove the plugs, a glass crashed to the floor spewing splinters, incidents inducing a lesson on foul language only Jordan thought she knew. Anxiously twisting knobs, and unplugging the drains, plucking weeks of dirty laundry piled in a corner, he scattered them everywhere hoping to sop up the water.

Thoroughly anticipating and prepared for the wrath of his retaliation, watching his amusing attempts, pleased with her success, Jordan's eyes bored through him with the force of her rage. As expected, when everything was under control, he turned on her fully prepared to administer punishment. She had nerve to look at him wide eyed as though a victim of an innocent accident.

Fumbling with a hand full of keys, at last Margaret found the one to Jakes apartment. Hearing foul language, and commotion coming from the bathroom, she hustled down the hall fully intending to help instead, stopped short at the threshold. In stunned surprise, she observed the chaos, and the god-awful looking, whatever it was, soaking wet hand cuffed to the sink leg.

Regardless of the rush of sympathy, knowing Jake, she presumed such precautions were necessary.

Speechless, she stood scrutinizing the escapades. Not only was the bathroom a disaster, but Jake had a swollen red eye, scratches all over his face, and blood dripping from his nose. He appeared as though he had come up against a wild cat, and she could only assume it was the pitiful looking person in rags, the reason for the handcuffs. Any moment now, she expected the police to arrive, the intensity of the vile language volleying back and forth loud enough for the entire building to hear. A scene suddenly becoming so comical her hand came quickly to her mouth to conceal an unexpected smirk. Women's intuition told her Jake had finally met his match.

It was not until he raised his fist, and she felt certain he would punch the day lights out of the wretched looking thing that she wedged herself between them. With both palms flattened against his chest, she warned tersely, "Don't you dare, Jacob Morgan, or you will answer to me."

Roughly, grabbing Margaret's beefy arm, Jake escorted her into the hall. Unable to contain his urge to kill, when he kicked the door slamming it shut, it created new cracks on an already worn plank of wood. As far as he was concerned, the bitch could lay in drenched clothing until she saw fit to do something about it. Long determined strides marched him toward an over flowing wastebasket to chuck the plugs. Neither made its mark.

Despite Jake's childish tantrums widening Margaret's grin, arms folded across her bosom, a stern look said she anticipated an explanation.

"Don't ask," he snapped impatiently.

Although admittedly confused, surprisingly Margaret felt warm all over as if wearing a fur wrap. For the first time in two years, Jake had completely lost control. Anger was good, she decided, better than brooding, and drinking.

Wagging a finger in his face, like a mother scolding a child, "Jacob Morgan, if you touch a hair on that person's head, I will have yours. Do you understand? I assume you have a good explanation, and I expect to hear it first thing in the morning, or I am calling McMasters." Knowing the threat alone would tie a knot in his tale, due to the lateness of the evening Margaret believed it best to leave. Once on the other side of the door, she gave into the chuckles shaking her chest.

Holy Shit, now Margaret knew about his hostage. Always meaning what she said, Jake knew she would call McMasters. In the past, despite McMasters allowing him to bend, and often break the rules, he would not condone a hostage. Somehow, someway, he had to convince Margaret that what he was doing was the right thing. Brooding over how he would explain the mess he had gotten himself into, he paced the floor, smoking, and drinking.

It was not until the hostage had been quiet far too long, that Jake thought about the possibility of suicide. A sudden rush of anxiety reminding him he was never lucky brought him quickly to the bathroom door. Forcing his back straight helped to regain his composure. Nose pressed against the wood, the edge to Jake's voice said he meant every word. "You have information I want. One way or another, you are going to give it to me. Until you do, you stay where you are."

Growing steadily angrier from each word, pain jabbed Jordan's temples as she listened. Her ears' were pounding, and her head felt as though it might explode if she did not start crying soon. Bravely pulling her wits together, spitting venom like a reptile, her response was sharp, and decisive. "Well, you can kiss your ass goodbye, Mr. DEA agent. I strongly suggest you do not turn your back on me. The first chance I get I will spill every ounce of your blood."

As her threat hung in the air, whatever the sensation was running along Jake's skin, raising an abundance of hair, told him this female was not going to be the airhead he presumed, the possibility stretching his nerves beyond the max. Heatedly he shot back, "Have it your way, bitch! Believe me; you are going to get mighty uncomfortable with no bed, no food, and no fix."

Though the roaring in his head made hearing difficult, he did not miss the echoing weird, bitter laugh piercing the cracks of the wooden door that said wait, and see, Mr.

Chapter 4

With water dripping from his hair, a plush maroon towel hugging a trim waist, for long moments Scorpio admired the well-toned muscles reflecting from the floor length mirror. Except for pale blue eyes, with jet-black hair slicked back, and dark skin, most would believe him to be Italian, Mexican, or possibly Latin. Even Scorpio did not know, nor did he care. Nationality, or little else, mattered when you were, the entrepreneur of a multi-billion dollar drug industry, influential, and revered, accomplishments never failing to bring a smug smile to thin well-shaped lips.

From a row of cologne, he selected a favorite costing one thousand dollars splashing an extravagant amount over his face, and neck, hands lingering much too long smoothing over his hairless chest. Flexing sculpted muscles, eyes running the length of his slim figure were finally satisfied. He believed he was indeed the most magnificent creature in the world capable of turning both men's, and woman's heads. A well-fed ego carved a gratified smile on his lips as he moved toward the door.

It was the view through the partially opened portal giving him pause. A substantial master bedroom-expressing wealth, the décor, imported carved wood furniture, drapes of tapestry, and fine art costing millions. Yet the nude body sprawled on her stomach on the bed, a position he preferred, brought on a surge of triumph. Unknown to anyone, Marla was his most treasured possession.

Scanning the form stirred a powerful urge of lust that began melting ice like eyes, and a steel heart, a rising desire parching his throat that only Marla could quench. Whenever he ravished his favored trophy, it was like a cold drink of water on the hottest of summer days. Savoring her well-proportioned body, slender waist, perfect buttocks, and the most luscious legs ever wrapped around his haunches, was never enough, his appetite for her frightening, and ravenous. Coming in waves reflections of their past sexual encounters dancing before his mind's eye fed his passion.

Although there were plenty of other women, and men, more than willing, none ever came close to gratifying his lusty needs. Indeed, the best of them, Marla never bored him like the others. Not only did she make him feel strong, and potent but most importantly never tired of his enormous appetite for sex, nor questioned or refused his perverted ways of committing the act. Whether she condoned them because of love or fear, or because he gave her everything her heart desired he was yet to learn. The reason did not matter as long as she willingly continued to share his bed whenever commanded. At least that is what he told himself despite knowing if the time came when she refused, or defied him, as much as he would prefer not to kill her, he would with his own bare hands.

Like a panther on the prowl, he closed the distance. Opening the drawer of an ornate marble top nightstand, well-manicured fingers sifted through a menagerie of erotic toys sure to bring a blush to anyone's face. Retrieving four gold silk cords, he secured each of her limbs to one of the giant bedposts taking the liberty while doing so to explore his mistress. Though Marla never moved or made a sound, he knew she was aware of his intentions.

A flick of his fingers tumbled the towel in folds to the floor. From the same nightstand, slender fingers retrieved a bottle of fragrant oil. Worked into a heated lather, straddling her buttocks, he slowly dripped oil onto her flesh. Skillful fingers followed firmly kneading flawless skin to a glowing pink as he moved rhythmically along the curves of her haunches.

Little did Marla know Scorpios' mind was elsewhere plotting malignant plans to exterminate a DEA officer, slowly, painfully, without the slightest touch, reflections serving to escalate his passion? Recalling his success over the past two years, he swallowed the silent chuckles intensifying his movements. Soon, very soon, Morgan would be nothing more than a shell of a man, a time when, as though possessing a poisoned stinger, Scorpion would make his lethal strike.

Nothing more than an, irritating, over confident prick, Morgan had cost him millions of dollars. Although Morgan had been unable to terminate his business altogether, he was indeed annoying. His insatiable thirst for revenge required a continuous change of distribution locales to allow staying one step ahead of the bastard. Playing the odds, on several occasions, Scorpio purposely arrived hoping to face his meritorious opponent, almost succeeding just hours ago. Now, considering how close he came before changing his mind, he wondered if it was his love of money preventing him from giving up or his love for the game of cat, and mouse.

Reflections of Morgan's trials suddenly swamped him. He had managed to strip Morgan of all his worldly possessions, among them his best friend, and the greatest trophy of them all. Reveling in his accomplishments engorged Scorpios' fantasy making him eager to seek fulfillment. Glancing down at the round, golden buns beneath him, he imagined he was about to plunder Morgan. Having complete control over a partner never failed to fuel his virility that rapidly increased his momentum bringing within seconds instant, and intense gratification.

Having been summoned by Butch over an hour ago then escorted to Scorpio's bedroom, Marla knew the reason for her command attendance. Still, over time having survived numerous occasions, when Butch turned, and locked the door behind him, the slightest amount of fear brought on perspiration making her lace robe more difficult to remove.

Listening to Scorpio shower, fighting the sickness rolling in her stomach, she stretched out on the bed in a position Scorpio favored splaying her long black trusses on the pillow as added enticement. She learned the more aroused he became, the less time it took to satisfy his hunger. Knowing of Scorpio's excessive, appetite, and how he thrived on control, Marla willingly surrendered, enduring whatever was necessary, thankful for the frequent breaks when he plundered other women, and men, who frequently shared his bed.

Scorpio's ravishment rarely lasted long, a span of time when her mind drifted to a, walk in closet, meticulously arranged, where rows of extravagant designer clothes, shoes, and exotic furs awaited selection. To the wall safe protecting her exquisite jewelry, the dressing table where rows of imported colognes competed for her attention, the garage storing her

Mercedes convertible, and, one by one, the villas around the world. A whimper or a pout, an occasional quick romp between the sheets was all that was required, after which Scorpio would whisk her off in a private jet to any desired paradise just to see her smile. Never once did she wonder if he loved her, far from naïve, Marla knew a demon like Scorpio was not capable of loving anyone other than himself.

At last, Marla had everything she ever dreamed of, except love. She paid that price long ago by destroying the one true love she had ever known, one that had wrapped around her heart, and still refused to let go. Time convinced her she would forever remember the enormous cost. To think of that brief period now was suicidal, for none of Scorpio's mistress' ever lived to tell the story due to the body-guard just outside the door, Scorpios' second set of eyes, ears, and occasional bed partner.

Eventually everyone involved with Scorpio got screwed one way or another. Faithful to the very end, as though attached by an umbilical cord, Butch, and Scorpio were an inseparable pair. Willing, and very competent, Butch fulfilled any order, easy tasks for an x navy seal with a body of steel and hands capable of snapping a neck like a toothpick at a simple nod from his master. Rumors about others mysteriously disappearing, kept Marla's nerves perpetually stretched taut.

Chapter 5

Before leaving for the precinct, for three days Jake left Jordan a bag of fast food. She could drink water from the plastic cup provided if need be, he sputtered inwardly while slamming the bathroom door behind him.

Each evening upon returning, it angered him to discover not only did she refuse all nourishment, but continued to refuse to clean up. She rejected, the clothing offered, the pillow, and blankets, tossed into the room, and Jake thought he was stubborn.

Frustrated by her mulishness, along with his fruitless attempts at interrogating Scorpios' thugs had Jakes nerves stretched taut. Known for his atrocious temper that could erupt without warning, Jake could not be alone with a prisoner. Particularly when after an entire day of unsuccessful interrogation, Billy had to peel him off the last prisoner to prevent bodily harm.

This morning, it would not have mattered what side of the bed he got up on, nothing would have improved his mood, not even a fraction of an inch. Today, would be his last attempt at both, Jake hissed between gritted teeth.

When the day ended, a stormy mood following him to his apartment hurled the door shut. He never noticed the keys flung on the kitchen table almost crushed a cockroach. Jerking open, the refrigerator door he grabbed his customary can of beer, not a difficult feat considering the appliance rarely stored anything else. Popping the top, angrily swishing a stray cat off his chair, constantly coming, and going at will through the open window, he settled down to guzzle the nerve numbing liquid as he smoked a half pack of cigarettes.

Much later than intended, confident the fire in-side had been smothered, he checked on his hostage. Discovering once more she had refused nourishment sent his blood pressure skyrocketing into the danger zone. Despite all the vulgarities sputtered, she never once uttered a goddamn word. Making matters worse, he knew she was not a junkie, surely by now she would have done anything for a fix, anything. A full-blown case of anxiety was a reasonable expectation considering if his hostage died his ass was grass and McMasters the lawn mower.

If he were honest, he would admit his mood swings were due to brewing over two long grueling years that had been futile in collapsing Scorpios' empire. So much for blood, sweat, and exhaustion, he fumed. No wonder he gave Jordan dark, glaring looks that in its self would disintegrate any living thing. Retaliating, tiger-eyes, now sunken, and cloudy, flickered with wild insolence, captivating, and frightening golden globes capable of tugging curiosity to the forefront. So hypnotized was Jake, he did not move, could not move from wondering what demon lurked behind those eyes.

Since the first day he delivered food, he learned to keep his distance. Upon placing the bag on the toilet seat, she lashed out slicing his arm wide open with a razor blade, an attack that knocked his competence right on its ass considering he believed he had frisked her thoroughly. Retrieving the sharp edge weapon was a feat yielding a multitude of bites, scratches, another black eye, and bloody nose. Despite the fact, he considered her a vicious animal; an unnatural force drew him to her. If it was the last thing he did, he had to know what turned her into such a barbarian.

Jordan was as stubborn as Jake was. In only twenty-one years, she had endured a lifetime of heartaches, and tears, cruel lessons that made her, street smart, strong, and a force to reckon with. She had no other choice, having a roof of cardboard and a mattress of cold, hard concrete, her address any street or alley with sufficient space for her tiny huddled body.

In view of her plight, one might find it difficult to believe that Jordan became a friend to every home-less person she encountered. In doing so, death became no stranger. She watched the black knight of death strike in the form of, aides, drug overdoses, alcohol, muggings, and suicides, helplessly observed friends selling their bodies, cried for the numerous children who died in their mothers' arms from the lack of food, warmth, and medical attention. Even now, whenever surrounded by quiet, Jordan heard deaths horrible shrill, the reason for her insomnia. Life's atrocities had gradually whittled away at a heart leaving only a small portion barely beating.

Experiences leaving no doubt in her mind she could cope with anything the arrogant, conceited, egotistical DEA agent dished out. He was, nothing more than a criminal, a kidnapper. What nerve he had, telling her she smelled when he was no different. Although he may have bathed more, his clothing was far from clean, and reeked of body odor. He never shaved, never washed the straight, oily hair pulled into a ridiculous ponytail, a dirty blonde color with sun-bleached streaks mixed with gray. A wiry mustache, and a several day old beard made him appear a wolf man, and the hideous earring worn in one ear reminded her of a pirate, for God's sake.

There were other disturbing characteristics besides his gruff manner, like his hypnotic, emerald green eyes, and for an old man, the impressive way he filled out a pair of jeans, and tee shirt. Despite considerable effort, her eyes continuously found his bulging arms with numerous scars possibly from knives, and bullets. Unable to determine his age, she guessed maybe forty or so. Considering the years of obvious wear, and tear, one second she found it surprising he continued to bring men to their knees, the next she remembered the ache in her jaw, testimony to a hidden strength, that had he chosen to use, could have crushed her. Was it possible he knew she was a female all along? Not liking for one second the direction her thoughts were racing, anger shoved them aside.

Who, in hell, did the maniac think he was? A DEA agent was not a God everyone worshipped. What did he think she knew? What could she tell him? To betray Scorpio meant the worst kind of death at the hands of his black bodyguard. Well, she would teach him to bend a knee. He would never break her, never! Someone tried years ago; a crippling memory making her repeat the vow uttered a billion times no one would make her do anything she did not want to ever again, no one.

All at once, she felt ill, hot one minute, chilled the next, her stomach queasy, as though she would vomit any second. Accustomed to not eating or drinking for days at a time, the weakness as she tried to sit up was puzzling. Her eyes magnified the food in front of her all she would have to do was eat, and drink. Spitefulness intervened. She would die before giving into this bastard, what else did she have left to lose, with, no future, no one, death would be a welcomed end to her misery. A rare bout of fear flashed high inside, never before did she feel so alone, so tired. She had suffered enough, why Morgan, why now?

Chapter 6

Shivering from the frightful darkness, clutching her doll tightly to her chest somewhat helped to ease her fear; all the same, desperate lungs sought air as a stream of tears' soothed bright red cheeks caused from suffocating heat. A rodents scratching, one large enough to gobble her alive should she dare to move, or sleep, announced she was not alone in the claustrophobic space. Each second intensifying the sound forced her trembling body deeper into the niche. Somehow, believing it would help, frantic hands stretched a torn cotton nightshirt over dirty bare feet. Face buried in her doll's sparse hair, Jordan cried, and screamed, and cried, quietly, very quietly.

Knees drawn to her chest, palms pressed against her ears she strived to block out the horrible reverberations of her mother's screams piercing the door, those of flesh striking flesh, a creaking bed, and animal like grunts. Trepidation increased as she wondered how long it would be before the monster came for her, a span of time depending upon their drunken state. The reason she must be quiet her mom warned each time before stuffing her into the closet, the only hiding place in the one room apartment her mother believed would provide safety whenever her clients were present.

For a few years, it worked until the time came, when the door opening, flooding the small space with bright light, replaced one nightmare with another. Each time small fists scrubbed blinded eyes as she, swallowed gagging lumps of fear, the silent screams, downed a cloak of bravery in preparation for what was yet to come. Plucked into bulging arms, she learned to do whatever necessary to avoid another trip to the hospital where doctors whispered, and nurses cried, years of abuse when unbelievably, no one came to her rescue, no one, not even her mother who lay close by high on drugs.

Illumination bleeding through a filthy window burst open golden nugget eyes. Thankfully, she had been proficient at halting the runaway atrocity sleep had resurrected. Masterfully her psyche stuffed vestiges of the demons back into their lair. Though she was shuddering, and her lips quivering, most importantly she did not make a sound or shed a tear. Once more she was proud of herself for learning well how to hide pain, and emotions at the tender age of ten.

Now she was hurting all over from the foreign softness beneath her bringing on an overwhelming homesickness. She longed to go home to her bed of concrete, walls of street noises, and roof of stars, her intention when jerking upright. Scanning her surroundings, she realized everything that happened was nothing more than a nightmare. The demons she believed had left replaced by another sitting all too close to the bed. Shock made her eyes bulge. So horrible looking was he, she thanked Lucifer for the sleep rendering him unarmed. Thought processes, briefly short-circuited, returned telling her she was no longer hand cuffed to anything hindering an escape.

Visions of freedom brought her fully awake, and allowed detecting the brush of cotton against her breasts, the sensation like a blaring alarm signaling she was naked beneath the unfamiliar shirt. Immediately, hands swept the quilt away. Anger dancing like flames lapped at hatred, both gathering velocity while she frantically searched her mind for answers. The only obvious conclusion, her captor disrobed, and raped her while she lay unconscious, and defenseless.

Fool that he was Jake did not know no man ever touched her, and lived. What kind of an infamous DEA agent was he she thought; only an idiot would have fallen asleep. How Scorpio could fear someone so utterly stupid she would always wonder? The moron was making it unbelievably easy to slit his throat, and escape. Apparently, no one knew of her kidnapping, or someone would have come to her rescue by now. Jordan smiled maliciously.

Other than occasionally closing his eyes for minutes at a time, Jake rarely slept. Granting the privilege plunged him into hell where the past seared him with its embers. Barely surviving the torture more times' than he cared to remember, he desperately tried to avoid sleeping.

His nightmare just began when, from out of nowhere, an unbelievable force landed on his lap sending the flimsy lawn chair he was sitting in backward with a loud crash to the floor. Before realizing he was the victim of a vicious attack, fists had already bludgeoned his face, nails clawed his skin, and fingers pulled clumps of hair from his skull. At last, the stunned surprise awakened the demon within.

As his mind whirled like a windmill, for a moment, he did not know, and then he did. An unholy light came to his eyes, fury burned like hot coals. "You insane bitch," Jake, yelled, having all he could do to fight off his attacker, the suddenness to the assailant's advantage. An orange crate toppled over shattering a glass lamp. His skull thudded against the floor, a numbing blow to his reflexes making it impossible to free his foot trapped within the collapsed chair. Before he could come to grips with what was happening, a hand retrieving a long, jagged piece of glass aimed it at his chest. Impending death rolled him to one side, the sudden move propelling his assailant to the floor. With an awful crack, Jordan's head connected with the corner of a wooden chest the instant silence making fear rise inside him like a tide of acid. Never before did Jake come up against a hellion quite like this one. Dazed, struggling to a sitting position, he tried collecting his wits scattered about like the glass on the floor. It did not help that every inch of his body was screaming in pain. When his vision cleared, what he saw scrambled what remained of his thought processes.

A witch that is what she was. Only a witch could make the legs extending from the cotton shirt shapely, enticing, too perfect to his liking, flawless, god dammit. Emotions speeding in the wrong direction brought relief that the surprisingly well-proportioned body lay motionless. With his feelings now far from honorable, he could not muster the strength to fight her off again. Desires he had not felt in a long, time, and vowed he never would again.

Yearnings that died like aflame doused with water upon noticing the blood beneath her head. Panic struck. Barely managing the stamina to crawl to her body, he sat admitting that he, of all people, was afraid to touch her, the reality a painful blow to his ego. No doubt, she was feigning the injury just as she had fabricated her illness earlier he rationalized. She was merely gathering strength for another surprise attack.

When long moments passed with no sign of movement, guilt, and anger, twining like vines, began strangling his insides. Holly shit he killed her. God dammit, one second, he was mourning the loss of an excellent opportunity to get Scorpio, the next watching intently for the slightest sign of life. When he finally mustered the nerve to touch her; reality slapped him in the face. She was not faking.

Fearful of the ramifications, gathering her into his arms, made him all too aware of how petite, pale, drawn and innocent she seemed, a victim, his victim. A reflection nipped at the bud when her body snuggled against his chest, and her warm breath began moving sprigs of hair. Pure poison, that is what she was, why would he believe her to be anything else, considering his life had become a gigantic roller coaster ride since they collided, the idea, making him release her less than gently onto the mattress. When her head turned into the pillow, relief coming in the form of a huge sigh eased the tension expanding his chest. Leaning over her, he examined the small cut thankful the bleeding had ceased. She stirred. Jerking back, he clenched his fists. Luckily, her disguise of frailty returned in time to destroy his urge to knock her senseless. "Shit" followed by more colorful expletives rolled off Jake's tongue. Angrily withdrawing hand-cuffs, he roughly secured one of her wrists to the bedpost. Hell would freeze over before he would ever trust her again, this time he meant

Chapter 7

Abhorring dust and dirt, Margaret vigorously vacuumed her apartment daily, an unbreakable early morning habit. It was not until turning off the switch, ceasing the humming noise, that she heard a loud crash, a thud, and a male voice uttering obscene vulgarities. "Lord Almighty," she exclaimed, as her robust body waddled across the living room to pluck keys off a table. Intuition told her, Jake undoubtedly had another confrontation with his captive. With horrid reflections bursting before her, she briskly covered the hall, and climbed the stairs all the while wondering if she made the right decision by not calling McMasters.

The morning after the bathroom disaster, Jake was at Margaret's door with an explanation. His job was to keep criminals like his captive off the streets leaving him two choices, protect her by bringing her to his apartment, or arrest her for delivering drugs. If he could convince her to cooperate, chances were she would receive a reduced sentence, or possibly be exonerated, her testimony alone enough to bring Scorpio down. Besides, if he put her in jail, the wild cat, that she was, if other inmates decided to do her harm, she would probably kill them.

Because Margaret trusted Jake, she agreed to give him the time he needed, sternly warning him she would be watching, and listening, and would not hesitate to call McMasters if he mistreated his captive in anyway.

Being the superintendent of the apartment building, having a key to every apartment was a blessing, especially during the past two years. More times then she cared to recall, just as the sun came up Jake would arrive home drunk out of his mind. Unable to find his keys, let alone use them, he would yell for her assistance, times when she, came to his rescue, undressed, and tucked him into bed.

From their first meeting, there was something about Jacob Morgan tugging at her heartstrings. Deep down she knew he was a good man, and although she had known few good men, she trusted her instincts. Back then Jake was blatantly handsome his short blonde hair immaculately groomed, his clothing professionally cleaned, and pressed. You could see your face in the shine of his shoes, and those enormous emerald green eyes were enough to knock a woman dead regardless of their age. That was when Jake knew how to use a razor, she sadly reflected, when he did not smoke or drink.

A year after Jake moved into the tenement he confirmed her suspicions, his confession did not come as a surprise. Residing at the run down complex was nothing more than a cover should anyone become suspicious while secretly working for the Chicago Drug Enforcement Agency. From the beginning Jake was not at all like the other tenants, Margaret immediately recognized the educated refinement. One day when flipping through a photo album he left on the table, she wondered how he could abandon such a lovely home in the suburbs with exquisite furnishings, and a professionally groomed landscape. She did not consider herself a busybody who had to know all her tenants business, the truth was she truly cared about them, Jake in particular. He reminded her of a lost puppy, who lapped up her attention as though no one ever fussed over him before.

Mature, and responsible, Jake became a good role model for her son, John. They were so much alike, full of life, full of hell, she reflected with a smirk. In no time, they became an inseparable pair. Youthful, and full of spunk, they thrived on outdoing one another with jokes, and pranks. She considered herself lucky to have two fine young men, fawning over her, always showing tremendous respect, and affection. Yes indeed, they were the two most important people in her life.

A tear strolled down her cheek. Now Jake was all she had. John's death devastated them both. On the day of John's funeral Jake vowed he would get the bastard responsible if it was the last thing he did. Her fear now, in doing so, Jake was losing his foothold on life, a sad reflection bringing her hand to a furrowed forehead as though a pain had shot there. John's death was not the only incident that changed Jake, woeful reflections that clouded over pleasant memories by the time she reached his door.

One hand on the knob, the other twisting the key, unannounced Margaret boldly entered Jake's apartment somehow, managing to duck in time to avoid a bag of garbage ripping wide open when it hit the wall scattering decayed garbage everywhere. Storming around the room like a wild cat, Jake kicked a stool with a bare foot, launching it into the air. It took a few seconds for the pain to register before he came to his knees. Hands grabbing a throbbing toe, he bellowed, "Jesus Christ, I'm going to kill that bitch. I swear nothing you do or say will stop me."

Though he was, wearing despair like a mantel, and showing all the signs of going through some kind of emotional crisis, Margaret had to bite her lips to imprison the laughter bubbling inside. Using her typical sympathetic, reassuring tone, Margaret said, "Calm down, Jacob, it cannot be all that bad."

Too angry for rational conversation, having all he could do to stand, he shoved Margaret aside snapping, "Get out of my way, she's dead meat. I am going to kill her, that is all there is to it." Two limping steps later, he yelped again.

Although Margaret was secretly admonishing herself for being so insensitive, it did not keep her blue eyes from turning to fire. Shaking a finger beneath his nose, she blustered, "You are staying right where you are, young man, until you explain what happened."

With disgruntlement written all over his features, the dam holding back Jake's inhibitions broke. "For a week I have been buying food, dammit, good food, like you said. I have even been cooking."

A quick glance at the kitchen turned Margaret pale. "She has the nerve, like she is the Queen of Sheba, for God's sake, saying it tastes like shit, and refusing to eat. I even removed the handcuffs so she can use the toilet, and clean up. Still, she refuses. Go check her out, she has lost more weight, smells and looks like the beast she is." Eyebrows crashing, crossing his heart as though a good boy scout, he continued to ramble, "Honest to God, Margaret, nothing more than a wild beast. She, attacked me, aimed a piece of glass at my chest, banged my head against the floor, and then punched me in the eye, and nose. Refusing to sleep on the bed, instead she sits on the floor twenty-four seven staring at me with a glare saying she will rip my heart out if I get anywhere near her. You have no idea what it is like to spend night after night in a broken lawn chair. My back hurts, my head is pounding and I have not slept in days. I swear I am going to kill her. I am."

The intensity in his eyes unnerved Margaret. Noticing where Jake's glance fell, Margaret managed to snatch the gun off the coffee table just in time. Abhorring guns, terrified of them, her hand began to shake uncontrollably when realizing never before had she held a gun.

Aware of Margaret's position on violence, of any kind, Jake was stunned. "Dammit, Margaret, put that gun down before it goes off, and you shoot my ass."

Trying to steady the hand holding the weapon at her side, Margaret shouted, "Your cursing is going to send you to hell, Jacob Morgan. Now, don't you move, you are not killing anyone, you big oaf."

When he defied her, bristling inwardly, she aimed the unsteady nozzle at him. "Now sit in that chair over there, while I go speak to . . . to . . . Well, I bet you don't even know her name, you probably never asked, did you? You just do not give a hoot. You are no better than she is. I ought to turn you loose on each other, and by the looks of it, I would take bets on that little thing in there. Shame on you, Jacob."

Jake was speechless, a loaded gun was dangerous in the hands of a mad woman. Margaret had been angry with him many times before, but this time she was trembling, her reprimands affecting him more than he ever believed possible.

Placing the gun in her apron pocket, Margaret stomped toward the bedroom like a mother about to administer much needed discipline. Upon opening the door, when offensive odors blasted her, she admonished herself for trusting Jake to handle things on his own.

The shirt his hostage wore was, sweat drenched, wrinkled, and soiled, her hair, a riotous mess her body filthy. There was no denying she resembled a beast. With a wrist cuffed to the rail of the bed, she sat upright on the floor, knees pulled to her chin, her back against the box spring and mattress sulking like a spoiled brat. Evidently, she was feeling much better than the last time Margaret saw her.

Fully believing an old-fashioned spanking was in order for both of them, Margaret stood tossing her head this way, and that. They were nothing more than stubborn, selfish, and conceited over grown children. Well someone had to end this vendetta before each killed the other apparently to her chagrin she was unanimously elected.

Knowing better than to invade the girls' territory, Margaret sat for a long time in the lawn chair, hands folded over the gun in her apron, staring at the mysterious urchin. She looked exhausted and utterly unapproachable as though a hidden seam in the fabric of life had given away. Appearing to be in her early twenties, somehow the girl had survived living on the streets for God only knew how long, a miracle considering her size, and weight would have limited self-defense. In conclusion, this girl was extremely, cunning, feisty, and brilliant, even for a man like Jake.

Deploring someone staring at her, having been the center of ogling eyes for longer than she cared to remember, bitterness shuttered through her making Jordan fidget under the intensity of the stranger's direct gaze. Something in the old coot's eyes said there was no other recourse but to spill her guts. Like an erupting volcano, she expelled pent up anger. "I hate him. He is a mean son of a bitch, just like all of them. He, smells, and has a temper to match that of a grizzly. I will not eat. I will not clean up. I will not tell him anything. I will not! Nothing you say or do will change my mind, nothing, so you may as well get your fat ass the hell out of here."

Margaret got what she was after. The girl had a voice all right, as foul, and ill-tempered as Jake. Wisdom, born from experience, told her, just like Jake, she was hurting, and Margaret wondered what awful things happened to cause a child to hate so much. Just imagining called up goose bumps that ran the length of her spine, and made her decide she was better off never learning the particulars.

"My name is Margaret. I am the superintendent. I live below this apartment. When you became ill, Jake called on me. I am the one, who gave you medicine, undressed, and cleaned you up. You have my word Jake did not touch or harm you in anyway."

Jordon's eyes, dull, and sunken, collided with Margaret's.

"May I ask your name? Of course, you do not have to tell me. I can give you a name myself if you wish." Supporting her chin with her thumb, her pointer finger pressed into a spongy cheek, Margaret continued, "Now, let me see, how about Cindy or Shirley?"

Horrible names, Jordan fumed. The fact her mother chose her name made it the only thing she liked about herself. "Jordan," she said so meekly Margaret barely heard.

"Jordan, Jordan," like a record, the name rolled off Margaret's tongue. "How lovely, my favorite name in the whole wide world."

Deciphering empathy in the strangers' eyes fanned the embers of Jordan's hostility. Hissing between her teeth like an alley cat, she countered, "I just bet it is. You are so old you probably never heard it before. You are no better than he is, allowing him to get away with treating me like shit." Awaiting the anger she was digging at, it caught her off guard when Margaret's features never wavered, and her voice remained calm, sweet, and sickeningly tender. Suddenly, like a turtle, Jordan withdrew within herself.

While listening to Jordan, Margaret's face appeared expressionless like a mannequins until a faint smile tilted her mouth. "Well now, you are a smart one. You are right, Jordan, I am old, and I have never heard that name before. Still, I like it; I like it very, very much. And whether you approve or not, it will be my favorite name from now on."

The woman was a wise old coot, Jordan scoffed inwardly, now convinced she was not going to get anywhere with "Mary" herself sitting at the pulpit. It was perplexing how her gaze fixed on the intruders' grandmotherly appearance, her pure white hair, shiny, each wave, and curl meticulously groomed. She had an oval face, the skin translucent and so well cared for her cheeks glowed. There was a splash of lipstick on her delicate lips. Her soft blue, global eyes were hypnotizing. Wearing a floral housedress, freshly washed, and pressed, Jordan could only imagine how beautiful Margaret must have been when she was young. She still was.

Calm settled over Margaret's features turning her voice into an almost tangible caress. "Whether you want to admit it or not, Jordan, we have something in common. We are females, much smarter than the male gender. From the day, we draw our first breath we know how to manipulate. I cannot help but think what a great team we would make if we joined forces. Jake would be a formidable challenge, don't you agree?"

While curiosity widened her eyes like an owl with over-sized glasses, astonishment made it impossible for Jordan to keep her lips firmly set. They turned ever so slightly into a trace of a grin, curiously bleak, and yet, yearning.

Margaret noticed. "You look so lovely when you smile, my dear. You should do it more often." The tender words floating from Margaret's mouth abruptly altered Jordan's mood. Cynicism twisted her lips. Cheek muscles twitched from grinding teeth, in her eyes a fleeting glimpse of pain, and longing. Head bowed, chin touching her chest, her emotions broke through the barrier. "I hate being a woman."

No one, other than Jacob, had touched her heart like the sight of this young girl who held her pride up like a shield. Margaret had to choke back tears riding effortlessly on the crest of her emotions. Having gained a smidgen of ground, she desperately fought to keep it from crumbling beneath her. "Well, my darling, you do not have to worry about Jake noticing your beauty, or the fact that you are a woman for that matter, if that is what is troubling you, and keeping you from cooperating. He, hates women, will not have anything to do with them. It is not because he prefers his own sex; a female worked him over good once. I think you both have more in common than you would like to admit, that is, you hating men, and Jake hating women, of course." With a quizzical lift of her brow, Margaret added, "Are you about to admit he is smarter than you?"

Despite herself, Jordan was beginning to admire the old fools' cunningness, her astonishing ease, and indescribable beauty. Reflecting on Jake's previous, cold, soulless, and ruthless behavior, with a look catlike in extreme, she expelled a pent up breath, "No way!"

An amused smile briefly lightened Margaret's expression. "That's the spirit. Just between us though, I must warn you regardless of sex, Jake will not surrender. Under protest, he may give a fraction of an inch here, and there, but he will never release you until he gets what he wants. Remember, he has a badge, so my hands are tied. Jake brought you here for a reason. I have to trust he knows what he is doing. Now, have I made the picture clear, sweetheart?"

Gag me with a spoon, Jordan whined. How dare the old battle-axe call her sweetheart? Just as instantly, her mind switched to the topic at hand, so Jake hated woman. Good, Jordan decided, thinking how much she would love to shake the hand of the female who put him in his place.

Aware of Jordan's spinning thoughts, Margaret decided to barter while she could. "Have you considered compromise? Just maybe the two of us can get what we want by working together. You see I would like my old Jake back and, you would like your freedom, right?"

Although Jordan's frown deepened, and her brow's collided, her eyes took on renewed clarity, gleaming like gold as she gave Margaret her full attention.

"Don't look so suspicious, darling, trust me, Jake was not always mean. It is a sad story, one I would rather have him explain someday. Life has done a number on both of you. Why don't we see if we can give it an old kick in the pants?"

The old coot was either a nut case, or "Mary" herself Jordan decided, wondering how Margaret knew how badly she hurt. One way or another, Jordan wanted out of this prison with its roof over her head, the uncomfortable mattress, and the putrid food.

Unable to think of another plausible way to gain freedom, desperation erupted. Giving Margaret her full attention, lips curled into the cutest pout, "What's the plan," Jordan asked.

Bingo, Margaret gloated, yet, she did not want to make the mistake of counting her laurels too soon. Smiling inwardly, she explained, "What if I tell Jake you will cooperate with certain stipulations. For instance, when he asks something of you, insist he does something in return."

A plan so simple, it robbed Jordan of coherent thought. Face jerking toward Margaret she asked, "Like what for instance?"

My dear, as I said before, women are rarely the, shy, retiring creatures we like men to believe us to be. We know exactly what we are doing, and why. I am positive you will come up with something."

Having planted a seed now was the time to allow it to grow. Making her way to the door, Margaret reassured Jordan, "I am right downstairs and can hear more than anyone knows. Should you need help, stomp your feet. Good luck, my dear." With a sly wink, she left.

The scheme was almost complete, Margaret mused; a boiling sense of triumph distending her breasts, now another person needed convincing before leaving the two alley cats at the others' mercy. Jake had a long overdue lesson coming on how to get more with honey than with fists, and guns.

Finding Jake on the couch, with futility, and exasperation contorting his face, Margaret stood in front of him like a rock. "I am telling you right now, Jacob Morgan, it will not work. Believe me; you have met your match."

Vaulting to his feet, he barked, "Well, we will just see about that!"

Having been already irritated to a screaming point, her temples throbbing, with the palm of one hand, and surprisingly little effort, Margaret shoved Jake backward onto the sofa. The force of her words like static cracking in the air, "Now, you listen to me, Jacob Morgan. Some people are cattle who require direction, told what to think, what to believe therefore they willingly surrender. This girl is not. With her, you will get further with sugar than vinegar. You have no choice but to compromise because that child is determined to be carried out of here in a black bag."

Child, like hell she is. Tell her that," Jake sputtered, folding his arms across a massive, very virile, chest before adding, "She probably drinks vinegar for breakfast."

A wave of pink engulfed Margaret's cheeks, her heart raced like a piston. There was no time to pray for patience, she was plumb out. With her eye's poaching Jake, she bellowed, "And you, Jacob Morgan, drink rattle snake venom. If you allowed the alcohol to evaporate from your pea brain long enough, maybe you could think for once. Be nice for a change. She is not the only one that smells. Maybe if you cleaned yourself up, took out the garbage, and. . . . and . . . aired this place out it would not stink so badly."

Like a hurricane, Margaret reached the door, halting; she spun around, "Her name is, Jordan." Hoisting her nose in the air, she left in a huff, the banging door verifying her anger. Leaning against the hall wall, Jake's gun still in her apron, Margaret inhaled much needed air. Squeezing her eyes shut, she made the sign of a cross across her bosom, and said an enormous prayer.

Shame curled inside Jake. What was there about Margaret that made him feel as though he should bend at the waist, and kiss her feet, he wondered. Her words ripped through his heart like a dull knife. Could she be right? He cringed at the thought. God, how he hated it when she called him, Jacob, doing so meant she was angry, and it seemed she had been angry with him for a very long time. Dammit, he wished Margaret were a man so they could duke it out.

Like, a dark foreboding cloud the room filled with smoke, ashtrays overflowed with cigarette butts, six empty cans of beer cluttered the floor before Jake cooled down enough to attempt reasoning with Jordan. With a black mood following him into the bedroom, he found her sitting in the same position she had been in for several days.

Reclaiming the dilapidated chair, he sat, greatly relieved when her glance did not find him for her looks recently were like lasers disintegrating him. Using what little will power he could muster, staring at the ceiling, he steadied his voice, and lowered the tone. "Jake! Jake Morgan."

Moments stretched as Jordan struggled with her retort, "Jordan."

"No last name?"

"Even if I had one, I would not be stupid enough to tell you."

Leaping to his feet, "That's it," Jake shouted. "You are impossible. This is not going to work."

"Fuck you," Jordan howled.

Her smells inundating the room moved him to the window. Explosive strength flung it open, the force shattering glass into a trillion pieces. "Son of a bitch," he bellowed, loud enough for all of Chicago to hear. With one trembling hand on his hip, the other angrily gripping the window casing to support his quaking body, drawing in deep breathes he counted to ten trying to steady what remained of his nerves. "O.K. dammit, what do you want from me," he barked.

"Remove these damn hand cuffs."

"Oh, sure, so you can kill me?"

"Don't tempt me."

"I will only remove the cuffs if you take a shower, brush your teeth, and put on clean clothes."

"I don't have any."

"I put some in the bathroom days ago."

"Yours? They are no cleaner than mine."

"You obviously prefer men's clothing. Look at you."

Why she found his retort hurtful, she would never know. Forcefully folding her arms over her chest, Jordan directed her nose upward before countering, "Fine with me."

Shocked by her sudden willingness to cooperate, Jake faced Jordan, his features showing every wrinkle etched by frustration combined with a full-blown migraine. Directing his pointer finger at her, he vowed, "I am warning you, if you try to escape I will slit your throat, and dump you into an alley. No one will know, or care. Chicago will be pleased to have fewer criminals on the streets. Besides, before anyone discovers you, your carcass will rot, and be eaten by rats."

Terrified of rodents, horrified by the idea, spiking Jake with dagger eyes, Jordan drove her point home. "Aren't you forgetting about Margaret?"

Margaret! Holly shit he could not handle much more of her disappointment, the thought alone admonishing him for such morbid threats. Whether she loved him or not, she would have his butt in jail in seconds if he harmed Jordan. What did he ever do to deserve to be sandwiched between "Mary" and the "Devil?"

Approaching cautiously, his glare never leaving Jordan's eyes, he literally yanked the keys from his pocket. Holding his breath, he, leaned over to unlock the cuffs, the sight of blood dripping from her wrist a mighty blow to his stomach. She flinched in pain, her reaction so startling, he jerked back as if expecting a knife out of thin air.

As if she could read his mind, Jordan's brittle laugh, devil like in extreme, made matters worse. "Oh, don't worry, cop, when I kill you, you will never know what hit you."

Jake was standing too close as she wobbled to her feet, poor nutrition and lack of exercise taking its toll. For a split second, he felt a surprising need to help her, empathy snatched by the fact that if he did surely she would scratch his eyes out.

Intending to hurry from his sight, the lack of strength made Jordan move like a snail toward the bathroom. Closing the space brought new dreads, not of Jake she could handle him but, the very idea of soap, water, and shampoo removing the remnants of her disguise. Terror rearing its ugly head increased her hatred toward Jake. Having put her through hell, first chance she got, he would be the one found in the alley.

There was no doubt in Jake's mind Jordan conceded under protest. As if a mind reader, his voice on the testy side, he added, "Don't forget to use soap, and shampoo, and brush your dam teeth."

Lighting a cigarette, puffing wildly, he secretly prayed his sentence with Jordan would be short, or surely, he would be arrested for murder. For some reason the possibility niggled a smile of great satisfaction.

Chapter 8

Anxious to put something solid between herself, and the barbarian in the adjacent room, Jordan shifted a heaping laundry basket in front of the door before fumbling with the bathroom door lock. Eyes wildly searching for something more to re-enforce newly won freedom found nothing other than the grimy toilet, tub, and sink. Luxuries, she wishfully reflected, that if they were hers would be spotless. What a fool Morgan was to take his blessings for granted.

Feeling a panic attack coming on demanded she seek other means of escape, discouragingly, the window in the shower, was too high, and too small. As disappointment inundated her, she leaned against the wall, eyes tightly sealed, breathing in, and out, in, and out, trying to calm the swelling apprehension making her tremble. When her lungs began to function somewhat normally, and her blood pressure lowered, new reflections charged. However claustrophobic the room was it provided a temporary respite from the wickedness of the world, and its terrible inflictions, one of them Jacob Morgan. Tough as it was to admit, the short-term security felt good.

Resonances of Morgan's incessant pacing on the other side of the door rudely reminded her why she was ordered into the haven. Left no other choice, torpidly she unbuttoned the shirt she assumed belonged to him. It had been years since she had seen her body naked, the trepidation seizing her making her feel she was about to expose herself to the entire universe. Feelings that were so overwhelming, she wondered if it was the chilly air, the ice-cold tile floor, or the act about to be committed making her shake so uncontrollably. Convincing herself such torture would only be a onetime deal, her shoddy attempt at calming otherwise jittery nerves.

Bravely stepping into the shower, she quickly gave the knobs a twist immediately jerking back as though they were cobras' about to strike. Mesmerized by the steam swiftly filling the room, she searched suppressed pathways of her mind for memories of the last time she, experienced the warmth of hot water, smelled the sweet fragrance of soap, felt the richness of its lather. Sensations repressed so long, her memory failed. Attempting to numb her senses, she avoided the warm spray convinced leaping off a cliff would be easier than what she was about to encounter.

Wise beyond her years, Jordan knew wallowing in such luxuries would make it difficult to return to the outside. She would of course there was no other way to survive the world she shunned. The pain would be unbearable. To counter attack the searing thoughts making her want to bolt, she reasoned, in life there was either one persecution, or another, Morgan or the shower. Choosing the lesser iniquity, she torpidly moved forward, mortified by the path she was treading.

The instant the warm mist touched tender skin; her body wrenched back, moved forward, and wrenched back. Despite the tentacles called upon to strangle her mind, the pleasant feelings inundating her moved her forward where she finally lingered. Raising the bar of soap to her nose, she briefly inhaled its fragrance while betraying fingers coaxed lather like a child captivated by the sensation.

Sadly, as she began to shower, it was not the soap that felt peculiar, but the touch of her skin. She was gaunt, almost desperately thin, nothing more than, a ghost in human form. Ever so slowly, she explored her body, deliberately avoiding private areas for touching them would unleash a monstrosity so deep seeded she would be led to a place offering no mercy. Filling her palm with shampoo, she scrubbed her scalp sluggishly at first, wallowing in a sensation so delightful, she repeatedly shampooed until the water turning cold thrusted her from the abyss alerting her she had made the mistake of lingering much too long.

Quickly drying with a scratchy, once white, towel, she examined the jeans, shirt, and socks tossed on the toilet seat, apparel, apparently belonging to Morgan, wrinkled, and not much cleaner than her own, worse yet, they smelled like Morgan. Upon picking up the shirt, she was shocked to find a piece of rope that fell to the floor. At once, she wondered if hanging herself was the answer to ending her crucifixion. It was not until later, after weaving the rope through loops, and tying it, she realized Morgan made certain it was not long enough, After brushing her teeth several times, Jordan's eyes examining the room one last time forced her to admit; her short stay in the sanctuary had been so enjoyable new dreads expanded her chest. Prepared to exit, though a tad bit curious as to her appearance, she avoided the mirror. There could be no reminders of the little girl who once made everyone stare and to this day, she still wondered why.

The aroma of freshly brewed coffee awakening drugged senses abruptly returned her to a time her mother allowed a sip from a favored mug. She could, taste the peculiar flavor, feel, her mothers' hand smoothing back her long blonde curls the tender lips never failing to place a kiss on her fore-head. Trembling returned. Thankfully, hands slicking back short, golden sprigs forced the pleasant memories into remission.

Brew in hand Jake sat in one of two-ripped vinyl chairs placed by a small chrome, and porcelain kitchen set. Eyes glued on the bathroom door, holding a gulp of high test in his mouth, he watched as Jordan languidly moved toward the kitchen, each advancing step increasing his heartbeat, and causing long forbidden warmth to rush his body. Feeling suddenly weak, and vulnerable, he began to perspire, the tiny droplets making him crazy as they trickled down his, sides, chest, and back. Jesus, she was turning him on, the very idea making him swallow the lump of liquid going down like cement. "Better," was all he croaked out before his gaze quickly lowered to the table?

Sitting at the opposing end of the table, head erect, her challenging eyes' boring through his, said he was staring. He, tried not to, did not want to, but a force more powerful than his will, commanded. Despite the baggy jeans dragging on the floor, the shirt, swallowing her torso, sleeves extending well beyond her fingers, shirttail past her knees, hair plastered to her skull, any dummy could see with proper nourishment, and rest Jordan could be an extraordinary looking woman. High cheekbones drew attention to a flawless, creamy complexion, and although there were dark circles under her eyes, one would have hardly noticed due to the gold compelling attention. Moreover, damn those lips for being irritatingly well shaped, full, and provocative.

Becoming uncomfortable with her filling his field of vision, restlessness eating at him prompted an urge to move to the coffee pot. Filling a cup, placing it before her, he swiftly put distance between them as though expecting her to hurl it at him. When her gaze found her lap instead, and she remained motionless, he returned to his seat.

Jordan could no longer look at Jake's eyes, radiating from them was an unmistakable message. Men were alike, nothing more than rutting bulls whose only purpose in life was to mount, and ride every heifer, damn him to hell for demanding she remove her disguise. Well, he would soon learn she would never lie beneath another man as long as she lived, never!

Trance like, she stared into the dark liquid conjuring up visions of her mothers' face, unsettling reflections hastily expunged by taking a sip. A time when her delicate hands slipping past the cuffs of the shirt exposed, cracked, and sore flesh, creases still embedded with dirt, nails broken, and stained, bruises on her forearms callously administered by him. He cringed.

Shit what was there about the monster, sitting across the table appearing a slip of a girl continually making him feel like a mean, heartless bastard. Not liking where his thoughts were meandering, he abruptly stood, the suddenness startling Jordan splattering coffee on the table, littered with crumbs, papers, and bottles, sticky from syrup, and grease.

Moving to a half opened drawer, stuffed with who knows what, Jake rummaged for a jar of salve in the process, spilling the contents on the floor, some on the counter. Finding what he sought, returning to the table, without thinking, he reached for Jordan's wrist.

"Don't touch me," she screamed, her eyes flashing red-hot fire.

Her reaction hardened Jake's facial expressions, his eyes emitting a blast of arctic air.

"Have no fear, I would not dream of it," he blustered, tossing the jar of salve onto the table. "You can suffer or put some on, either way, I don't give a shit." Spinning around his foot propelled an empty can of beer into the air crashing it against a cabinet door. Mumbling his favored four letter words, he moved as far from Jordan as possible hoping leaning against a short stretch of chipped countertop, fingers gripping tightly, would help him regain the control Jordan always managed to obliterate.

Taken back by Morgan's short spurt of humanity, unable to handle the silence that seemed somehow worse than fighting, Jordan attempted conversation. "What makes you think I can help you," her voice all at once childlike in extreme.

Staring blindly at the floor, his voice level, and soft, surprising even him, "Simple, the packages you deliver lines the pockets of the man I am after."

Aware of the tension crackling between them, that Jordan did not know how to dispel, and wondered why she even wanted to, warily she examined him. "I know nothing. Someone drops the packages off in the middle of the night with an address attached. I deliver them. I could not identify anyone even if I wanted too."

Jake's eyes altering to biting clarity swung to hers. "Maybe you don't think you can, but I am willing to gamble you know more than you realize."

In an instant, Jordan's features, radiating contempt, transformed into fear. "Considering the way you have treated me, you are crazy for thinking that I am going to risk my life just so you can get your man," her retort icicle sharp.

Emerald eyes', hot, and liquid capable of melting flesh, and bone, held hers. With blatant effrontery, Jake fired, "Whether you want to admit it or not, one way or another, your life is on the line. You are between, a rock, and a hard place with no way out. It is either Scorpio or me and if you know anything about your precious drug lord, compared to him, I am Jesus Christ."

A long lapse of silence followed, during which Jordan was unable to peel her eyes off Jake. She could not help but consider how awful he looked, tired, disheveled, as if he had been living on the streets. How could he insist she clean up when he was no better, she seethed. Even though the intended quick appraisal stretched out interminably, making her want to squirm, she continued to challenge his stare wondering, how old he was, if he were ugly or, the least bit good-looking. Disturbingly, her eyes could not leave his trim physique, and corrugated abs visible through a tight tee shirt, the bulging forearms, and heavily veined hands that spoke of strength the dimples in his cheeks, his wide mouth, and captivating full lips.

Jordan measuring him made Jake so self-conscious he began prowling the kitchen like a caged animal, wondering why he felt so ill at ease, why every follicle of hair on his body began to tingle under her direct stare.

Their confrontation nothing more than a Mexican standoff, Jordan sipping her coffee, hatefully peering at Jake over the rim of her cup, Jake with his, fingertips pressed against his hairline, eyes' squeezed shut one second, the next opening to reveal hard, cynical globes stealing glances at Jordan. It seemed nothing would bring them together on common ground until Jake noticed Jordan's hands shaking uncontrollably. "You are weak from not eating," he barked.

Trying to still her hands by cupping them around her mug, Jordan's words struck their mark. "Why do you care? You just said you did not give a shit, remember?"

Hard on his heels, Jake grabbed his cell phone brandishing it as he sputtered, "You are the key to putting an end to a crazy man, and like it, or not I am going to provide for you until this is over." To her utter shock he added, "Now tell me what you want to eat, dammit."

The mention of food made Jordan's stomach grumble. "Pizza," rolled off her tongue before giving any conscious thought as to what she wanted, "with peppers, onions, and mushrooms."

"And, mouthwash, if you intend to eat such garbage," Jake, reiterated, her request reminding him how much he detested pizza.

A half hour later, sitting across from Jordan, Jake watched in total amazement as she unabashedly plunged right in, slopping sauce on her lap, nosily devouring most of the pizza along with a half litter of pop, her eyes closing tight as she licked fingers in ecstasy. Never before did he see a human eat like a wild animal, as if she may never eat again, as if the horrid stuff she was consuming was caviar. Angering him more, while she chewed, and her tongue licked at traces of sauce, he felt twinges of arousal.

Mulling over his plans to get Scorpio abated the anger, and managed to keep his mind off the creature becoming all too fascinating. Simple, Jake thought, rather than risk one of his men he would allow Jordan to do the dirty work. Under his surveillance, she would return to her world at night, continue to receive the packages, and make deliveries. This would buy him the time and additional information he needed to organize another raid.

Stomach hurting from all she consumed, striking a melodramatic pose, Jordan sat wide-eyed trying to control the odd sensation flurrying in her mid-section. Jake just finished explaining his plans ending the conversation by repeating the warning he had issued earlier. If she refused to cooperate, authorities would find her dead in some alley, Margaret or no Margaret. This time the look in his eyes' said, he was serious. Something gave way inside her; fear filled its place.

Wondering why he suddenly felt sleepy, glancing at his watch said it was two a.m. Attempting to fight off the luxury, he escorted Jordan to the bedroom convinced he would be fine if he rested for a little while.

Jordan ate so much it hurt to walk an overloaded digestive system inducing lethargy. Dutifully, she sat on the floor, and leaned against the mattress, disbelief flaring her eyes wide when Jake neglected to handcuff her. Instead, he sat in the lawn chair a few feet away gripping a gun placed on his lap. Weapon or not, Jordan patiently waited for him to close his eyes for more than a few seconds.

As Jordan slept fitfully Jake, scrutinized her facial contortions, listened to her whines, her mumbling, and watched her tremble. Though there were no tears, he heard her shallow breathing, saw her chest rise, and lower rapidly as though she was sobbing inwardly, behavior making him wonder what horrible atrocities she endured.

Jordan's discomfort brought on a barrage of childhood memories when shuffled from one foster home to another following the death of his mother when struck by a drunk driver on her way home from work. For the billionth time, Jake vividly remembered waiting day after day never leaving the apartment wondering, where she was, if she would ever return. A week later, he gave himself up to grief, it was only then that neighbors heard his cries, and came to his rescue.

Jake knew nothing about his father; his mother never spoke of him or of any other relatives. At the age of five, he learned what it was like to be, alone, unloved, and unwanted, physically, and verbally abused by foster parents. Such was the course of his life until he ran away at fourteen. The summer and fall spent wandering the streets of Chicago, sleeping in parks, under porches, in garages, and stealing food to survive. That winter, lacking the money for food or shelter, a priest found him lying beneath a bridge almost frozen to death.

Father Mahoney promised to provide food, shelter and odd jobs for spending money as long as Jake attended school. Due to Father Mahoney's age, and physical limitations, their relationship was nothing like a real father, and son, then again, it was as close as Jake would ever experience. Shortly after graduating from High School with honors, Father Mahoney died leaving what little money he managed to save to Jake. Thanks to his heavenly guardians influence, and inheritance, Jake chose a future in serving, and protecting others.

Possibly Jordan experienced the same abhorrence's in life, Jake decided, a consideration that increased his heartbeat, and made old wounds fester as he thought how much more difficult it would be for a young girl with no choice but to sell her body, or deliver drugs. Instincts, making him want to, protect her, care for her, and help her, but mind you, only temporarily. Wholesome thoughts tugging on the lids of his eyes snapping them closed.

Chapter 9

Jake's eyes sprung open. Despite the fuzz clinging tenaciously to his mind, he sensed Jordan was gone. The sound of running water jerked him to his feet. Overpowering the urge to sprint, he stuffed the gun into his waistband, and crept quietly into the living room.

The kitchen light illuminated Jordan as she stood at the sink on her tiptoes. Even with her arms stretched to the max, her reach fell short of the upper cabinet. A quick glance, assessing the room found her jeans draped over a chair, then wrenched back to the shirt scarcely covering the creases of her buttocks. A scrutiny that, halted him in his tracks and, lasted a few heartbeats too many as it went from accusatory to damn interested.

Will power substantially weakened, Jake could not help gawking at the legs beneath the hem, shapely limbs leading upward to what he imagined to be firm round haunches. While male anatomy entertained the delusions of a lunatic, for the briefest second his breath caught. Impulsive feelings nipped at the bud when he remembered the vow made long ago never again to allow a female to bewitch him too strong was his theory women were witches who, once within their clutches, consumed every fiber of a man.

Having honed her sense of hearing, and smell, into that of an animal, Jordan was instantly aware of Jake's presence. Slowly lowering her arms, one hand reached for a dirty glass, the other for a butcher knife lying on the counter.

Certain his presence went undetected, Jake sneakily closed the distance purposely crowding her, his glare drilling through the back of her head summoning a shocking response.

Temper, rising from the ashes of exhaustion, spun Jordan around bringing the tip of the knife against Jake's bare chest. The audible click of two sets of eyes' clashing left no mistake she pushed the ogre well beyond mild annoyance, a realization brightening the color of her cheeks. Survival instincts pressed the knife against flesh watching as the point made an indentation meanwhile struggling not to notice, the taut skin covering swelling muscles, the blonde, kinky curls spreading across his chest, and upward to a cluster at the indentation of his Adam's apple. The warmth rushing through her body, collecting in her throat, making it feel parched, and raw, was nothing more than a trace of apprehension, she reasoned. Ignoring the pulsating heart clanging about in her chest, her visage exhibited no visible signs of distress.

The look Jordan gave him filled with reproach, her spunk so amusing; Jake had to fight the smile threatening to curl his lips. Damned if he did not admire her fearlessness that kept exploding when he least expected. Damned if she did not arouse him again. Nevertheless, he made no motion, no sound, never even blinked.

A verbal response was not necessary. Struck dumb she was by spearing eyes, his gaze as sharp, and steady as the beam of a laser, emerald orbs that never moved, or abandoned the gold threatening to paralyze him. Mesmerized by his features becoming fierce, and disdainful, Jordan missed entirely his hand raising slowly, the rough, calloused fingers curling around hers, seizing control of the knife.

Even though her disguise was cold, and deadly, it was impossible for Jake to ignore the soft flesh, and fragile bones beneath his touch. Thankfully, reality arrived in time igniting sufficient rage goading him into pressing his chest forward into the knife. Eyes' dueled, his dark, and inscrutable, hers glistening bright nuggets worthy of a lightning bolt.

The instant their flesh touched, Jordan felt swallowed by her heartbeats. Aghast she was when she felt the knife sink easily into soft layers of flesh, and muscle, the shiny steal tip becoming lost within brawny depths. Horrified, she watched crimson fluid trickle through kinky curls downward to the gun tucked into his belt. There was no stopping her heart careening like an elevator fifty floors. Enlightened eyes flicked back to his boring through her, piercing her with the force of his rage.

There was no shadow of doubt; Morgan was as stone cold dead inside as his features were outside. In the churning, ever changing depths of green, there was no trace of fear, or pain, only an outrage lurking, the kind Jordan recognized, and understood, causing the length of her to shudder.

Bone crushing bone, Jake diverted the blade upward ever so gently positioning the bloody tip against the tender skin beneath Jordan's chin. Vexation increased his breathing, and fanned the blazing furnace of his soul bringing beads of perspiration to his forehead. As unbearable moments lingered, Jordan was convinced that even carefully screened quaking would cause the air between them to burst into flames.

Like an earthquake, his voice rumbled, "This is the third time you have threatened my life, and the last. If you are stupid enough to consider a fourth, I strongly suggest you make it good."

Directing the blade with slow purpose, he traced her chin, the translucent flesh of her slender neck, down to the base of her throat where her heart was racing. She felt, the deadly edge, its sharp apex, and her predator's moist blood dripping sickeningly onto her skin sensations bludgeoning her lung's, and escalating palpitations that screeched to a halt the instant the weapon came to rest between her breasts.

Like frostbite, the breath from his words. "Fearing no one, I welcome death. It would end my miserable life. But, allow me to make myself crystal clear." Deliberately pausing to heighten her fear, he pressed the knife sufficiently to make a slight dimple in her skin. "I will not die alone. Should you decide to gamble the odds you had better be precise, and swift, take no time to think or bat an eyelash or you will never draw another breath. Keep in mind, vixen, for a long time I have fantasized about killing a woman. There is a first time for everything. For you to be my guinea pig would bring me immense pleasure."

Stunned by his words, Jordan rocked back on her heels, the floor seeming to dip beneath her feet. It was incomprehensible as to what paralyzed her. Her eyes transfixed, she stood stiff, as though charmed like a snake. When his breath touched her skin and, his presence became suffocating, pent up anxiety expelled in a rush. Thrills shot the length of her. Wondering why, as quickly as the questions roamed her mind the answers came. Morgan was a mortal who had conquered fear, and pain, someone pulverized to the core, just like her.

Insight struck full force without a doubt he could, and would do what he said, just as she would.

As green globes dove into caves of molten, gold even though they saw no fright no remorse, only hatred, and guts the discovery confirmed what he suspected, Jordan did not possess the killer instinct, or surely, she would have thrust the knife into him. The thought he had placed himself in such a position to do so, churned his stomach. His oppressive need to uncover her capabilities could have been the death of him.

Amazing, he thought, that only moments ago as Jordan slept, she seemed nothing more than an innocent child, her frailty so convincing it brought forth the need to protect. Truthfully, Jordan needed no protection, needed no one, therein lay his greatest misery, and confusion. What caused that child to vanish right before his eyes? What were the elements to her she guarded so carefully?

Like a swipe of an eraser across a blackboard, Jordan's defiance obliterated those reflections, the expression on her face hard, and unyielding, her voice as stiff as her back was. "Go ahead, do it. Make my day. Get it over with," and, instead of relinquishing her grip, she shoved the knife.

Jake's quick reflexes barely prevented slashing her throat. Repulsion filled him. Fury burning like hot coals flung the knife across the room. Freed hands, instantly found her arms easily lifting her to her toes, pressing her body hard against the cabinets.

Holding her awkwardly with an iron grip he maintained a distance between them that would prevent her knee from connecting with his vulnerability, surely if given the opportunity, she would. Color crawled up his throat as fear shaking him spilled from his mouth. "Jesus Christ, are you crazy? Why do you dig until you bring out the worst in me? Why do you try me so? Dammit, this has to stop." Shaking her like a rag doll, "Now tell me why you left the bedroom. Tell me."

So furious, and out of control was Jake, he would have continued, but his tongue became thick, and numb by the closeness of their bodies. It was impossible not to look at her a huge jolting mistake juggling feelings already mashed. Wandering eyes examined the, multi-shaded strands of dried hair haphazardly falling about a sweet face, thick arched eyebrows, and long lashes, the pug nose. Considerably thrown off guard by whatever he was feeling, he would always wonder how he managed to avoid kissing her, he wanted to, desperately wanted to, but intuition sensed it would be his undoing.

Eyes skipping over her chin found instead the shirt pulled open exposing sizable delectable breasts pitching, and grazing his chest, the dark nipples only he knew were visible through the thin material pulverizing his vulnerability. Unmistakable was the desire drawing him up tighter than a string of an instrument, damn her.

Becoming embarrassingly aware of the frailty of his emotions eased the pressure of his hands, though there was no ignoring the chaos she caused, pride forced him to honor his pledge never again to need a woman. Besides, Jordan was too young to permit a flicker of lust to streak his mind. Hell, it was more than a flicker, much more and he knew it.

Jordan watched Jake's dark look lighten, the pain seeming to drain from his eyes as his forehead unwrinkled, the grim line of his lips, soften. At first, she wondered why his expression turned from curiously bleak to yearning then, to her dismay, remembered her bare skin tingling when the edges of the shirt slowly parted. A pleasant feeling inducing a languor spreading over her making, her cheeks so hot they stung, her heart race. When Jake's eyes traveled lower, and his face flushed, watching his mood change reminded her of men's disgusting wants. She had all she could do to control the knee wanting to bring him to his; the only thing stopping her was, without flinching, he would strangle her.

Knowledge born from experience told her she could not physically win against his strength. Still, she had to do something, anything to get rid of him, and cleanse herself of the flustering feelings. Frantically digging through the pile of her beliefs crashing at her feet, she plucked her voice. "Why do you care? I am nothing to you. With my help, you may win, but without me, mister, you lose. Believe me, there is nothing that would bring me more pleasure, even if my death insured it."

Shame slapped her full force when Jake flinched from her words. For the life of her, she could not understand the overwhelming compulsion to explain, in fact, she did not recognize her own voice. "I am not accustomed to a hot, stuffy apartment. I needed air, a drink of water. That is all." Vulnerability, running away, changing the subject altered the pitch of her voice into a scream. "Just look at this mess, you cannot get near the faucet, there is not one clean glass, there is shit growing in the sink, and you have the nerve, the audacity to criticize me? You are nuts, mister, plan, and simple, nuts!"

Tight fisted, Jake desperately fought his urge to punch her silly whether the compulsion was due to her insinuations or what she made him feel sexually, he did not know. Needing to get away from her, he stepped back. Wandering eyes scanned the kitchen, the living room, trying to visualize what she saw. Why suddenly what she thought mattered was preposterous, but it did, and the fact filled him with hate. The very idea, raking his nerves, made his fist raise and get lucky as it punched a cabinet door that sprang back in retaliation barely missing his head. Stomping from the room he shouted, "If you don't like it, if it does not suit you, Miss Prima-Donna, clean it up."

Jordan loathed the fact she winced when he raised his hand. Nevertheless, she almost gave into the urge to laugh, or, was it the urge to cry? Suddenly, she realized there was more to learn about Morgan than his exterior exposed. Was he truly unique, or like the other men she had known cruel, deplorable, self-indulgent cockatrices. He would not deliberately hit her, would he? He would not rape her, would he? Then again, maybe he would, but, so far, he had not, and she knew he possessed the strength, and lack of morals to take anything he wanted, when he wanted.

Even a blind person could sense he wanted her. No, it was more as if he was hungry for her and she wondered just when she would be on his menu. She had pushed her luck too far, the next time he would kill her or worse expect sex. Anger with the slightest trace of fear, and a smidgen of admiration screeched forward. "Go to hell," she screamed at his back.

In the kitchen below Jake's, Margaret stood, her hands in dishwater, head shaking, tongue clucking, ears straining to overhear the commotion above. Relief floated over her when she heard Jake's footsteps retreat to the living room. She waited for the phone to ring, knowing he would call. He did. Finally, he admitted he needed help. Poor soul, he actually pleaded with her to supervise Jordan. His excuse got her undivided attention. If they were together much longer, he would strangle her on the spot. Thundering thoughts of the formidable challenge ahead made Margaret say another prayer.

Chapter 10

Jake's mood had not cooled one degree since the incident in the kitchen with Jordan. Certain he had lost all control, Margaret stood stunned as he barked orders. Jordan was not to, leave the apartment, use a phone, stand near a window, or snoop into his private things. Both were to take every precaution to keep her existence top secret. If Jordan disobeyed or made the least little threat, Margaret was to shoot her. Reclaiming his gun from Margaret, he demonstrated how to load, remove the safety, and aim before stuffing it back into her apron pocket.

However anxious to leave the apartment he seemed, Jake stopped abruptly at Jordan's feet. With a frown bending the lines on his forehead, gritting his teeth he lectured, "If you hurt a hair on that old woman's head, you will not live to tell about it, there will be nowhere you can hide that I will not find you. Got it?"

Bristling inwardly, Jordan fought hard not to bite off finger wagging an inch from her nose.

Two stairs at a time, Jake descended four stories some-how missing, roller blades, a football, and a doll abandoned by careless children. In the four by four foyer, angrily tossing aside a neglected bag of garbage he kicked a stroller that was blocking double doors to assess the knob requiring a special technique to gain freedom, minor incidents serving to exasperate his mood.

Entering the bright light, the boastful sunshine went unnoticed, as did the people gaping at him from opened windows. So preoccupied was he loudly uttering colorful, explicit profanities proclaiming his frustrations, he never noticed the pedestrians on the sidewalk who stopped in his wake. Worsening matters, his attempts to open the car door were fruitless. Enraged, his foot came hard against metal, the blow adding another dent to the multitude of others. Once inside, he frantically searched his pockets for keys fearful he would have to reenter hell to claim them. In doing so, he managed to crush his last pack of cigarettes leaving only one worth lighting now hanging from his lips. More anxious than ever to light up, he punched the cigarette lighter, the sparks flying defining his mood. It was then he noticed the keys already in the ignition, a sign he was losing his mind. Receiving the blunt of his abuse, the engine protested with, a groan and a whine before spitting, and sputtering as he wildly pumped the accelerator, and repeatedly twisted the key. Radio blaring, teeth gnawing on the end of an unlit cigarette, with a squeal the Mustang sped away from the curb. A thoughtless move met by, a blaring horn, and a volley of obscenities spilling from the mouth of another driver, vulgarities Jake matched all the way to the precinct.

A bang from two palms swung wide the doors to the drug enforcement agency. Charging like a bull, he covered the length of the hall, defying signs prohibiting smoking by continuing to puff on his cigarette. Climbing the stairs to the second floor, he marched down the aisle lined with desks.

Though smirks twitched his co-workers lips, no one lifted their head, or ceased their activity. Accustomed to his, odious moods, and aversion to rules, and regulations, no one dared to question Jake's smoking.

As if his appearance alone commanded, a young, handsome lad stationed behind a desk instantly stood to follow the giant of a man. Both disappeared inside an office, the glass on the door boasting bold black letters identifying Jake's private domain.

Typically watching his idol intently, Billy waited patiently for Jake's temper to cool. Jake was unaware in many ways he reminded Billy of his father, intelligent, strong, cunning, determined. Decoding Jake's mannerism's that said he had a plan, Billy sat across from his hero, the first man in twenty-five years who meant anything to him, whose very existence demanded respect, and admiration. While the hands on the clock ticked maddeningly, Billy's thoughts wandered down a dark, forbidden alley etched indelibly in his mind.

Raised by a single parent, Billy's mother never spoke of his father. Despite his curiosity, not once did he dare to question, not even when the monthly check arrived enabling her to, afford a meager apartment, and sensible furnishings. Working as a server part time provided her time to spend with him, and the extra cash to grant the needs of an average child.

It was not until his thirteenth birthday that the answers he longed for turned his life inside out. The day the stranger meeting him at the door introduced himself as his father, a handsome man whose demeanor and designer clothing spoke of wealth, and position. The stranger did not waste words or sugar coat the conditions of an agreement made between his parents the day of his birth. A phone call earlier in the day reminding his mother had caused her visible distress, and robbed her of all coherent thought, and mobility. Suitcases packed, and placed alongside a chair, told Billy he had no say in the matter like it or not, he was leaving to live with his father until he turned twenty-one.

Forever he would remember the candles on the cake melting his heart instead of wax. The beautifully wrapped gift from his mother he was not permitted to receive. Haunting Billy to this day how her gorgeous face turned pale, and her normal wide smile became nothing more than quivering lips, how her breath taking blue eyes clouded over from pain. A stunning woman whose model perfect figure, and features made her look ten years younger than she was, far from the image of someone abandoned by a man to raise a child alone. Inseparable over the years, the love they shared made it impossible for Billy to believe his mother would willingly agree to such an arrangement. Later, he learned there were no choices when dealing with wealth, and ruthless power. Permitted no goodbyes, their stolen glances spoke of mutual torture. All too often, Billy recalled his mother's fingers balled into tight fists at her sides, how she trembled, how anger flushed her face. Never did he imagine from that day on they would only share a monthly phone call, and a yearly visit on his birthday. As his father intended, through the tides of change they grew apart. By his twenty-first birthday, his mother remarried, had two daughters, and relocated on the West coast. Sorrowfully, long before then, the calls, and visits ceased.

Military school, martial arts, fencing, and sharp shooting consumed his life, each challenge, and new honor, worthless accomplishments when he had no one to share them with, so cold, and meaningless was his relationship with his father. In time, Billy accepted his choices, either succumb to his father's wishes or face the brutal consequences. Today, what mattered most, he had forgiven the mother who had forsaken him, a delicate sweet women she could never have fought such a force.

Made strong and brave by the course of his life, upon turning twenty-one, Billy dared to defy his fathers' will by accepting a position on the Chicago Police Force. Shortly after the death of Jake's best friend, he proved himself worthy of a commission as a DEA officer under Jake's command. It took two long years to gain Morgan's trust, and confidence. For some unexplainable reason that meant more to Billy than anything, he had accomplished.

Habitually rubbing his beard whenever he was deep in thought, Jake paced the dark, gloomy office littered with scattered books; papers piled on a marred metal desk, a wastebasket overflowing with scraps of idea's, and plans. Hell would freeze over before Jake would allow anyone access to his private domain, whether to clean it or otherwise, Billy the only exception.

At last, Jake acknowledged the lad who made him wonder why someone as handsome, astute, and brave would waste his youth on drug enforcement, in his opinion, a losing battle. Tall, extremely well built, with dark skin, black hair, pale blue eyes, and a rogue's smile capable of melting any female's heart Billy could make a fortune as a gigolo, Jake often chuckled. So why would he waste his attributes on a life of hell?

Oh, Jake tried hard not to like Billy. The kid was nothing more than a damn, hotheaded hero who one day would be in the wrong place at the wrong time. It would not matter that Billy could out draw, out shoot, out fight anyone he knew, with the exception of himself, of course. What worried Jake was unquestionably the day would come when the young fool would make a rash decision. Nevertheless, Jake admired Billy's guts the kid had literally knocked himself out to earn his favor, and as days passed, despite the pain of wounds festering now, and then, Jake shoved aside memories of John. Today was one of his weaker days.

Staring at his young sidekick, reflections skipped over Jake's mind of the day Billy prevented him from killing a prisoner by wedging his body between them ready, and very willing to take him on unless he backed down. Never before did someone dare to interfere with his methods of justice, a confrontation proving Billy to be a respected, valued partner, until now. Jakes' new plans did not include Billy. Paranoia had set in. Knowing there was disaster lurking, he did not want the kid involved. Working alone was imperative. After days of mulling over the last raid, plaguing uncertainties made him wonder why Scorpio was there, why there was a convenient escape hatch, reasons he suspected a spy within the agency.

Unable to stand Jake's pacing another minute, Billy dared to ask, "What is it, pops? What's on your mind? Tell me, for God's sake."

"I am putting you in charge of the men. Figuring this mess out is going to take some time. Until I can come up with a plan, I am laying off Scorpio. I am tired and need a break in hopes that a leave of absence will clear my thoughts. The next time I will not fail."

Struck immobile, let alone speechless, Billy's mouth seemed to dangle on hinges. Knowing Jake, he was certain his hero had not lost his marbles. There was something up his sleeve; Jake never considered taking time off. Pushing for answers now would only prove futile. Wisely, Billy decided to bide his time until Jake was ready to explain the real reason. "Yes, sir, what should I tell the men?"

"Have them continue the stake outs, keep their eyes, and ears open. Pass any information on to me either by pager, cell or text. I will be in, and out of the office." Withdrawing his pager from the desk drawer, Jake clipped it onto his belt. Moving to the door, he held it open, Billy's signal to leave.

Billy was several feet away before Jake's voice stopped him. "Be careful, kid. Don't get too hot headed." It was there, in the exchange of their knowing smiles defining their uncommon bond. Offering up a salute, "Got it, pops," Billy said wearing a wise-ass smirk.

Chapter 11

No fat, old, woman was going to stand in her way, Jordan fumed. The instant she heard the unmistakable clatter of Jake's car drift away, with a stature of purpose, she headed toward the apartment door, and wrenched it open. Before a limb crossed the threshold, a faintly menacing tone from behind instantly halted her and brought her erect. Fully prepared to challenge her assigned guardian, she spun around.

In a knife like tone, a familiar voice warned, "I would not do that if I were you, my dear." The gun in the old woman's hand was surprisingly steady, her eye's round as quarters, uncommonly hard. A dark expression flashing across her features cautioned she was not at all amused with Jordan's intentions. Bright color came to Jordan's face as if a misbehaved child.

Though a faint smile, neutral without hostility or triumph, curved the old coot's mouth, and her tone was mild, there was a ruthless purpose tainting every word. "I do not know anything about you, my dear, but I do know my Jake. When he feels strongly about something, he is rarely mistaken. However apposed I am to holding you hostage you must understand I will follow his instructions to the letter until I am convinced he is wrong."

Pausing delicately, with a lift of an eyebrow, Margaret's eyes returning to normal size, softened as they shifted over Jordan. The smile Margaret offered was so warm, Jordan felt touched by the sun. "Now, our time together can either be pleasant or unpleasant, the decision is yours. What will it be, my dear," Margaret said with a roguish look.

Feeling like a bucket of broken fine china, Jordan conceded. Surrender was advisable, there was no fighting "The Devil" and "Mary," an absurd combination. Like it or not, the only way she would escape the mess she was in, was to cooperate, the certainty making her very sick to her stomach. Bewildered, and confused, in retaliation, she resorted to a sarcastic loud snap. "All right, I will do anything you say, just put that damn gun away."

Margaret returned the gun to her apron pocket as if they had been talking in a companionable way. With admirable warmth she replied, "I may be old, fat, and ugly, but I am far from deaf. In the future, darling, please lower your voice. I would also appreciate it if you did not use vulgar language, it is quite unnecessary."

Uncertain as to the woman's intentions, when Margaret approached, Jordan shifted nervously to grant space. Stepping into the hall, Margaret looked both ways before signaling with her pointer finger for her to follow. Jordan was positive the smile of conspiracy jerking on the old fool's lips was that of lunacy.

"Well, come on, dear. We do not have all day. What Jake does not know will not hurt him?"

Long before Jake came home that evening, as if the day had been uneventful, Margaret and Jordan returned to his apartment to watch television. In truth, it had been a day of enlightenment.

Upon entering Margaret's apartment, she was encouraged to explore while Margaret secured the door and placed the key in her apron pocket. Entering the kitchen Margaret began fluttering around the galley-sized space opening the refrigerator, shuffling through cabinets, and several drawers to prepare the food she deemed necessary for a young girl to regain her health.

Sunshine beaming through two sparkling clean windows greeted Jordan as they entered. The ray's filtering through white lace curtains, tied back with ribbon, twisting in the wind, was painting patterns on everything they touched, a minefield of knick-knacks, and fussy little pieces of furniture. Worn wood flooring, polished to perfection, peaked from beneath a tattered but thoroughly vacuumed hooked, rug. Facing a portable television was an earth tone sofa, and matching chair both boasting crocheted doilies on their backs, and arms to camouflage wear. Small wood tables accented both ends of the sofa. Freshly painted cream color walls exhibited several diverse shaped, creatively arranged country scenes. On the short wall, open bookcases held neatly arranged paperback, and hardcover treasures systematized according to size. An upright piano fit perfectly between two windows facing the street, its top adorned with lace doilies, a menagerie of dissimilar sized picture frames, none matching, revealing Margaret's life story.

While becoming enchanted by the photos, surprisingly, Jordan made a conscious effort to avoid the windows where wafting from the street below she heard horn's, children's screams, and giggle's, women's gossip. As if robbed of the one thing she desperately needed to survive, she took in deep breaths of the fresh air continuing to toy with the curtains.

Her mind flashed from one photo to the next, a kaleidoscope of sight mingling with the sounds, and smells from outside. Watching the subjects change one of Margaret when she was young, and indeed beautiful, and a man the image of perfection, she presumed to be her husband. Several baby pictures, and group pictures, and then, one impossible to ignore for there was no mistaking those eyes. She knew before asking, the photo was of Jake, and another young man, year by year, one by one, she examined the images. Possessed with a feverish need to know more about the image holding her transfixed, lifting the picture, she brought it closer to inspect the immaculate stylish suit, shiny shoes, and handsome face beneath a hat. As her thumb unconsciously eased across Jake's face, her chest heaved, and weakness inflicted her knees. Despite the man next to Jake, who was younger, and better-looking, Jakes face captured, and held her attention as she wondered what terrible things happened to alter the handsome persona?

Margaret touched her shoulder; she jumped, and almost dropped the photo. "Yes, it's Jake. I am sure you agree he was handsome. Though I took it only two years ago, you would never know he was thirty-three then, would you. Next to him is my son, John, the two of them inseparable, and such monsters, they drove me wild."

Like a cloud floating over the sun, Jordan watched as the past enveloped Margaret how her warm, sunny expression turned dark, and brooding, then thankfully brightened again as she painstakingly returned the photo. "There is a lot you do not know about my Jake. Now, come on, breakfast is getting cold."

Her Jake, Margaret said the softness in her eyes, the sweetness in her tone, said she loved him. Curiosity niggled Jordan's mind as to who was the real Jacob Morgan.

The smell of Margaret's omelet would have sent a heathen to heaven, let alone the taste. Jordan ate until her stomach felt as though it would burst. Determined to enjoy the luxuries of food, as long as she could, she topped it off with toast, smothered with butter, and jelly, washed down by several glasses of milk, and juice. It had been much too long since Margaret had someone other than Jake to pamper. Sipping her coffee, delighted by her guests' antics, she believed in no time she would have Jordan on her feet looking healthier and more beautiful every day.

Margaret had secret plans of her own firmly believing Jordan just might be the long overdue answer to her prayers. She had, already made Jake, sit up, and take notice, jarred the grizzly from a long winters nap. Whether he knew it or not, Jordan was beginning to breathe life back into a hollow man.

Hours passed while Margaret's tales of her son, and Jake's friendship, of John's addiction, and death, enthralled Jordan. Regretfully, as if on purpose, she skimmed over the person in Jake's life responsible for stealing his reason to live.

The full extent of Margaret's shrewdness was not apparent until Jordan finished lunch when she was marched toward the bathroom with, a towel, a wash-cloth, and a new toothbrush. Her instructions were, in return for her meals, she was to bathe, and scrub herself spotless. Parting at the bathroom door, Margaret warned that if she did not pass inspection, she would personally see to it. Inwardly Jordan chuckled; Margaret managed to implement her concept of compromise quite successfully.

An hour later, spit polished, Jordan entered the kitchen surprised to discover a snack spread before her, and Margaret insisting she eat again. Ice tea washed down a giggle as Jordan wondered what the old coot would request in return.

When Jake entered his apartment that evening, and his eyes converged on Jordan, Margaret had to chew her bottom lip to prevent a smug smile from curling them. Though unable to see his eye's flash in her direction, there was no mistaking the heat, the intensity making her quickly gather her belongings, and exit before Jake collected his thoughts enough to scold her.

Chapter 12

Stomping into the bedroom, Jake tossed a garbage bag onto the floor. Like a tidal wave, he moved to the kitchen jerking the refrigerator open, retrieving a can of beer, and then slamming the door closed so hard the appliance shook. The long swigs of beer, the deep drags on a cigarette, his idea of anger management, neither working in eradicating the sight of Jordan he was trying hard to suppress.

It was not the oversized shirt, the jeans hugging her legs slightly tighter, the slouch socks, and sneakers, the workings of "Mary" herself, but Jordan's face. Polished clean, her skin shined with fresh color, the dark circles beneath gold, somewhat faded, fine strands of multi colored blonde hair definitely puffier, her hands clean, her lips. . . He should have known better than to trust two conniving women, it was a conspiracy, for cripes sake.

Demented he was for bringing Jordan to his apartment the admission crushing the empty beer can in hand then tossing it on the floor before retrieving another. Angry he was for wondering, why Jordan was the first thing he looked for the moment he opened the door, why he was so relieved to find her there, why he did not miss the slightest detail of her, why he even noticed.

The only conclusion, he had lost his marbles, the result of exhaustion, malnutrition, and too much overtime. Still, he could not stop. Tonight, he hoped, would be a fresh start at toppling Scorpios' empire, mulling over the prospect obliterating reflections of Jordan.

With elongated, obstinate strides, stopping in front of the television, with a determined flick of his wrist, he switched it off. Turning to confront Jordan, like a General, he bellowed, "Your clothes are in the bag in the bedroom. Put them on. There is a jar of camouflage on the top of my dresser for your face. You have ten minutes." When Jordan immediately stood, her willingness to cooperate inflated his chest.

Sauntering toward him, using exaggerated movements, instead she reached around him to flick the television back on. "I was watching a program, if you don't mind."

Goddamn, she knew just how to light his fire. Almost breaking the knob Jake angrily twisted it off again. "Oh, but I do mind. Now you heard me, move!" The last word, said with enough gust of wind, it separated the strands of what few wispy bangs covered her forehead.

Despite the fury evident in his furtive eyes, digging her feet in, Jordan stiffened soldier straight. Again, she had the nerve to turn the television back on. Arms crossed, chin raised in defiance, her posture stiffer still, she countered, "Make me!"

In a flash, Jake started to raise his hand fortunately reconsidering in time. Like bulls, measuring each other, analyzing their next move, both stood their ground.

The nearness of Jordan's skin blasted him with a spring fresh fragrance while golden nugget eyes', sparkling with renewed vitality radiated revulsion. Feeling the ice inside him beginning to melt, ever so slightly, he wanted to move, but could not. Giving into her would be a grave mistake. "That's it, isn't it? You want something in return, don't you, what, the White House, glass slippers, or, a castle perhaps?" He was screaming of course.

Jake's pitiful expression and ridiculous insinuations were indeed humorous. Choking down an unexpected giggle, searching his face for a trace of the man she had seen in the picture found only eyes barely recognizable. Hands propped on hips she took a step closer bringing them nose to nose. "If you think for one minute I am going to help you for nothing, you are a bigger fool than I thought, Morgan. I am not sticking my neck out just for freedom. If I survive, you are going to make it worthwhile."

One of Jake's hands went to his hip, the other stretching up, as if he were going to smack Jordan senseless, began rubbing a neck stiff from tension. In desperate need of fresh air, he put space between them wondering what was worse, Jordan's clean fresh aroma, or the old stench. A migraine was threatening, if it got out of control, he would not be worth a shit. Getting rid of the thorn in his side was necessary, the sooner they began, the sooner they would finish then, she would be out of his life for good. Desperation erased all conscious thought. "Name it."

Surprise collided with disappointment Jake gave in so easily Jordan was tongue-tied. What she wanted, she had no I idea. Margaret confused her by exposing her senses to a foreign but pleasurable way of life. The time spent with Margaret made her believe that, if an old woman could manage alone, meagerly, and survive, possibly she could as well.

"You are to stop shouting at me. I hate yelling. You have to shower, and shave, as often as you expect me to. When we are through I want ten thousand dollars, and a first class airline ticket to where ever I want to go." Jordan's face registered wonder, so astounded was she by such unleashed demands she had no idea where they came from.

Jake felt the heat, climbing up his face, and frying his eyeballs. Hands thrust into the air, he bellowed, "Where, in hell, do you expect me to get that kind of money? Do you think I have a counterfeit machine hidden under my bed, for Christ sake?"

Emotions threatening to boil over made Jordan's mouth feel papery dry. It was best, she decided, to walk away. Plopping into the chair, she folded her arms, and legs, Indian style. Pretending indifference, she studied the television screen, breathing in, and out, trying to calm her anger. Once her emotions were under control, she spoke confidently. "You will retrieve a thousand times that in drugs when you get Scorpio. My requests are a drop in the bucket compared to the notoriety, promotion, and raise you will receive when you get him."

Completely at his wits end, in no time, Jake reached the chair leaning over his fingertips practically penetrating the padded arms brought his nose within inches from hers. The dark looks he gave should have made her flinch; instead, she gave them right back. Her dainty tongue slipping slowly between her lips, extraordinary long lashes, and the dancing gold flecks of her eyes pinning his, were weapons capable of winning wars. The woman child filling his field of vision was sure as hell intriguing enough to ruin any man. Reflections, plus another whiff of her sweet, clean, fragrance, catching him completely off guard, forced him to seal the deal. "You've got it." A tentative smile, so quick as to be almost nonexistent flashing across her features made him wonder whether he imagined it.

Dumb struck that she bargained, and won, Jordan felt skeptical, and reluctant. His willingness to accept her conditions toppled her whole world like a row of Domino's. Now she had no choice but to do what he demanded.

Standing slowly, she walked woodenly to the bedroom. Opening the garbage bag, she dumped the contents onto the floor every item of clothing she was wearing when he found her remained untouched. Sluggishly she dressed, layer after layer, gagging on the odor. If Margaret's, apartment had not been so orderly, and clean, towels, bleached white, smelling like a bouquet of flowers, her hair shiny, and well-groomed, Jordan probably would have never noticed the filth on the clothing, or smelled the stench. For the first time in her life reality slapping her in the face made embarrassment, flash high inside.

Hesitantly smoothing the camouflage, on the palms of her hands, over her face, and into her hair, she tugged at the short sprigs forcing them into spikes in varying directions. Finally satisfied, she listlessly entered the living room.

Leaning against a wall, arms crossed, Jake waited impatiently wearing layers of clothing, resembling hers, and an old battered hat pulled snugly over his head. Camouflage disguised his face his hair remained in a ponytail.

Before embarking on their dangerous mission, Jake re-minded her of the weapon in his pocket, its sole purpose to shoot her if she made one wrong move a warning ending with the chilling fact he had a reputation of being deadly accurate.

Exiting through the bedroom window, down the fire escape, and into the alley, they entered Jake's car. All too soon, they arrived at the forbidden South side of Chicago four blocks from where Jordan lived. Walking on opposite sides of the street, they covered the remaining distance, passing prostitutes, pimps, and drug pushers, windows, and doors protected by iron bars. Polluting the night air were, boom boxes screaming rap tunes, people shouting expletives, tires screeching, revving engines, motorcycles racing up, and down the street, and an occasional gun-shot.

With his heart beat resonating above all the tumult, Jake watched Jordan, her head held high, undeniably brave, cross-hell's invisible forbidden borders. Gang members glanced at her nonchalantly then returned to the mischief they were planning the scene playing out increasing the thudding of his heart. Blood gushed into his skull when abruptly he wondered if they ignored her presence due to her being unworthy of their trouble, or, because they revered her courage. He chose to believe the later.

No man in his right mind would enter the alley she turned into, desolate, crawling with danger, with its sinister-looking recesses deeply shadowed. For a brief second he wanted to run to her, pluck her from Satan's jaws, and return her to the safety of his apartment, It was too late. Out of nowhere, the alley took on life like insects seeping from cracks; people converged on Jordan, a colony of varied shapes, and sizes, all ages, dressed in unseasonable heavy clothing. Wide eyed he scrutinized them, as they scrounged in garbage cans, as mangy looking men relieved themselves against brick walls, revelry's battering his mind. Suffocating, sultry air made him perspire profusely. Beneath his feet, the pavement moved bringing his back hard against the brick wall behind him. Any second now, he would vomit if not for his throat closing up forcing him to rush to catch his breath. Silently reprimanding himself for being so hell bent to get Scorpio, unexpectedly, he wanted to know all about Jordan, where she came from, how long she survived hell, and how. The vigil dragged on as, through the haze forming over his eyes, he observed homeless people crawl inside cardboard huts to lie on scraps of this, and that, as Jordan did the same awaiting her delivery, a time when his chest twisted into a gigantic, agonizing knot. Why had he not noticed all of this before?

It was two a.m., and two packs of cigarettes later, before a figure carrying a package entering the alley tossed a parcel inside Jordan's hut then disappeared through the veil of darkness. A few minutes later, with Jake a safe distance away, Jordan made her way to a sinister looking apartment complex. After she entered, the minutes seemed to drag on interminably as anxiety lashed him. Never did his heart beat so loudly, so fast, that it sounded like a drum in his ears never did he, know such trepidation, smoke so many cigarettes, or experience the inability to breath. Guilt had raised its ugly head and was staring him in the face.

Whipping himself mentally, he wondered what kind of monster he was to expect a woman to do his dirty work a task few men would do. His plan was insane. A glance at his watch said it was taking her too long in his opinion. Envisioning the worst God only knew what was happening. Just as he was about to enter the building, to pluck Jordan from what he believed to be the jaws of death she reappeared unscathed.

It was dawn before they returned to the apartment in impenetrable silence. Without a word or expression, Jordan hurried into the bathroom to peel off, with frantic haste, the clothing clinging to her damply. Eagerly stuffing them into the bag, she dutifully showered before slipping into the clothing Margaret claimed she secured from a teenager in the complex. Trance like, she quietly entered the bedroom resuming her position on the floor by the bed pulling her legs tightly to her chest, her arms encircling them, offering a resting place for her pounding head. Thoughts were racing through her mind of her hungry friends who lacked shelter, and hot water. Exploding shame churned into nausea, never before did she feel so alone, so frightened. She wanted to cry, but could not, do more to help, but could not. Reality had rudely invaded telling her when this insanity ended she would return to the life that only today, thanks to Margaret, she began questioning. Counter attacking the thought, she decided it was very possible tomorrow would never come, thankfully life as she knew it would finally be over. Feeling exceptionally lethargic, she forced new fears to join the multitude of others deep in the crevices of her subconscious until sleep became a savior.

Jake sat in the kitchen, no beer in hand, no cigarette, all too aware of the risk he was asking Jordan to take. Feeling like the cockroach running across the table, he decided a long hot shower was overdue.

Draining the hot water tank, scrubbing his body red, did nothing to alleviate the shackle's remorse placed on him and, for the first time since John died, he struggled with an overwhelming urge to weep.

Positioned in the folding chair, he no longer questioned its hardness, tonight especially he felt fortunate to have it beneath him.   Self-examination began turning his eyelids to steel.

Chapter 13

Wearing a negligee of white silk and French lace, with coordinating high-heeled slippers, Marla looked cool, and sophisticated, like a model from out of a magazine. Standing at the portable bar, she was preparing a Martini for Scorpio, staring out the French doors at the lucid blue sky promising a beautiful day with temperatures to reach ninety, according to the weather forecast.

Out of the fifteen rooms in the modern brick mansion, the garden chamber was her favorite. Encompassing glass windows were open to emit the late morning warm breeze. A white Polar bear rug accented the multi shaded green tile floor, his opened mouth, and sharp teeth, threatening to nip any bare foot daring to tread upon him. Realistic, and life size, a ceramic Bengal Tiger guarded one corner. Rockers, settees, chairs, and glass top tables, of white wicker added their share of charm. Professionally placed, as if the outdoors was a guest, gardens bloomed in pots over flowing with various flowers, and greenery, potted trees, and tropical plants. Four sets of French doors offered access to an elaborate patio surrounding a kidney shaped pool, its turquoise, shimmering, water perpetually luring Marla's attention. Swimming, and sun bathing, maintained the body tone and tan that enticed her lover, occupations consuming many a glorious hour. Providing the privacy necessary for savoring such luxuries in the nude, tall shrubbery, blossoming bushes, and large urns crammed with colorful bouquets, circumscribed all but one end the unobstructed portion offering a breathtaking view of Lake Michigan. Lounging in her favorite place allowed Marla's imagination to take on wings, as though sea gulls surfing the wind currents. Safety was not a concern, the estate crowning a knoll, was protected by, eight foot, ivy draped, concrete walls', and a state of the art security system. No living thing could penetrate the lofty mansion, the only entrance an ostentatious iron gate at the end of a coiling driveway guarded by a sentry, while several others, with German Shepherds in hand, roamed the rolling five acres twenty-four seven.

Butch was the only predator Marla feared, never knowing when or where he might appear, his cat like, piercing, eyes forever raping her as they traveled the terrains of her body. She knew he lurked, every second of every day, somewhere scrutinizing her, as she swam, and sunbathed, savoring every inch of her physique. Suspicions she reported often to Scorpio only to have him laugh. Butch was harmless, he said besides, it flattered him when other men desired what was his. If Butch ever dared to touch her, with a flick of his wrist, he would castrate him Scorpio's scenario always ending with a reminder there was a big difference between touching, and looking.

In the background, a cell phone rang. Phone pressed to his ear, Scorpio stretched out on a settee, cushioned in a bright floral pattern of green, and peach. A silk bathrobe, of navy and maroon stripes, draped his body, the mid-calf length exposing long, hairy, legs. Freshly showered, and shaved, his raven hair slicked back, with his expensive perfume tainting the air, he was perfection personified.

Though Marla only heard one end of the conversation, she knew better than to show interest, Scorpios' affairs far too dangerous to claim any knowledge. Nevertheless, as her red, manicured, fingers stirred the Martini, hateful reflections became riveted on the person on the other end, the snitch spying on Morgan. Uncomfortable with the treacherous road her thoughts were wandering, prompting the empty, sick, feeling encompassing her, she was greatly relieved when the call ended.

Within seconds, Scorpio's deep, gravely, voice penetrated the silence. "Come here, darling. I am thirsty, and very lonely. You have been away from me much too long." Martini in hand, hips swaying, Marla dutifully complied.

Plucking her empty hand, Scorpio pressed the soft palm to his mouth while the other hand retrieved the drink, and placed it on a table. With an unholy light in his eyes, "Sit with me, my love," he ordered, directing her to the space between his legs, her back against his chest. "You look beautiful today, darling, you always do," his voice as smooth as whiskey, and as dangerous as a scorpion. Immediately he began to explore a breast, an act that soon made his arousal obvious against her back.

Sipping his drink, Scorpios' fingers continued to fondle her, his lips briefly resting on her thick tresses, breath hot upon her skull, as manly hips rhythmically moved heightening his excitement. Becoming lost in memories of the past, Marla became a puppet, prepared, and eager to comply, whenever he decided to pull the invisible strings. She was floating on a dream cloud that turned dark, and foreboding, and then dissipated, when he spoke words dripping with venom.

"Can you imagine that, my love?"

Bewildered, she innocently asked, "What, darling?"

"Morgan claims he is giving me a break for a while."

Trying desperately to act dumb, Marla replied. "He is?"

"You act surprised, my pet. Didn't you hear the conversation?"

Feeling the level of evil enveloping him increase, aware he was testing her reaction, she wisely replied, "You know I pay very little attention to anything that goes on around here, darling."

Appearing satisfied with her reply, Scorpios' hands, traveling up her arms, over her shoulders, curled around her neck, pausing briefly, threateningly, before fingers combed through her hair. As his body slowly undulated against hers, fingers locking together allowed palms to apply pressure to the sides of her skull. "Tell me, my darling, do you believe it?"

Marla felt the dangerous part of Scorpio trying to intimidate her. "No," she choked out; her throat, filled with trepidation, narrowing from knowing Morgan would never give up. And yet, in the deep crevices of her mind, she couldn't help but wonder if miracles still happened now and then.

"Well, I don't either." One hand filled with hair, began twisting, and pulling, the other clutching Marla's shoulder, turned her bringing her stomach against his. His mouth covering hers, gently sucked briefly before his tongue forced her lips apart to probe the inner depths of the warm, moist cavern. Releasing her lips, an index finger replaced his tongue, a command to suckle it. Marla's expertise, and willingness to obey, closed his eyes, and tilted his head back-ward. Gasps spilled forward. Heightened desire quickly brought his hands to her shoulders pushing downward until her lips were even with the part of him aching, and throbbing. Obediently she began fulfilling unspoken wishes, she had no choice, when fingers clutching her hair tightened and began wrenching the delicate threads controlling the motions.

Through a blur of tears, Marla noticed a shadow move in the bushes, as always Butch was watching. Embarrassment, and shame, scorched her body. Blinking back tears of frustration, and fury, brought forth a feverish need to become invisible

Chapter 14

The sly manipulator that she was, in no time Margaret tunneled her way into Jordan's heart. Her compassion, and loving ways, warm, and cheerful apartment, made it wearisome for Jordan to return to the filth, and stench of Jake's flat.

Having earned Jordan's respect, Margaret entrusted her with the freedom to come, and go between apartments providing she returned to Jake's before he arrived each evening. A devious arrangement to be kept top secret she warned. Each day, in return, Margaret insisted Jordan consume two nourishing meals to make up for the cold, greasy, fast, food Jake brought home nightly for supper.

Jordan looked forward to visits with Margaret each experience informative and pleasant, a host of confidences satisfying her enormous curiosity, and providing a solid foundation for their friendship. The handsome man in the picture with Margaret was John's father, the only man in her life. Due to years of verbal and physical abuse, it was a long awaited blessing when he ran off with a younger woman never to be heard from again. The shattering, emotional years, were enough to last a lifetime, Margaret relented. Now, old, and alone, the many males, who pursued her over the years, often came to mind leaving some regrets of remaining single to maintain her independence.

A divorced mother, left with a seven-year old son to raise alone, required working two jobs to survive. As if overnight, John grew up, graduated from high school, and was in a great deal of trouble.

Jake was God sent. Finally, her son had a male role model he could respect, and admire. At the time, John had a lengthy arrest record involving drugs. With Jake's encouragement, and support, he entered rehab, and managed to stay out of trouble. That is, until both began socializing at a new nightclub.

Reminiscing caused pain to streak across Margaret's eyes, the unbearable kind that ages the face, and weakens the heart, a visible agony troubling Jordan. Margaret had, taken up stitches in Jordan's heart, and opened her senses to an assortment of emotions, and revelations. Life had at last blessed her with the friendship of a very special woman someone who believed, sunrises were daily chances to chase dreams, that laughter painted sunsets, and turned rainy days into holidays. To her humiliation, Margaret's stories also reminded Jordan she had no pleasant memories to share with anyone. Twenty-one years had come, and gone like the seasons, filled to the brim, and frothing over, with unspeakable secrets'.

Each afternoon, Jordan sat in a rocker, close to the window, yet far enough away to remain undetected, soaking up the healing powers of the sharp summer rays, breathing in the fresh, reviving air. Listening to the melodies of the street, and stealing glances at the phenomenal woman Margaret was, a person void of idle moments so occupied was she tending to others misfortune, Jordan began assimilating her philosophies. Regardless of striving to see the beauty of the sunset through Margaret's eyes, it signaled the time had come to return to Jake's apartment. The thought of dealing with

Morgan filled her with dread, times when she missed Margaret the most.

Tonight, once inside Jake's apartment, the clicking latch brought reflections of him. Leaning against the wooden door, she thought about their times together how they would go on their missions night after night returning just before dawn how he would be gone before she woke. Habits convincing her he never slept, or ate. The nightly tasks were the only times spent together, hours when he, incessantly battered her with barking orders one minute, then unbearable silence the next, all the while puffing on cigarette after cigarette. Actions he justified by keeping his end of their bargain by showering. Nevertheless, his unkempt hair, beard, and earring remained, and his odious moods never wavered.

The first morning she woke in his bed, Jordan was furious, and unnerved then, as the occurrences continued, she found comfort in the soft, lumpy, mattress, the warmth of the covers carefully tucked around her. Though she had no memories of how she got there, she knew he was responsible. Why each evening he did so, she often wondered. Possibly, a ploy to make her feel guilty about the inconvenience, and discomfort she was causing him. Well, hell would freeze over before she fell into that trap.

With his continual absence, Jordan began to feel as though the apartment was hers, the idea inflating her chest. All too quickly, she grew accustomed to the security the warm showers, and Margaret's fabulous meals, luxuries tugging at yearnings to one day live a normal life. Runaway yearnings occasionally straying down sugar lined avenues until halted by realities stop signs. Lacking the education and finances to secure the necessary status made them nothing more than pipe dreams requiring admirable stamina to end such invasions of foolishness.

Tonight before Jake arrived, once again the cloak of darkness wrapped around the city. Without a word, he tossed onto the table a, grease soaked, bag of food that would go to waste. After changing his clothing, together they entered a world that now seemed a space age away, where she dutifully delivered a package then returned before daybreak.

Ritually, the evening withered away, and the hands of time unleashed another dawn. This morning the sky had turned inside out displaying a dark interior plundering the earth with thundershowers. As usual, Jake was gone and Jordan was alone. Obediently prepared to visit Margaret, she paused at the door, then turned, and as though she was seeing through Margaret's eyes, inspected a living room that had become a battlefield of life. Desperately she searched for answers to pick up her spirits, every fiber sulking from anticipating another day of monotony. Continuing to scrutinize the apartment, she concluded, it was in worse condition than the first time she saw it. Inhaling a whiff of gagging smells made her hastily exit and descended the stairs two at a time. With newly found excitement bubbling over, she charged into Margaret's apartment

Margaret did not have the heart to refuse. Arms laden with rags, cleaning products, and tools, they embarked on a formidable project. Singing, and dancing to music on the radio, they washed windows, opening them to the rain as if inviting the moisture to cleanse the air. They scrubbed the kitchen, and bathroom, organized shelves, and drawers, took out bags of garbage, vacuumed, swept, rearranged, and polished furniture, washed clothes, and bedding. With excitement overflowing, Jordan dared to think of the day as a celebration, a new beginning.

Everything was going well until Jordan opened a closet and found Jake's bulletproof vest tossed into a corner. Upon picking it up, with intentions of hanging it on a hanger, bludgeoning questions twisted her stomach into knots. Margaret releasing a deep sigh behind her prompted the need for answers. "Why doesn't Jake wear the vest?"

"He did until John died." Regrouping distressing thoughts, Margaret paused. "He thinks he is "Superman" I guess does not care anymore and feels if anything happened he would be better off."

Disturbing sensations made Jordan turn, her wide-eyed glance finding features swamped with a sadness embedding wrinkles on Margaret face she had never noticed before. Moisture turned Margaret's blue eyes pale, a problem erased by a quick swipe of her forearm. Moving away, she began busying herself with something she had no thought of doing.

The sadness consuming Margaret dampened the excitement of the day. Calm paraded on until Jordan approached an old wooden trunk, tucked into a corner of the living room, the lid piled high with books, and magazines she planned to organize.

"Jordan, no please do not touch Jake's things he would be very angry if we disturbed anything. Trust me; it is best to leave the dead where they lay."

At the time unable to comprehend Margaret's implication, Jordan went on to challenge another project.

It was seven o'clock before the pair stopped to admire their handiwork. Facing each other, for the first time, Margaret saw what a genuine smile could do to Jordan's exquisite features a smile quickly erased when she offered Jordan a hug. With a cold look of distrust, radically changing her features, Jordan withdrew within herself. Though deeply saddened by her reaction, Margaret dismissed her despondency, said goodnight, and returned to her apartment.

Jordan hated herself for wounding Margaret's feelings. She was not accustomed to affection. Having forgotten what it felt like, it frightened her. The last time someone hugged, or kissed her, she was ten, the night they carried her mother away on a stretcher. Little did she know then, she would never see her again. Jordan clamped down on the tears almost reaching her eyes, almost. A long hot shower eradicated those memories, along with slipping into another set of clothes Margaret claimed a girl in the building outgrew. Jordan knew better, Margaret neglected to remove a few price tags.

Entering the kitchen, she placed a kettle of stew prepared earlier on a burner, and began stirring, the circular motion's brewing visions of Jake's pleasure over their efforts.

Hearing his footsteps, certain he would be thrilled with the surprise, she stepped back to witness his reaction.

The instant the door swung open; at a glance, Jake was convinced his drunken stupor caused him to enter the wrong apartment. Stepping back into the hall he tried focusing on the apartment number, it was his all right. Reentering, he scanned the living room the sight instantly clearing his vision. Nothing was recognizable, as if a hurricane touching down had removed the bad. Never before was it so clean, the air so fresh, as though purified by the storm outside.

Though Jake's pride prevented him from admitting it, what his eyes sought first was Jordan an acknowledgment of eagerness he cursed. The instant he saw her in the kitchen, with relief cleansing his fears, he staggered to the bedroom. There he found, the bed neatly made, clothes put away, a new lamp sitting on the crate, drawers no longer spilling pieces of mashed clothing, the folding lawn chair replaced by a small stuffed one that once belonged to John. Emotions becoming bubbling acid churned, and filled his stomach, his throat.

Doubled over from excruciating grief he walked heavily into the bathroom clutching the sink to steady a body shaking uncontrollably the brightness of the sparkling porcelain forcing his head level. Staring back from a mirror otherwise streaked, and dull, was a crystalline image of a stranger. A man with, long, stringy, hair tied back, unkempt mustache, and beard, an earring, lines creasing a face, smudges under blood shot, and dim eyes. There in the caverns of the strangers, eyes Jake caught a glimpse of the young man whose life was once so full of purpose, of youthful mischief someone that, ages ago, he believed had everything. Abhorrence provoked his fingers to bite into the hard, cold, mass that seemed to be moving. How was that possible when he killed him? That spirit could never rise again. He could not allow it, could not take the chance the pain would return, so convinced was he, if he did not allow anyone back into his life, no one could ever hurt him again.

Pain, that retaliates when we are least prepared, brought on a violent urge to empty a stomach abused by alcohol. On his knees, holding on to the toilet basin, his stomach turned inside out as reality lashed him and ripped open his heart. With sweat drenching his clothing, head spinning, he prayed to the heathens possessing him to let him go.

Truth was staring him in the face, he spent too much time, in the arms of memories, and regret's while drifting on a lonely sea of self-pity. He was much too young to be feeling so goddamn old. It seemed forever before he could stand, when he did, he caught a glimpse of Jordan in the doorway with concern displacing her features.

"Are you all right? Is there anything I can do? Anything I can get you?"

All too quickly, his mind registered that her pale blonde hair had grown out considerably, and shined with luster. Her gold eyes were clear, and bird bright, her cheeks, rosy, lips a darker pink than before, lush, sweet, kissable lips. She had gained much needed weight and, although her blouse was colorful, it remained too large, the short sleeves revealing creamy skin too enticing to his liking. Her jeans, not the same as before, slightly tighter, hugging legs he remembered naked all too well. If she quit becoming more beautiful each day, he could erase her from his mind, his dreams. Only a witch possessed such powers. Damn her to hell she had, ambushed him, taken him completely by surprise, and annihilated his control. How could he, of all people, allow her claws to dig in so deep?

Face turning crimson, body trembling, eyes radiating the fire of self-disgust from wanting her saturated emotions too numerous to separate or censure. "Get out! Get to hell out of here, out of my life. I do not need this shit. I do not want it. I do not need you. Do you hear me? You have nerve disturbing my things, uprooting everything. What do you want from me?"

An almost audible crash said Jordan's mood sunk to the dregs, so much for spending the entire day agonizing over the apartment's appearance and, unbelievably herself. Galvanized by his words, anger poking at startled senses turned her blood cold. The man she was beginning to think of as different, from all the others in the world, was not at all, the realization convulsing her whole body with agony. Despair clamped its icy grip around her throat, turning her breath into the coldest wind of winter, crystallizing each syllable cracking with scorn, and emptying her mind.

"You are nothing more than a barbaric, pompous, ass-hole; all you do is wallow in self-pity? Look at you. Take a close look. You are nothing. You will never be anything. You will never win; you cannot, because Scorpio has proven himself a better man. Look at what you have allowed him to do, he has turned you into a looser, Morgan. The bitch that finished you off must be something. She deserves an award. You want me out of here you have got it, mister. And, if you dare come after me I will cut your balls off, destroy what little manhood she left behind."

Jake blinked, and yanked his head back as though her verbal attack thoroughly thrashed the hell out of him.

Jordan was aghast over the words spewing from her mouth leaving her throat cooked. A heart pounding a tattoo against her ribs heaved her chest. Any second now, her head would explode. Every speck of her, vibrated, hurt more than she ever believed possible.

Never before had her emotions been so tied in knots that she wanted to shout at the top of her lungs the string of curses colliding in her throat. She did not understand what there was about the beast making her want to kill him one second, and hug him the next? Unable to swallow the sob growing in her throat, she spun around barely able to see where she was going through the moisture splashing her eyes. She cursed her disappointment, for believing Jake was different from other men, for expecting more from him. Why, when she already knew men were no good bastards? Why did he make her want more out of life, want to change, climb out of the gutter? Could it be because they were sharing the same gutter?

The door opened, and banged shut she was half way down the hall before Jake caught up with her. When he grabbed her wrist, she turned it this way, and that until his grip somewhat relaxed. To her shock, his fingers began moving, almost absently against the skin of her arms, rather as though he were stroking the fur of a Tiger. Yanking her arms away from him, she hugged herself tightly beneath her breast, attempting to calm her shuddering. Turning, she faced the wall so she would not have to face his sharp gaze. Pressing her forehead against the cold plaster helped keep her upright. Biting quivering lips to maintain her anger prevented her from blurting an apology, bludgeoning her teeth, threatening to escape, and leap into midair.

The sounds of his opened hands coming hard against the wall, one on each side of her shoulders, blocking her escape yet, not touching, made her jump. He was dangerously close, his hot breath on the nape of her neck, the power of his arms, and hands, encompassing.

Despite the space, he maintained between them, the molecules of air trapped, snapped, and crackled like an inferno penetrating her clothes, skin, muscles, and bones, her heart. She wanted to move, shove him away, run, and deny the sudden feeling of delirium setting up residency within. The essence of him exploding entered every pore, bringing to life sensations she never weathered before. Senses that were frightening, yet magnificent, that if she breathed would surely evaporate. Moving was impossible, he would only touch her again and, the powerful bolt of lightning surging through her only seconds ago, this time would surely strike her dead.

She heard his heavy breathing, his mind shifting gears, grinding and yet for unbearable moments he did not speak. Then, when she thought she could bear no more, he gave her heart, pounding like a captured bird, wings when, he whispered into her hair. The heat of those words separating the fine strands, burning through her skull, and melting the armor, she built around her mind.

Jake felt certain words would not get past the ball of choking emotions, occupying his throat, obstructing breathing. Drawing in a deep breathe he began to speak conversationally, hoping to set the tone at a rational level. "Don't, don't go, please. Not like this. I do not like myself much these days so; I do not blame you if you hate my guts. It stops here, Jordan, it has to. We both have been through too much to do this to one another. I will try to make it up to you. I do not make promises; they only get broken in the end anyway. I will not ask you for anything, and do not ask me, because I have nothing left to give. You are my last chance to get Scorpio. He took two people I loved from me. Help me; help me, Jordan, but this time, only if you want to. I know you are scared, and I am too, but together we can be a force to recon with."

Tears pricked Jake's eyes as he fought an impulsive urge to press his mouth into her silky, fragrant hair. While he spoke, he did not have to touch Jordan, he was so totally, so intimately aware of her sweetness, her softness. He marveled how his body covered every inch of her, how it came to life in her presence. Trying to fight memories of her body, awareness struck full force it had been a long dry spell and his male anatomy was screaming for the pleasures only a woman could give. Despite desperately wanting to feel the power of him fill Jordan more unbearable was, he knew, with alarming certainty, he wanted her more than he had ever wanted any woman. On the other hand, reprimanding him were dangerous thoughts, she was much too young, she had been hurt too badly, and both were powerless to erase each other's past.

Jordan's attempt to face him scared the hell out of him. His arms dropped. He stepped back.

Jordan was shocked when Jake made no move to claim what he wanted, considering his arousal was a visible sheet of flame. It was there in his eyes earlier; still he did not touch her. She did not understand why his control meant more to her than anything in her life. She had grown accustomed to his, ruthlessness, and lack of conscience, his violence. Now standing before her was a stranger. She not only felt but also saw the same vibrant current of sexual tension flowing between them that suddenly leaped to life. His, tears falling unchecked, his features, dazing, melting, were brutally battering her senses. She did not know how to handle a man that, one moment wanted to kill her, and the next seemed afraid to touch her.

Suddenly, wanting to reach out to smooth his haggard face, reassure him everything would be all right, she could not. She knew all too well, what would happen. She could never touch another man, ever, men expected, wanted, demanded, and she despised them all. Jake was no different. Oh, but he just proved he was, a frightening revelation tugging her voice from the pit of her stomach, one that sounded less than steady, lifeless, a monotone. "You hurt me."

The shame of the world seemed to weigh down Jake's shoulders, his head, and his eyelids. "I know. I am sorry."

Somehow, Jordan's mangled mind tripped over her heart, flip flopping over his apology, and mustered the nerve to reply, "Don't do it again."

In silence, they returned to the apartment, sat at the table, ate Margaret's stew, and shared the job of washing dishes, and putting them away. Though there was no conversation, it was there, draping all around them, invisible, intangible, compassion linking two kindred spirits.

Jake showered, took over an hour to cut, and shave off his mustache, and beard, a feat rendering his face red, and sore. Tossing the earring in the waste-basket this time, when he looked into the mirror, he saw a rebirth.

Jake took great pains to leave the bathroom as orderly, and clean as he found it. Returning the clean towel to the rack brought reflections of Jordan. A rare smile twitched his mouth as he marveled how one woman could have a temper like a tigress and a forgiving nature like a tranquil sea at low tide.

When he entered the bedroom, he was surprised to find Jordan had willingly climbed into bed, she was asleep, curled up like a kitten, wrapped in a familiar comforter, John's.

Positioning himself in John's chair, with the soft padding hugging his weary body, as though John himself were holding him, Jake gave into grief making him shudder, and drain his tears.

Margaret stood with her back against her living room wall, arms hugged across her chest. She heard the argument, the slamming door, and the footsteps in the hall. She waited for Jordan to descend the steps, and prayed Jake would stop her. When he did, and she heard them return to the apartment, the door close, and silence follow, she exhaled the breath she had been holding. Eyes squeezed shut she muttered another prayer.

Chapter 15

Children's squeals echoing in the hall woke Jordan with a start. Wrenching upright, she listened intently until verifying the sounds as playful giggles. Swiping anxieties moisture from her brow, she slipped weary legs over the edge of the mattress.

Frozen by the sight, she tried focusing on the stranger occupying the chair in the shadowed corner. Fists found, and scrubbed film coated eyes, so positive was she a dream had lingered. Scrutinizing the scene thrust her into the real world; someone was there all right, so sound asleep he was, undisturbed by the commotion outside.

Disbelieving, she remained paralyzed until a photo of Margaret's came to mind the stranger, clean-shaven, looking ten years younger and magnanimously handsome, was indeed Morgan. Quizzically measuring him, she pondered what else there was about him appearing unusual until noticing his earring was gone. Long, blonde hair all that remained of the man who had become disturbingly familiar.

A squall of peculiar feelings, chilling, yet warming at the same time, made her exceedingly uncomfortable. How in the world was she going to fight the new Morgan? Not amused by the only probable answer, she felt an urgent need to put space between them before the labyrinth woke, and con-summed her for breakfast. On tiptoes, cat like in extreme, she snuck out of the room.

Starving, she entered the kitchen searching the cabinets, and refrigerator for something to eat. Rest was good, and food certainly would not hurt, possibly even rid Jake of the poison in his veins, she reasoned. Besides, Margaret's mothering convinced her balanced nutrition was necessary to maintain health, and vitality.

Considering last night's events, she wondered why she wanted to do anything for Jake. Briefly, she thought maybe his new image was to please her. Jake Morgan? How absurd, and yet, she was pleased, more than she wanted to admit. God, her mind was in such a jumble, it never registered that during the cleaning process she threw out everything resembling food.

Occupying the archway, Jake observed Jordan his senses taking leave of his mind. Startling her with his casual good morning, Jordan turned to acknowledge him seconds passing before she could cage fluttering thoughts. The man, the very handsome man, that sat sleeping, immobile, therefore, not a threat, was now awake, and on the prowl. For the life of her, she wondered why her gaze could not meet his, why her knees seemed to be clicking together. She felt light headed. The rumblings, once in her stomach heaving into her chest alerting her to a peril she was powerless to handle.

"Good morning," somehow garbled out. She could say no more her fascination of him, pushing through her mind, propelled all other thoughts into oblivion. A bleached white tee shirt sandwiched his rippling torso, his jeans, fitting like a glove, revealing more than she wanted to see. Stinging embarrassment leveled her eyes with his, the mere glimpse of his features radically destroying her countenance. Not only was Jake rugged, with a temper of a grizzly, but also strikingly good-looking. Most unsettling were his well-rested eyes, the whites no longer pink, and the green, like sparkling emeralds. Panic, pushed to the max, caused warming color to rush her cheeks her gaze careening to the floor searching desperately for what was left of her wits.

Sensing Jordan's uneasiness, Jake became soldier erect, seconds stretching as he waited for her to say something, anything. Unable to control himself, his inspection of her, stretching the limits of time, sent an unfamiliar smoldering need directly to the part of him suddenly coming to life. He took in a long, refreshing drink of her, tasseled hair, wrinkled blouse, and properly fitted jeans, her sweet, adorable, face. Right now, if he got closer, even by a microscopic inch, he would sweep her into his arms, and hold her until they broke and that could not happen, not now, not ever.

Masterfully flipping the switch capable of reversing all pleasurable sensations, Jake reminded himself when he got Scorpio, she would leave, she had to, and he would let her besides, he wanted her to go. She could not stay; there was no reason why she would. He would never trust her or any woman, he would never fall in love again either, but right this second, physically, God, how he wanted her.

Facts began to rally, what if something went wrong, and she did not survive. No, he screamed inwardly trying to abort such perilous reflections she was too young, too innocent, and too damn beautiful. It would be his fault for implicating her. No woman deserved to be in this cataclysm. Just a few more days, and then he would send her away, before the worst happened, before he was tempted to beg her to stay.

Measuring her toes, Jordan mumbled, "I was looking for something for breakfast."

The growling anger Jake was accustomed to calling upon whenever befuddled came to his rescue. "You do not have to worry about me, Jordan. I rarely eat," he snapped.

Gold eyes reached their target, and before she could halt her scalding lecture, words came boiling out, "You should," her words just as clipped.

Now angry about the obscene amount of alcohol he consumed, that had transformed into the worst hangover ever, he sputtered, "Do not push me. I have been on my own a long time. I do as I please, when I please, that will never change. No one has ever taken care of me, no one ever will. I do not expect it. Nor do I want it. Do I make myself clear?"

Jordan could not expel the words seizing her features, turning expressions into a boulder tossed toward him, threatening to crush his banging head. Expressions that said, back off, mister, and get to hell out of my life.

The next move he made, the next word he spoke, could be his Waterloo. Frantically he was trying to mollify a major portion of him wanting to carry her off to the bedroom, and remain there for a year, somehow knowing sampling the tiniest portion of her would mean never letting go. "I will leave some money with Margaret to order some groceries, and have them delivered. I will be back, at ten, tonight. Be dressed, and ready."

Spinning around, he measured the floor with giant steps. There, he had done it. He was safe now, as long as he kept advancing in the opposite direction. If he hurried, the darts' her eyes were shooting would not meet their target.

Jake was gone before Jordan could remove the invisible knife slicing through her ribs, and puncturing her heart.

Chapter 16

A hush fell over the office as astonishment filled the eye's trailing the intruder. A stranger passed Billy's desk, leaving him dubious as to whether or not to stand. There was something familiar in the man's long stride, his build tough, and sinewy, and lean like a cowboy, the blonde hair tied back dangling between shoulder blades, the cigarette spewing smoke, that said it was Morgan. Caught off guard Billy was, he had never seen Jake so well groomed.

Sounds of casters on chairs rolling on the tiled floor, mingling with whispers, turned Jake. Eyebrow raised his austere look sufficient intimidation to return everyone to work, and reposition Billy into his chair.

Solemnly entering his office, closing, and locking the door, Jake tugged on the cord to the blinds to block the view of onlookers from the outer office. Settled at his desk, he unlocked a drawer to retrieve, an envelope filled with information, and photos collected over the past few weeks.

In disguise, he trailed, and recorded every move of all known couriers delivering packages to Jordan, as well as, everyone assigned to his team. Spread before him documented proof of, places frequented, their friend's, and acquaintances. Leaving no stone unturned, Jake dug into each man's past, their, childhood, old girlfriend's, schools, Church's, military records', searching for anything the least bit suspicious. Spreading the data before him, littering the entire desk, like a blind person seeing the sunrise for the first time, it occurred to him the information would not have been possible without Jordan's help.

In a few weeks, he had accomplished more than in two years thanks to a young girl who ran away at sixteen putting her life in jeopardy by delivering drugs. Funds earned not intended for, buying dope for her own use, to get off the streets, or to provide sustenance, or insure a better life. Using his badge, he procured answers from unwilling couriers that sat him on his haunches. A dull ache, leaving his heart, became a shooting pain joining the multitude of others in his skull as he pondered the reasons Jordan jeopardized her life. Never in a million years did he suspect the money helped support a shelter for run-a-way teens that Jordan was living the way she wanted to, the way she had to, the only way she could survive each day.

Picking up a glossy, colored, photograph sticking out from all the others, for the hundredth time he reviewed the attached missing person's report filed five years ago. The young girl, dressed, and groomed to appear much older, was the most striking young woman he had ever laid eyes' on, her hair, well beyond her shoulders, was thick, and wavy, her complexion flawless, her mouth capable of tempting a saint, and her eyes, as bewitching as a tigers.

Unable to look any longer, the photo, slipping through tired fingers, fell to his lap. Closing his eyes, Jake's head came sharply against the back of the chair. His hostage made one huge mistake by revealing her real name. Enlisting the help of experts who owed him favor's, in no time, the thousand pieces of Jordan's puzzle were pieced together. Now, that the picture was crystal clear, God, how he wished he had allowed the past to stay buried. The death of Jordan's mother raised suspicion when, a day after she contacted an agency for battered women, she reportedly took an overdose of drugs. Records disclosed, she feared for her life, and that of her young daughter. Two weeks later, due to the lack of conclusive evidence, the authorities closed the case and returned Jordan to her father.

Over a period of years, hospital accounts revealed treating a Jordan Montgomery for questionable cuts, burns, bruises, and fractures. Although there were, no tests permitted by her father, doctors' suspected sexual molestation a theory leading Jake's investigators to X-rated photos, of Jordan as the primary subject. Feeling like the slime of the earth for probing, Jake could not bring himself to view them. Vowing he never would, he sealed the information in an envelope, and placed it in a drawer securely locked until he could destroy them.

Lids' flicking open allowed green eyes' to find the key lying on top of the information. Yesterday, he secured a safety deposit box containing, a first class airline voucher and fifty thousand dollars, all the money he had left. Little did Brenda know she did not get everything? Somehow, knowing one day the funds would come in handy he decided Jordan had earned, and deserved every dime. It was worth that, and more, to get Scorpio, to settle a feud going on too long.

As though a ricocheting bullet, and as painful, Jake's thoughts returned to Jordan's scarlet past. Again, he wondered how such a young girl garnered the guts to flee from a beastly father. Reflections of the past confrontations between them brought a twitch of a smile to the corner of his mouth, a grin lost the moment his glance found, and scanned, the missing person's report her father filed. Frank Montgomery was a no-good alcoholic, who never worked, who had a lengthy list of arrests for pornography, drugs, and prostitution. It was fitting he died of a brutal knife attack in his apartment during an orgy. His demise saved Jake from, hunting him down, and making him pay for what he had done to Jordan.

At once, the guilt over his confrontation with Jordan the previous night pried apart his ribs. It was his fault, knowing the hurting side of pain, he should have understood when people are most troubled they crawl within themselves where they become something they are not. That day he received the details of Jordan's past. Disgusted with himself for snooping, nauseated by the world, and the people in it, who harmed, and defiled innocent children, he drank, and drank. Coming home to discover Jordan's efforts, the goodness remaining inside a human stripped of everything since a small child; he despised himself for meddling, for knowing, for the sexual fantasies she provided in his dreams.

Despite the hell he went through as a youngster, it was not a level even close to, what Jordan survived, regardless she went on with her life, maybe not headed in the right direction, yet she did not give up, not as he did. She was doing the very best she knew how, and if it was the last thing he did, he would make up to her for all the bad of the world.

Lowering the report to his lap, his head draped in shame, eyelids sealed, he shuddered at the possibility the horror would never be over for Jordan. God, how could a father condemn his child to a life of hell, of distrusting, and hating men, a life without love, or someone to care, and provide for her, a home, and children?

Never before did he want to scream his anger, and frustrations. The worst part of knowing was he could never tell her or anyone, they were dark secrets that would become his private hell. On her own, Jordan became a proud, stubborn, and self-sufficient person. If she ever suspected he knew, he would never see her again. Right now, the wringing of his heart, the emptiness in the pit of his stomach, told him he would never survive. Adding to his suffering, he was no better than her father was, he had used her by drawing her into a mess that could cost her the life she deserved to live in any manner she chose. Determination raised his head, straightened his shoulders, one way, or another, he was going to get her out of this mess alive. At least, when she walked away, and he knew she would; maybe, just maybe he would get to see her, if only from a distance.

Feeling the need for urgent remedies, he reassured him-self soon his vendetta would end. Plans for a raid, certain to make Chicago tabloids, were almost complete. The problem was, to insure its success Jordan had to make one more delivery before giving her the freedom he understood she needed. Right now, suspicions as to why the thought of her leaving felt like a ton pressing on his chest became an unbearable pain.

Not for one minute did Billy like being left out of what he knew Jake was planning. Something was going down, something big; it filled the air all around Jake. Just as he accumulated enough nerve to reach Jake's office, McMaster's, the head of the agency, halted him, "Get Jake and both of you get your asses in my office, pronto," his bellow bringing everyone to attention.

"Yes, sir," Billy replied. Before his knuckles met wood, Jake jerked the door open.

"Sounds like he is pretty pissed," Billy said with a smirk.

Patting his young sidekick on the shoulder, Jake reiterated, "What else is new. Come on, let's get this over with." Together they entered McMaster's office.

With shirtsleeves rolled up, tie loosened around his broad neck, McMaster's sat forward in his chair, beefy arms propped on his desk. Not only did his fifty something years, and experience demand respect, but also his six foot two, two hundred, and fifty pounds. Once riled, no one in his or her right mind would challenge him, except for Jake.

"Sit," McMaster's demanded. Billy complied. Jake re-fused.

Tossing the pencil he was tapping wildly on his desk, McMaster's commanded. "Dammit, Jake, sit your ass down."

Again, Jake refused.

"Have it your way, you stubborn jackass but, before you leave this office I want to know what in hell has been going on during the past few weeks. Your team has made no raids, or arrests, I have received no reports, in fact, have no information at all as to what you jerk offs' have been doing. Pray tell, did you declare a vacation? It is a, Goddamn, jungle out there. Almost as if the gangsters think, we have given up, given them carte blanches" for Christ's sake. There have been five unsolved murders, three drive-by shootings, and two gang fights."

Stopping short as if he just noticed, McMaster's exclaimed, "Dammit Jake, what, in hell, happened to your earring, beard, and mustache? Don't tell me this is your new idea of a disguise?"

With defiance oozing from every pore, Jake shot Mike a heated glance of displeasure over his comments. "You can let Billy off the hook. I put him in charge, and asked him to lay low for a while. He followed orders. This is between the two of us, let Billy get back to work."

"He is your partner, just in case you have not noticed you are not God, Morgan. As much as you would like to, you cannot shut out everybody and work alone. I realize you have a personal grudge against Scorpio but, your men are your responsibility, they need your guidance. I want Billy groomed to take your place because sure as shit you are determined to get your ass killed." Raising a beefy fist, he pointed a finger at Jake. "You are the best I have, Morgan. The head honchos are on my ass, and as long as they are, I will be up yours. Got that?"

Jake's eyebrows shot up, his look harder if anything. Gritted teeth made the muscles in his cheeks ripple. Face flushed, eyes boring into McMasters, opened hands slammed the desk as, he leaned over to shout, "Stick it, Mike. You will get nothing out of me as long as Billy is in this room. If Scorpio wants me, he can come get me. I am not risking one of my men until I perfect my next move. The next time I go after Scorpio, he is going down."

Thoughts rushed Billy he had what he was after, Jake no longer trusted him, or anyone, which meant only one thing; Jake suspected a spy among them. It would be better to lay low, allow him some time, and space. There had to be a way of finding out what his plans were. There had to be.

Mike's face became a twisted scowl his eye's never leaving Jake's as he spoke to Billy, "Go ahead son, leave."

Through the windows in his office, Mike patiently watched as Billy returned to his desk. When it was safe to speak, he said, "You think Scorpio has a spy within the agency, don't you, who for God's sake?"

Chapter 17

Who did Jake think he was, ordering her around? Well, he had another guess coming Jordan fumed. There was no excuse for an old man to be so grumpy. Old man, hell, he was far from an old man. Lacking the beard, mustache, and earring, he was eye catching, and never before did any man mesmerize her. Embittered by the attraction, yet, curious as a kitten, she could not help but wonder about the female who shattered the life of someone as strong, and determined as Jake, who was she? Speculating brought about various expletives. Deliberately defying Jake's warning, she moved to the window watching as he entered his car, and speed away. This was her chance; all she would have to do is exit through the bedroom window, and climb down the fire escape. It was so ridiculously easy she wondered why she had not done it before. What was stopping her?

Finally convinced she could do it, she turned, her eyes unintentionally staling on the trunk in the corner. Inquisitiveness erased all thoughts of escaping. "It was better to leave the dead where they lay, Margaret warned. How could she leave without knowing more about what ate at Jake's insides causing him to be so mean, and miserable?

Etching to memory the exact position of each item re-moved from the top, she placed them in neat piles. Not yet ready to open the lid, she sat back on her haunches, fingers trembling as they hesitated on the latch remembering word for word, what Jake said, "Don't go snooping through my things." Right now, she was nothing more than a spy was. Why was she interested? Why did she care?

Sitting Indian style, glassy eyed, an undetermined length of time passed while Jordan stared at the memorabilia strewn on the floor. Among the debris several pictures of John, and Margaret, a church, a Priest, and Jake. Peculiar, she thought, there were no traces of a man old enough to be his father in fact; the majority of the photographs were of a, compelling, beautiful, woman holding a child at various stages of growth, the last, when the child was probably no older than four or five. There was no mistaking the child resembled his mother, except for his eyes.

Once more Jordan's attention returned to a newspaper article pertaining to the death of Jake's mother, the tragedy unearthing too vividly her own experience. Feeling anguish, for Jake, for herself, she frantically searched the stack of information for clues as to what happened to him after she died, finding nothing until his teenage years. Jake's life seemed to stop until high school when he played on the football team, a photo of him in uniform she purposely turned over. Daring a second glimpse, she flipped over another snapshot, a colored depiction of Jake that stole her breath, and made her wonder at the feelings rushing her veins. Despite the fact, it was of an entire group of Police Academy graduates, meticulously groomed, and proudly displaying their uniform, she saw only Jake a man who had an arsenal of alluring smiles she had never seen, one who could charm his way through life with a wink, and a grin.

The photograph, only one of the disturbing discoveries in the pile of treasures, she kept trying to ignore. Too many others were of a breathtaking woman with striking features bringing envy and jealousy into prominence. She had raven color shoulder length hair, bronze skin accenting eyes of coal, generous eyebrows, and thick lashes. Jordan sighed; she was model perfect, her elaborate wardrobe flaunting a trim build along with other unspeakable attributes.

Jake apparently had every poster advertising Brenda Star's performances in themselves announcing the success of her singing career. Plucking a packet of matches from the array of bittersweet memories, Jordan recalled Margaret saying everything was fine until John, and Jake, started going to a nightclub, no doubt the one named on the packet. Drawing her knees to her chest, hugging them tightly, she studied the photos of Jake, and Brenda together one of Jake wearing a white tuxedo, his hair short, well groomed, with his cheek pressed against Brenda's, another of them kissing, and another, and another of the captivating pair, obviously in love. In the end, he learned his life with her had been nothing more than smoke, and mirrors that enemies came with smiles stroking with one hand while the other plunged the knife in deep.

Love, she reflected, meant nothing but pain, even Jake found that out. Then again, if that was true, why did people hold hands, hug, look at each other with stars in their eyes, kiss, marry, have children? On the streets, while observing men, some appeared to be gentle, kind, and caring still, she could not help but compare the love she had known from her mother to that of men. In conclusion, there was no such thing as love between the sexes. Men were nothing more than Neanderthals who thought, women's willingness came down to a few inches of penis. Her mother made a huge mistake of trusting a man, so did Margaret, both paid the price, and as a young child so did she, one she would never pay again. Loathsome memories replaced the brief reflections of kind, gentle, loving men. "No!" Jordan screamed aloud, her hands quickly covering her face as if they could block out the horror's parading before her. She could never love, ever, especially Jake. Then why did she have all she could do to keep from ripping every picture of Brenda to shreds'.

So overwhelmed with grief was she, she did not hear the footsteps, coming up the stairs, down the hall, the door knob turn, the door open, nor did she see the person standing behind her. She heard nothing until a voice slammed her heart against her ribs.

"Oh, no, Jordan, my dear, mercy, mercy, you should not have, you simply should not have." Coming hard to her knees, Margaret hurriedly began picking up the clutter; there was no mistaking the tears of fear, and frenzy in her eyes.

"Margaret! I am sorry, so sorry. I did not mean."

"Help me quickly, Jordan, quickly. If Jake finds out you snooped, God only knows what he would do. Dear me, dear me he has not looked at Brenda's pictures in two years, if he did hurry Jordan, hurry."

Returning to Margaret's apartment, terrible silence brewed along with a pot of coffee. Over several steaming cups, gradually Jordan learned about the woman who stole the life, and spirit from Jake, the only woman he ever loved, the woman he sacrificed everything for to keep her in the manner she craved, one whose features remarkably resembled his mother. They were together a year before Jake proposed, a diamond

Brenda returned making it clear it was not good enough. Afterward, he learned the awful truth about Brenda, and the other man.

There in Margaret's eyes was a hatred Jordan thought only she held the copyright for, a tangible hatred capable of making anyone do anything. She wondered if Margaret was just like her, capable of murder, like a strobe light, she saw it flashing in her eyes each time Margaret spoke of Brenda.

Clumps of tissue's lay on the table, and though Margaret continued to sniffle, her eyes' red, and puffy, her nose sore, Jordan envied her discomforts. Feeling so much sympathy for Margaret, for Jake, she wanted to cry, desperately wanted to, but could not, her mind a mass of confusion with questions running amuck. Why did Margaret care about Jake? Why did she love him so? Why did she feel as though Margaret loved Jake more than she did her own son?

Answers came when Margaret retrieved a scrapbook containing all the front-page newspaper articles since she had known Jake, interpreting how many times he survived, gunshot wounds, stabbings, beatings, and yet, persisted. Jake was a real life superman, an all American Hero, Margaret's hero. Jake tried to save her son, Margaret continued, but John took after his father who possessed a self-destruct button. John lived longer only because of Jake, the first man Margaret ever knew that was worth a grain of salt. She loved him, loved him with all her heart. She did not have to tell Jordan, she knew, she felt it, saw it, a powerful love Jordan wanted desperately to believe in, yet was beginning to resent.

The day drained Jordan both emotionally, and physically. When Jake arrived, he never spoke nor did his eyes meet hers. On his way to the bedroom, beneath lowered lashes, she stole a glimpse of him for the first time seeing a different man. Yes, she reflected, they were alike, having weathered the same storms. How could she hate someone that had leaped the same hurtles as she, someone Margaret loved? For whatever reason, she felt compelled to help get Scorpio, maybe then Jake could go on with his life, Margaret could be happy, and she could be free.

Ever so slowly Jordan began dressing, cringing with each layer of clothing smothering her skin, and gagging at the odor churning her stomach. While applying the camouflage, when repulsion crawled over her skin, the only thing staying those feelings was imagining the day, she would finally burn the clothes as a symbol of freedom, the day she would embark on a new life.

Earlier that morning standing, kiddy corner, in the alley across the street from Jake's apartment building, someone watched him drive away, a thirty five-millimeter camera with a telescopic lens in hand aimed at his apartment window. As Jordan stood framed by glass, there was a series of clicks. That night waiting for Billy under his door in a manila envelope was several enlarged photographs with a note attached saying, "Investigate."

Flipping through the photos, Billy thought how breath-taking, the woman was, how remarkably beautiful. For the longest time he was, stricken deaf, and dumb by her tiger-eyes. Curiosity made him wonder, whom she was, where she came from, how she fit into this mess. It was not until his eyes strayed away from her features that he recognized the apartment building. Like a wad of crinkling foil, his heart became a shriveled ball.

Chapter 18

The library was awe-inspiring with floor to ceiling mahogany bookcases adorning three walls, on the other, a life size portrait of Marla wearing a black, strapless, evening gown. In front of the painting, an elaborately carved mahogany desk embellished with typical office items, among them several preferred snapshots of Scorpios' adored mistress. A burgundy leather sofa added to the masculine ambience beneath which impeccably clean parquet floors glistened.

Stretched out on a window seat, nestled between the bookcases, Marla gazed out the only window grand enough to permit an unobstructed vista of the, rolling green lawn, brilliant flowers, and abundant trees. In the background, sailboats seemed to take on wings against the blue horizon. She was listening to the bird's chirping welcoming the sun, and warmth, or, as she elected to presume, offering their thanks for the seed she distributed earlier in assorted bird feeders. Satisfied her only friends were well fed, she smiled as they frolicked, and bathed in their grand marble birdbath.

As her thoughts meandered, as if a child in a cosmos of make-believe, she was unaware of, the ringing phone or, the conversation-taking place, Scorpios' flushed face, his mashing teeth. She heard nothing until he hurled the phone against the wall, a shattering sound jerking her from revelry. The calm that before had sprawled around her in sunny innocence now held an ambience of expectation.

Positioned in a chair in the hallway awaiting orders, the same noise jerked Butch instantly to his feet. Standing in the doorway, his overly trained muscles bulging from adrenaline signaled, he was alert, and ready.

"That son of a bitch," Scorpio roared trampling the Aubusson carpet in front of the desk, his exaggerated movements commanding Marla's attention.

"What is it, darling? Why are you upset?"

"Morgan, who else, he has cleaned up his act, and is looking better than when we first met, wouldn't you know, just when I am ready for the kill, a broad enters his life, a young, beautiful woman, who is sharing his apartment."

Scorpio now held Marla's undivided attention.

Coming swiftly to her feet, Marla walked heavily to the mini bar, and threw open the doors. Fumbling with the contents, "Impossible," her thoughts stampeded there had to be more to the story Jake, would never, and could never. The barest reflection of Morgan, that once caused her heart to rumble, her body to perspire with want, instead, made profanities curl her tongue. One hundred percent jealousy, governing her actions, poured an excessive amount of whiskey into a glass that she gulped in one swig.

Mind swimming in boiling thoughts, Marla became frightened Scorpio might see or hear her Richter scale reactions. Although outwardly, she was working hard at remaining calm, hateful reflections, ranted, and rallied controlling the toe of a shoe tapping the floor to heart palpitations. Who was the slut? Where did she come from? What did she look like?

With words as sweet as honey, yet, tainted with sarcasm, Scorpio asked, "Something troubling you, my love?"

Biting her tongue to keep anger stashed inside, "Certainly not," Marla answered much too quickly. Trying to regulate the emotions soaring like a rocket she purred, "What makes you think that, darling?" Training lips into a, sweet, false smile Marla turned, shock realigning her features upon discovering Scorpio mere inches from her face.

Suddenly, strong hands securing trim arms just below the shoulders held them rigid. An off the shoulder bodysuit, clinging to heaving, braless breasts, exposed the magnitude of her fright. Greedily, Scorpios' mouth found hers crushing, and grinding whiskey tainted lips. His body pressing forward, securing her hips, and buttocks against the cabinet, permitted his arousal to heave roughly against tender flesh, and fragile bone. Releasing their hold, fingers snatched the stretch material of her bodice, and with one quick tug downward exposed her breasts.

"What's troubling you, my dear? Are you thinking about Morgan? How he once held you, kissed you, screwed you? Was he such a stallion I haven't erased him from your mind?" Pressing harder against her his, hands crushing her breasts, nails practically piercing translucent skin, he continued, "You are mine. You will always be mine. Do not forget it? He will never have you again, never. I will kill you both first."

One hand held her buttocks securely against him, the other, sliding between her breasts, grazing her collarbone, and neck, stopped to clutch her chin. Menacing vice like fingertips began crushing the delicate bone beneath. "Kiss me kiss me as you would, Morgan. Show me you have forgotten what it is like to lay beneath him, convince me or I will choke the life from you."

Left no choice but to comply, opening her mouth, Marla obeyed, her tongue slipping past Scorpio's' lips, dancing, teasing, and tormenting. Thin, feminine, fingers coming between his legs caressed as mouths continued to devour. Finding his zipper she lowered it, in response, he raised her skintight mini skirt to gain access to black, silk, panties, that he ripped from her body.

Just when she believed the battle was in her favor, abruptly raising his mouth from bruised lips, Scorpio summoned fears' staph. "Come here, Butch. I do not want you to miss the entertainment." Hands balling into tight fists, Marla had to reign in the urge to panic.

Butch did as commanded stopping a few feet away, his shocked expression saying what he could not.

Scorpio's eyes stabbed Butches. "I know you watch, and listen. I want you to see up close the sumptuous body I have claimed." Out of the corner of his eyes he saw what Marla's fingers were struggling to reach. "Most importantly, make sure my darling mistress does not stab me in the back with the ice pick she seeks."

Terror, and disbelief, widened Marla's eyes, within; one could see her mind adrift, flashing memories of long ago when she believed Scorpio's million lines, his empty words of love. If he truly loved her he would not have done all the cruel things he did to her in the past, but then, she should have expected a man like him would. A man she grew to care about, the one she did everything to please, in truth was insane. She was no different from the others, just like them it was just a matter of time until he left her in the dirt. Before she was too blind to see, what had been happening to her, what kind of clown she had become? During the past two years, allowing Scorpio to seize her identity, never did she think the day would come when all she wanted was a life of simple pleasures.

Every road eventually ended; Scorpio's betrayal indelibly marked her life. The time was here to put on her goodbye shoes. Enduring the hollow churning feeling in her stomach, gagging on the need to cry, even as she ruthlessly denied herself the privilege, she prayed for the power to summon a lightning bolt that would strike both men dead.

Continuing to heave his body against hers, Scorpio persisted, "When I am through, maybe I will give her to you, Butch, then, you can do all the things filling your dreams. Am I right, Butch? Right now, you would like nothing better than to do what I am doing."

Drained by the thoughts racing endlessly through her mind, all Marla could do was, stare at Butch with wide blank eyes. She watched as Butch's jaw clenched shut, as vacancy and a coldness hinting at a temper came to his eyes, reactions she never witnessed before. Concentrating solely on Scorpio, his brows scaled his forehead with undisguised contempt.

During his five years of faithful service, Butch never witnessed Scorpio, so enraged, so demented. What terrified him more Scorpio knew how he felt about Marla? "Yes, sir," he wisely answered, not daring to say anything else.

The hands on Marla's buttocks, kneading them, suddenly lifting her directed her legs around a narrow waist. "Are you watching, Butch," Scorpio taunted.

In quick succession, Butch saw the pain on Marla's face, the terror, the shock, and cowered at her stifled scream cut off by Scorpio's smothering lips. Cringing, Butch watched as Scorpio grabbed her waist to direct, rapid painful moves. He was only human the color of his skin did not mean he was not a man with the same desires as any other. Of course, he wanted Marla, wanted every part of her, and as Butch scrutinized his master seeking pleasure, he could only imagine the ecstasy of changing places. Still, he despised Scorpio's manipulation, for knowing how much he loved Marla, and what he would give to have her.

Scorpios' last thrust, slamming Marla's body against the cabinet knocking the wind from her, bashed her head against the wall. Wanting desperately to hide from the horrified expression twisting Marla's face, Butch did not dare. Clenching his knuckles at his side was all that prevented him from plunging a tight fist through Scorpios' back to rip his heart out.

Regaining composure, Scorpio jerked the teeth of his zipper closed. Without raising Marla's top to cover her breasts, or lowering her skirt, he grasped her shoulders. Turning her, holding her back firmly against his chest, allowed Butch a better view. "Look, Butch, look at her! Never forget her beauty, and fantasize of the day you will have her. She will never live to screw Morgan again I will give her to you first. She thinks I am dumb, thinks I do not know she still loves the bastard, and you, if only you could see your eyes." Laughing fiendishly, Scorpio rambled on. "Look, Marla, see what you have done to poor Butch, his arousal evident along with the sweat on his brow."

Meticulously manicured nails dug into Marla's skin as Scorpio shook her. Pressing his mouth hard against her ear, his sick torture continued. "Before I am through, Morgan will lie at my feet begging, and you, my precious, will watch him die. Then, I will give you to Butch and, with great pleasure, watch as he makes you his sex goddess. Oh, believe me; he will do everything I tell him." Scorpios' eyes that of a mad man, speared Butch. "Won't you Butch, because if you don't I will put a bullet between her eyes."

A forceful shove sent Marla hard against Butch's chest. Feeling the heat of his lust made her sick to her stomach and her head whirl. The urge to vomit, buckled her knees beneath her.

Grabbing Marla Butch barely prevented her from falling. Waiting until Scorpio stomped from the room; he carried her to the sofa where he, gently raised the top of her body suit to cover her breasts, lowered her skirt, and brushed back sweat drenched hair from her face. Plucking his hanky, he dabbed at tears flowing in a steady stream.

Shock prevented Marla from speaking. Her mind was riveted on Scorpios' determination to kill Jake. Apparently Scorpio did not know, in the past she would do anything for him, did, but, today he made the biggest mistake of his life, again he made her choose. This time, he lost.

Brenda Star was the Parakeet Clubs featured entertainer. For several weeks, each time Jake drove past the Club, the billboards outside drew his attention to the most beautiful woman he had ever seen. Curious, one night Jake, and John decided to check the club out. Spending the evening listening to her sing convinced him she was the woman he had been waiting for all he had to do was persuade her.

At the time, Jake did not know Scorpio owned the Parakeet Club. Using her stage name of Brenda Star, following Scorpios instructions, Marla lured Jake into a relationship purposely meant to win his love, and trust, and to enable Scorpio to strip him of everything.

Unintentionally, Marla fell in love with Jake, despite the magnetic force drawing her to Scorpio. Later, she did not know if it was Scorpio's, power, money, or fear of him, but somehow, he convinced her, Morgan would never be good enough for her. If his attentions were not testimony enough, his lavish gifts were. By the time she realized who, and what Scorpio was, it was too late. Knowing too much about Scorpio, he demanded she prove her loyalty. What he asked her to do made her no better than he was.

Tonight, it was clear; Scorpio was a hateful, murdering monster. She was not a complete idiot; she had lost his favor. Just as quickly as it began, their relationship was over. Scorpio meant exactly what he said, after killing Jake; he would give her to Butch. Just imagining the orders he would give Butch, sent shivers of alarm up her spine.

Unable to bear the possibility of Morgan's death, Marla could not allow Scorpio to win. She played a big enough part in destroying Morgan. In the past, she was secure in knowing Jake would eventually bring Scorpio to his knees, now after what just happened, she was not at all sure. Somehow, there had to be a way to protect the only man she ever loved.

Butch carried Marla's stiff, sore body to her bedroom. Adjusting the pillows beneath her head, somehow he endured her sobbing while covering her with a comforter. Descending the stairs, he moved to the bar previously forbidden to him to pour a good amount of whiskey. Stirring treasonous thoughts into a whirlpool, he made a secret vow, the day Scorpio dared to harm a hair on Marla's head; he would draw his last breath.

Chapter 19

In disguise, Jake, and Jordan climbed out the bedroom window, and down the fire escape routinely permitting access to the alleyway. They entered a car that, as an extra precaution, Jake consistently made certain was never the same. Normally, a monotonous, routine, except tonight, as they rode in crushing silence, each heard the clamor of the others beating heart.

Two worlds colliding created a current, each tiny ripple telling them nothing would ever be the same. Now, as static cracked in the air, even the wind paused for a moment. Having lost its memory, the moon refused to shine leaving the dome overhead dark, the air stagnant. Breaking all records for the month of July the temperature was hot, and excessively humid. Opening the car windows emitted a slight breeze doing little to relieve the perspiration dripping irritatingly beneath layered clothing.

Looking beyond the windshield, Jake noticed the clouds swirling, and twisting, in the ever-rising wind. In the distance, a loud angry rumble of thunder warned of a pending storm. Flashing lightening made the clouds blink. A light mist began coating the glass. To him, it seemed as though Mother Nature was mimicking how he was whipping himself mentally.

Jake's brooding quirks; eyebrows knitted together, end-less smoking, thumbs drumming the steering wheel, mumbling to himself, made Jordan squirm in her seat. At every stoplight, and everyone that just happened to be in his way, even some that were not, he screamed profanities followed by flipping the bird. Four times, he swiped his forehead with his sleeve.

Sheets of rain began blasting the car the windshield wipers swishing back, and forth trying to hold it back. The brewing squall, reminded Jordan how much she hated storms as a child, how she ran and hid under her bed whenever it thundered Lost in those frightening memories a blasting horn jerking Jordan upright made her nerves stand on end. Making matters worse, the driver responsible made an obscene gesture as he veered around their car, and sped on.

As if a demon possessed her, from out of nowhere, a quick thrust of her hand plucked the cigarette from Jake's mouth, and tossed it out the window. "These goddamn things are going to kill you," she sputtered, suddenly horrified by the spontaneous act she just committed.

Wrenching the steering wheel hard to the right, their car barely missed another as Jake abruptly changed lanes. Squealing brakes pitched them forward, the tires hitting the curb bringing the vehicle to a jarring halt. All the while Jake wondered what there was about Jordan that continually irritated the hell out of him.

It appeared as though the back of his hand would connect with her face as he swung, his fist connecting with a powerful jolt against the seat instead. Eyebrows climbing into his hair, eyes ablaze, with the entire belligerence he was capable of, he bellowed, "God Dammit, do not ever do that again. Jesus Christ, Jordan, you will be the death of me long before my fucking cigarettes." In the face of her upset, his animosity became unstable.

Her hand finding the car door handle twisted and jerked. It took an iron grip to thwart her frantic attempt to exit the car; her eye's flaring wide pivoting to challenge his. Reacting like a cornered animal, her hand slapped his that held her. "Let me go! Now," she shrieked, and with full intentions of slapping his face, she swung again.

Jake's quick reflexes secured both wrists firmly in a warm, damp grip. "You are not going anywhere."

Trying to decipher whether his expression was as furious as his tone, even though it was not, she hissed like a rattlesnake. "The hell I'm not. You either let me out of this car or tell me why you are brooding. Why suddenly you seem so afraid? If you do not let go of me this instant, I will scream bloody murder, bite your nose off," the silliness of her last statement making her smile.

Jake's defense mechanisms seemed to go all to hell when it came to Jordan. At first, he smiled back unrepentantly, and then could not stop the genuine smile swiftly replacing it at the thought of what she said. Knowing she would do exactly what she said made his head shake expressing his wonder of her. At once he wondered when she became his only weakness.

As eyelids slowly shaded emerald gems, he eased his holds on her wrists. When the shades rose, there was no mistaking the raw desire flaring within, the kind Jordan was suddenly battling herself making it difficult to understand her crippling disappointment when his hands abruptly fell away. Although his hold on her was both firm, and singeing, beneath she felt a peculiar tenderness that, for some irrational reason, made her want to draw him into her arms, maybe even . . . kiss him.

Adding to her confusion, when he reached across, and opened her door she believed him to be an idiot. Penetrating the unbearable silence a voice capable of melting steel said, "Go ahead, get out, you are through. You are free to go. I have all the information I need." Returning to his position, arms draped over the steering wheel, provided a resting place for his throbbing forehead.

Baffled, for a moment, Jordan did nothing before impulsively slamming the door shut. At the same instant, her voice escaped the snarled web of her thoughts. "I will not and, you cannot make me. I said I would help you and I never go back on my word. Besides, until you get Scorpio, you will not be able to meet the terms of our agreement. Perhaps you have forgotten?"

Eyes tightly sealed; Jake tried valiantly to ward off the lust gathering all too quickly in his center, twisting his guts into one gigantic ball of heat. Jordan could not know he was hanging on to the wheel for dear life trying to calm the unpredictable component of him that, one second wanted to thrash the hell of out her, the next pull her into his arms. If he did, surely, he would kiss the, soft, luscious, lips he was dying to savor, draw them into his mouth, and spread them open, so he could search out the nectar within to see if it tasted as sweet as imagined. Hell, right now, he would walk fire, and brimstone to kiss every part of her, just once.

Instead, eyes, expressing amusement over her reminder of their agreement, glided toward hers. Clashing emerald, and gold gems turned into red-hot coals. No longer did Jake see Jordan's rags, camouflaged hair, and face, nor could he smell the stench of her clothing. She taught him to look beyond what the naked eye sees to where the beauty of one's heart and soul outshines their visible wrappings. Bravely trying to keep them concealed, she proved she had more heart, more guts, more love to give than anyone he had ever known.

To his exasperation, without terrifying her, there was no way he could express the emotions, inflating his head, and heart, making them ready to explode. No words, except for those he vowed he would never say again. Frightening him most, this time it would not be a game of make believe. An overwhelming, all-consuming awareness stabbed his stomach. Nothing ever touched his heart like the sight of this woman. Realizing his heart had abandoned his mind, and had fallen irrevocably in love, for the first and last time, made him tremble from head to foot. All at once, never did he have so much to lose.

Jordan could not make another delivery. The chance something might happen to her would kill him. Setting her free was the only answer. That was his plan before they dressed, before they left the apartment, before they got this far, the problem was, he could not find the guts to do so. It was not easy letting go of something, so rare, so precious. The time had come, now before he begged her to stay, and after tonight, he knew he would.

Reaching into his pocket, groping fingers found what he placed there. Holding it out to Jordan, he said, "I have Scorpio where I want him. I have enough to put him down. We do not have to go tonight. This is a key to a safety deposit box." With his other hand, Jake withdrew an envelope from beneath his clothing. "In here are instructions, as to where the box is located, along with a notarized letter granting you permission to its contents." A smirk realigned his lips into a Pirates grin. "After all, a bargain is a bargain. You may stay at my apartment until you decide what you want to do, and where you want to go."

Inflicted with stunned paralysis, the key lay in Jordan's opened hand. When her fingers refused to grasp it, folding them over with his, Jake gently squeezed them shut. His voice an almost tangible caress, "You earned it, Jordan. You deserve it. For God's sake, take it."

Though the touch of Jake's hand, and his verbal message meeting his eyes, made her want to bolt, she could not. The part of her he claimed would be lost forever. A portion she believed had shriveled, and died that never existed until he rudely entered her life. A heart bursting into prominence, partying crazily, was flashing as though a strobe light, gorging her brain with blood, and turning hurt, and pain into an antiquity.

Finally, she found someone, good, kind, and honest, who cared, enough to set her free, enough not to touch her, who gave her a reason, to wake every morning, to eat, to dream, to begin trusting again, a reason to live. The worst part, he was a man. The fist clutching the key came hard against her chest hoping to contain the heart about to rupture through her ribs. She jerked her eyes away that always seemed to cloud up, and mist whenever he was around. She could not cry, would not, damn it all, she would not.

Jakes drawl was like honey, and smoke, "Do not be afraid, Jordan. This is your chance. Take it. If you need me, for any reason, I will be there. I would never do anything to hurt you. I will always protect you; keep you safe, I promise."

Damn him, he must know he was hurting her now, tearing her to shreds. Tiger-eyes' filled with renewed terror struck his face. Her voice sounded very young, very small, as if a petrified child. "Don't say that. You told me you could not make promises because you do not have it in you to keep them that promises are only meant to be broken."

Moving closer, he looked as if he were going to gather her into his arms, and he was, so desperate was he to hold her, hold her close, and draw her inside him, where he could keep her safe forever. Kiss her, oh, God, yes, kiss those lips just once. Whisper the words pulverizing his chest. Words, she would never accept, that meant nothing to someone who never knew love from a man that would make her run.

Hands shoving his away concealed her face. Confronting her was a fear of a horrifying dimension. What would she do if Scorpio won and took Jake away from her just when she discovered the true man behind the disguise? Love always leached everything from you the only thing it gave back was pain. It took her mother, and now, it wanted her Jake.

Before she collected her senses Jake, started the car, turned around, and was heading in the direction of the apartment. Once they arrived, head pounding like a freight train, feeling beyond exhaustion, Jordan went to the bath-room, stripped, and showered until the water turned cold. Returning to the bedroom, she laid on the bed with the key, and envelope, clasped tightly to her breast. There was no way she could sleep, not tonight, not ever again.

Upon entering the kitchen, Jake never realized he did not reach for a cigarette, did not search for a can of beer.

Sitting in a chair, preoccupied was he planning his final move. Someone's investigation was unsatisfactory, his past a blur, his record too clean, someone who, never reminisced or, spoke of the future, and covered, all too carefully, his every move. All signs he was hiding something. He hoped tomorrow the proof of his suspicions would arrive.

Chapter 20

Mind whirling, staring at the clock on the orange crate, its black limbs pointing out three A.M., Jordan assimilated, and dissected the evenings' occurrences. If not for the key, and envelope still clutched in her hand, she would not have believed what took place.

Reflections of Jake, bringing on a powerful yearning to see him, bolted her upright her glance instantly searching out the chair he normally occupied. Finding it vacant, her disappointment became so oppressive her legs almost came from under her. Collecting herself, she ran to the open bedroom door. Stopping abruptly, sheepishly she peaked into the adjoining room discovering him asleep on the sofa. Relief coming as a tidal wave somewhat eased an anxiety she did not understand, and would never admit.

Astonishment's residue remained indelibly written on her features. She never expected Morgan, of all people; to uphold his end of the bargain, least of all set her free. No longer were any shackles binding her.

He had sufficient evidence to get Scorpio. She met her obligations, therefore earned her reward. It was time to leave, begin a new life, now while Jake slept, to do so any other time would be impossible. Damn his manipulating emerald eyes, their reflecting facets would not permit an in person good-bye without crumbling into a billion pieces, without crying.

Cunning as a prowler, she came beside him embedding to memory every minuscule detail. Despite the rags, his face was clean, hair brushed, the blonde threads, no longer in a ponytail, splayed randomly across the pillow. The master of sleep had erased the dark smudges beneath his eyes, smoothed the once deep lines etching his face. For the first time, since she met him, he seemed at peace and she wondered how someone so ruggedly dangerous awake could look so vulnerable, and princely asleep. A deadly blow struck her chest; a hand came sharply to her breast.

Never before did she want to, touch a man, feel the texture of his skin, eyebrows, lips. It would be safe now while the labyrinth slept, she need not worry about him, feeling, reacting, wanting what she could never give. Maybe one day she would call upon a memory of Jacob Morgan, then again, probably not. Why would she remember someone she believed she hated, but, if that were true, it would be easy to disappear?

As though blinded to the truth, her eyes flicked here, there, and everywhere, examining the room, every crevice, every detail before stalling on the trunk. How could Brenda do what she did to Jake? What kind of woman was she? Could women be as cruel as men could? Why did she despise a complete stranger?

"No," her mind screamed. There was too much unknown, and undone to cop out now. For the life of her, she had to make certain Jake got his revenge before writing the only ending to her story. She had to find the two people he hated and kill them. If she did not Scorpio would kill Morgan.

Determined to make one last delivery, ever so quietly, she tiptoed into the bedroom. Placing the key, and envelope under the mattress for safekeeping, she changed into her disguise, then cat like, climbed out the window, and down the fire escape. Maybe, if God truly existed, she would find Scorpio before Morgan.

An unbearable clanging shook Jake's skull, as though the demon inside was suffering the effects of alcohol withdrawal. Anxious for a remedy, blurry-eyed, he stumbled into the kitchen, and opened the refrigerator door, the only items remaining the workings of two conniving women. With a bang the door closed, the racket, tightening the tension, seizing his muscles, and escalating the velocity of the hammer bludgeoning his skull.

Hastily, moving to the drawer normally over-flowing with unimaginable junk, jerking it open, he saw the bottom lined with shelving paper, every bottle labeled, and placed in neat rows. "Damn meddling women," he sputtered while popping a handful of Tylenol tablets into his mouth. Searching out a glass to hold the gagging, tasteless, liquid needed to wash them down he tugged too hard on an upper cabinet door sending it crashing into another. The glare from sparkling clean glasses hurt his eyes.

Anguish in his head, plummeting to his chest, almost brought him to his knees. Guzzling glass after glass of cold water did nothing to dose the flame's Jordan kindled.

Jordan, he thought, her name surprisingly easing nerves twitching relentlessly. Dear God, tonight he made the biggest mistake of his life by, giving in too easily, granting her freedom. An ass he was for, purchasing a ticket, giving her money, not knowing where she would go, or when. What an idiot. Ridiculous as it seemed, he wanted to know her plans, where she would be just in case he wanted to, see her, and make sure she was all right.

With a smack, his palm connected with his forehead.

Jesus, he never slept, now all of a sudden he could not stay awake, he made it too damn easy for her to escape. Escape, hell, he ordered her to go.

Finding Jordan gone, sputtering curses he stared out the bedroom window at the iron offering refuge. Tremendous force brought his knuckles against drywall, caving it in, the action doing nothing to ease the fatal wound to his chest. Tears ran down his cheek so convinced was he it never was his destiny to love, or be happy.

The phone rang, and rang, and rang, a cruel but much needed reminder of his only purpose in life. McMaster's ordered a last minute raid, Billy said, he was to meet his team at the location

Chapter 21

Six of Scorpios' expert sharp shooters were assigned a primary target the success of their endeavors would gain his favor, and the sizable reward making the risk well worthwhile.   Positioned behind barricades, the assassin's eagerly awaited a cocaine delivery confident Morgan would strike the moment it arrived.   Hands holding weapons were ready, any minute, now, any second.

Why a raid now, Jake's mind shouted, just when his strategy was almost complete a plan that would organize Chicago's entire drug force into teams lead by experienced commanders.   One night, with precision, hard and fast, they would strike.   Raiding one location at a time was getting them nowhere.   Scorpio was, toying with them, making them appear fools, and laughing in their faces.

It was the biggest mistake of McMaster's career, Jake seethed. Successful raids required calculated moves of each team member combined with precision timing. Billy was too damn young, and headstrong, his lack of experience could cost his life, and those of his team. Anxiety told Jake, if there was a spy among them, tonight might be a trap.

Duty, and the safety of his men, banished all thoughts of Jordan.   Paying no heed to stop lights, traffic, or speed limits, with the engine of his Mustang revved to the max, Jake's car sped down side streets' barely missing parked cars, as it swerved around corners', and cut through alleys'. Each traffic light, each street light, each sign seemed to be flashing a fatalistic warning, as fenders hurled trashcans, as he prayed the short cut would get him to his destination on time.

Although the address on the package seemed familiar, Jordan rarely delivered to the same location twice. After worrying it around in her mind for a few moments, she decided there were so many deliveries over the years her imagination was working over-time. Besides, sweet reflections of Jake were adding to the state of confusion clogging rational thoughts.

It was not until rounding the corner that with bright clarity, the environment became familiar. Gorging instincts churning her stomach made her, heart sprint, and her mind wail, "Turn around, now."

Just like Jordan, the wind seemed to be holding its breath. The monstrous trees lining the street suddenly appeared as though they were moving, their arms, and hands reaching out threatening to pluck the life from her. Berries on bushes became examining eyes, weed's cover for lurking rodents, snakes, and deadly spiders, all waiting for sustenance. Jordan's eyes rapidly swished from one window to another to another, none in the rundown buildings bordering the street glowing with light. Broken glass from street-lights, crunched beneath her feet, the sky chalkboard black. Due to the uncommon quiet surrounding her, all she heard was the reckless beating of her heart, like a frenzied bird escaping a hunter and for the first time, she was terrified of being alone in a tranquilized world.

Preposterous sensations, she scolded herself, Margaret and Jake provided a false sense of security. Damn them, they made her soft. Naturally, in this neighborhood, alone in the earliest hours of the morning, anyone would be spooked, or, could it be, before tonight, she never cared what happened, nothing mattered, so convinced was she, she would be better off dead.

Tonight, dammit, it mattered more than she dared to admit. She needed to see Jake one more time. See his reaction when he learned of Scorpio's death. Reaching into a pocket, slender fingers explored the gun stolen from Margaret's apron. Thanks to overhearing Jake's instructions to Margaret, she knew exactly how to load, aim, and pull the trigger. Tonight, if Scorpio showed his face, she was determined to put a bullet between his eyes.

Behind, a garbage can, crashing to the ground, rolled toward her spewing refuse seeming to take on life. A cat screeched, gusting wind tugged at her clothes, shocking occurrences, affecting her reflexes making the package careen to the ground. Wide eyes jerked wildly, her legs becoming mush as she, slowly, cautiously bent to retrieve the parcel. Across the street, behind a tree, something moved, she was sure of it.

Now, she was not sure she knew anything about anything. Calling upon her ability to block out all emotions, inhaling several deep breaths, helped to shore up what little courage remained. Stepping over her heart that had careened to the sidewalk she continued to approach the structure twenty feet away, the dense silence magnifying footsteps seeming to be tapping out an S.O.S.

Awaiting his signal, all officers' eyes were on Billy. With a flick of a wrist, he turned the brim of his hat around, just as his idol always did just before a raid. About to give the sign, noticing a courier in front of the house stopped him instantly, an innocent victim caught between crossfire. Knowing the person did not stand a chance, he justified his actions by deciding the courier's death would be like crushing a cockroach only to have thousands of others take its place. An insignificant incident compared to eliminating a major contributor to the drug problem in Chicago.

Abandoning his car a safe distance away, Jake, sprinted, leaping over, overgrown bushes, fences, the hoods of cars', abandoned bikes'. Twice he tripped, and fell. Cursing up a storm, regaining his equilibrium, in quick succession, his eyes zeroed in on Billy behind the tree, the building, and lastly the . . . courier. At once, his body slammed into a brick wall built by the worst terror ever known. Visions of his mother, and John, sped across his mind forcing what oxygen remained in contaminated lungs upward into a shriek, "Jordan! No!"

Spinning around, Billy struggled to assess the man in rags running toward him. Who, in hell, was he? Immediately, he signaled the man in the line of fire to hit the ground.

Was that Jake's voice? Impossible, Jordan concluded it was merely a dream. Determined, stature erect, she, climbed steps that squeaked, walked around holes in rotted flooring, and faced what suddenly appeared to be a ten foot blockade. One, two, one, two, one, two, three, the knuckles of the hand, determined to send a bullet to its mark, rapped on the door. Receiving no reply, she tugged, and yanked, and tugged on the humidity swollen wood, a barricade refusing access until unadulterated anger shot adrenaline to her arm. When the door finally gave way, like a gavel in a judge's hand, she entered hell.

Billy raised his arm, a long awaited signal penetrating the air with sounds of exploding guns, and breaking glass scattering every living thing.

"Jesus, no, Billy," Jake roared stretching his legs, torso, arms, and fingers beyond the bounds of human ability, attempting to prevent Billy's signal. Despite the tips of his fingers grazing cloth, they fell short of their mark.

Billy heard his name, saw the eyes of the man charging past him on his way across the battlefield. There was no mistaking Jake. Billy cringed. So much for hoping his hero would not arrive until the raid was over.

A raid ordered by McMaster's more than a week ago that he instructed Billy to have Jake lead. Order's deliberately ignored until the last minute so optimistic was Billy his team could, out maneuver, out shoot Scorpios' men. After all, they received their training from the best, someone who always lectured never to take unnecessary chances then why, in hell, was Jake entering the war zone?

Torn apart by despairing choices, someone he feared more than life itself, and someone he loved, left Billy two choices, kill Jake, or face the consequences. Far too long, he succumbed to expectations hoping to protect his friend, and, as he raised his gun, and aimed at Jake's back, as his finger began squeezing the trigger, everything that was once black and white took on clarity. He could not kill, his hero, his best friend. Choosing the path forged by his leader, Billy fired providing Jake with the necessary cover praying a bullet would find him before facing Scorpio or, worse, Jake.

The moment Jordan entered the house, and the barrels of guns raised, she hit the floor. Ricocheting bullets hurled wood splinters, and glass, into the air, the roar tearing at her eardrums. Her fingernails seemed to be ripping from her fingers as she frantically clawed at the floor crawling, like a reptile, toward cover while the ghastly odor of gunpowder made, her cough, and her eyes water. A bullet lodged in the wall, less than an inch above her head, powdering her face with plaster. Even in her worst nightmares, she never envisioned dying this way, the way she lived, alone, filled with terror.

Engulfing pain slammed her eyelids closed as a hard-soled shoe came brutally against her fragile ribs curling her eyebrows into a tight ball, making her teeth bit her lips with such tremendous force she gagged from the taste of blood.

"Get, to hell, out of my way, bitch," a man snarled frantically attempting to escape gunfire.

There was a sickening groan, a thud. Hoping to avoid the demon of death chasing her, closing in, groping her clothing, tugging, tearing, natural instinct pried Jordan's eyes open. Staring back were eyes glazed with a veil of recognizable death as blood gushed from the man's twisted mouth, and his desperate last words gurgled from his throat. Snatching her clothing from his grip, threatening to pull her into a whirlpool of blackness, she bravely slithered over the body.

Brandish gunfire unmasked a doorknob an arm's length away. Twisting, and jerking, she gained asylum thrusting her into the nightmares of the past, as she crouched into the corner. Tugging her nightgown over bare feet, she pressed her palms against her ears to shut out the blasts of accusing bullets. Starved lungs sucked in quick breaths, every microscopic speck of her twitching relentlessly. Burying her face, into her dolls hair, rasping sobs, sounding as if torn from her, came in currents of screams, yet, her vocal cords never wavered, nor did tears give into the potential rising flood.

Crazed from worry left Jake no room for rational thought. All he envisioned was Jordan's face all he heard were her screams. Dear God, she was, in pain, suffering, bleeding to death, dying alone. After promising to protect her, knowing the results of broken promises, how they wring hearts, and drain life, he had to save her. Unable to protect his mother, and John, this time, if it cost him everything, he would find Jordan, and if he could not save her, at least she would die in his arms and if he lived he would summon the wrath of God to avenge her.

Jake, along with the door crashed to the floor, a shocking incident making Scorpios' men wide-eyed with disbelief. The person they expected was supposed to be in uniform, not in rags like the creature boldly entering. They could not waste their ammunition on a pitiful street bum, another courier; the idiot would not live much longer anyway.

The moment Billy informed the men it was Jake entering the fortress, like a swarm of killer bees; they closed the gap between themselves, and the enemy threatening their leader's life. Like cancer, bullets riddled the dwelling, lodging in drywall, penetrating wood, and tearing human flesh.

Having given his men the advantage, their raining bullets offered the protection required to crawl to safety.

As though a roaring fire engulfed the building, gun smoke became too dense to permit visual penetration making Jakes' eyes sting, and water. Depending solely on touch, with the odor of death encompassing him, he began searching for Jordan. When the tips of his fingers grazed a body he grabbed, tugged, and shook believing it was Jordan. Fear sifting through his body heaved his stomach, and tossed his heart into a savage sea of bile, until a flash of light exposed a man's face the sight jerking Jake's hand back. Insanity thrashed him with its invisible power as he continued his search through the darkness until a foot away he saw a door.

New hope banished the exploding sounds; the pungent smell of smoke, so busy was Jake praying Jordan found refuge. All that mattered was reaching her in time to say he loved her before it was too late. Resolve iced his blood. Chills shot the length of him. Intuition told him he was tempting fate for the last time. All at once, a great wave of relief, clawing at his resolve, brightened his countenance. Was it real? Did he actually hear muffled screaming, crying? Dear God, let it be Jordan, he prayed. The possibility she was still alive, made his heart beat to a different drum, and gave strength to determined hands wrenching the door open. There was a shrill scream. The door slammed.

It was time, again he was coming after her he would tear more of her dolls' hair as he ripped it away, and flung it against the wall. He would, take her to bed, strip her, and do all the horrible things done so many times before. Even through the terrible blackness, she saw the face penetrating hooded eyes. Survival dictated there be, no sound, no breathing, not even a flinch it was either him or her. Tugging the gun free, Jordan aimed, this time she would, win, end the madness forever. Finally, she would follow through with the plans her mind repeatedly envisioned.

Hovering over the invisible membrane separating sanity, and insanity, Jordan never heard a distant voice begging pitifully, "Jordan, Jordan, are you in here? Please, God, please."

Slapping at groping hands, she wailed, "No, no, don't touch me." So desperate, and terrifying, was the battle to survive, the old biological maxim of fight, or die, tugged bravery from the floor as Jordan wondered dimly if she would be sick before it was over. The monster's hand was now, clutching the mass of cold steel, tightening her finger on the trigger. How stupid of Jake not to know Jordan would think to protect herself.

"It's me, Jordan, Jake, it's me."

Before Jake claimed control of the gun, Jordan pulled the trigger, the hot cylinder burning his hands as he ripped it from hers, and flung it to the floor.

Like a mad woman, her fingers tore at the clothing suffocating her.

"Jordan, it's me, it's me," Jake yelled, his persistence barely preventing her from taking the final step into a world obscure to those who have never known true pain, true fear. Bracing his hands against the wall to hold her up was not working so his arms circling her, probably much too hard, lifting her, pressed her into a corner where his body was the only shield separating them from the war outside.

Magically, the Closter phobic space became a place with blue skies, and brilliant warm sunshine, where flowers dance in the pure, fragrant air and birds sing, where pain, suffering, and terror, are nonexistent, a space in time when love surrounds us with its pleasures, and gifts.

Jordan's hands on Jake's face, his shoulders, and his arms, making sure he was real, finally locked around his neck practically choking him. Accepting them, Jake prayed she would never let go while her head found his chest as if giving up all her burdens.

"Are you all right, Jordan? Are you hurt? Please, God, tell me you are not hurt." Shaking her head no was all Jordan could do in answer. "Thank you, thank you, thank you," whispers as he kissed an, earlobe, her neck, and cheek. Actions trying to block out the sounds of gunfire making her flinch, and tremble while inwardly he cursed the inability to summon the magic to whisk her away to a plateau where she would never again know terror.

"Don't be afraid. I promised you I would protect you. Keep you safe."

Jordan was frighteningly aware of, the strength of Jake's arms, the solid wall of his chest upon the softness of her breasts, his hipbone hard against her pressing her into the wall. As if to fight off those delirious thoughts, her head reared back, "You can't fool me; you said promises are made to be broken. We are never going to get out of here alive, but thank you anyway, thank you for trying thank you for every-thing."

Jake did not expect the earthquake striking when Jordan rose up on tiptoes to align her lips with his, lips, sweet, and soft, the nectar he never believed he would taste, more delicious than imagined. A kiss jerking his pulse crazily, as lips moved slowly, subtly, seductively, stirring his insides to boiling liquid. When she drew his lower lip gently into her mouth, gooseflesh followed making him certain he would fall flat on his face. Tentatively, at first, as if afraid of her, he obeyed the silent commands becoming a purring sound in her throat a lingering kiss, so debilitating, so sedating his sleek musculature pressed harder against her for fear of tumbling into an abyss.

Tasting Jordan's full lips was a sedative for the pain ripping through flesh, and muscle causing eyelids to squeeze tight, eyebrows' to furrow. Feeling his body nearly cave in from the pain, he fought to silence rising groans. Though his heart was breaking from the awareness little time remained to consume every part of Jordan, inhale her sweetness, make love for the last time, as if he never made love before, such thoughts were preposterous. Instead, guardedly, tenderly, he responded, not taking more than she offered, pressing his lips briefly against those trembling like taking tiny sips that could never quench the thirst she made him feel, each doing little to ease his pain.

Despite knowing he would not survive, to tell Jordan how much he wanted this, wanted her, he avoided touching the temptations beneath layers of cotton, and, while the two loves of his life bombarded him, ripped him apart, he shuddered. The anguish of the wounds nothing compared to the misery in his heart from realizing before he met Jordan, as he thought back in time, love had only been in his mind. For the first time in his life, he found love hanging in a closet, as if waiting to come back into style, the kind capable of shoving dangling skeletons' aside, a love that could never be.

Feeling, her kisses deepen, her lips open slightly, somehow soothed his anguish, and reinforced stability.

Unable to resist any longer, one of his hands cupping her cheek allowed his thumb to ease apart trembling lips, coaxing, and teasing until she innocently surrendered. All the while he prayed she was unaware of the passion he was feeling one so new, so breath taking, he was convinced she was the angel who had come to claim his soul.

At least, before she died, she knew what it was like to want a man, to hold her, touch her, and kiss her. Shockingly, Jordan loved the taste of Jake, so different, yet somehow familiar, as if she had been waiting for him all her life. Surprisingly comfortable was his pressing weight bringing with it invading sensations deep in her loins making her tense, warm, moist aches capable of shattering control and making her want to scream. Emotions, beyond reality, beyond comprehension, were tossing memories of other men over an imaginary cliff smashing them on the rocks below.

Now she, saw clearly, understood the kind of love that made people marry, have children. How fitting it was to die in Jake's arms while he kissed her still refusing to take what she would have willingly given. Unlike her, Jake would survive he was stronger, braver. Maybe, in some way, she helped erase his past as he had hers maybe, someday he would love again. She wanted him to. Jake deserved the best. Possibly, in another life somewhere, sometime, there would be a time for them, but not here, not now her past would never allow it. A man like Jake would never want a woman as tarnished as she, if he ever learned the truth, he would shun her, and that would rip her heart out.

Of course, he would, after all she had allowed it to hap-pen it was her fault for being, so beautiful, so desirable. Her father and other men who paid him for her favors said she asked for it. She should have, said no, fought them, but that was exactly what they, wanted, and enjoyed. Why did it take her so long to run away? Answers she may never know, but at least she had a few short years of peace.

As tears pooled beneath clamped eyelids, with Jake's arms surrounding her, Jordan allowed his warm lips, slanted across hers with tantalizing skill, to erupt foreign desires. She was, ready now, ready for the devil to make his claim. In answer, gunfire ceased, the door rudely opening returned them to the real world.

Deciphering Billy's shocked expression, Jake announced, "Take good care of her for me Billy do not let anything happen to her. Promise me." Jake's skin was pale, his clothes' blood drenched. Staggering brought his back hard against the wall as Billy, and Jordan watched with the same horror in their eyes'. As fear reared its ugly head, and tension pulled nerves taut, like cold wires touching skin, Billy begged for the strength to accept what was happening. "Call an ambulance," he screamed like a woman, his mist-filled eyes locking on his hero as Jake's feet came from under him, and his back left a red trail on the wall.

Dropping sharply to her knees, frantic fingers' tore at layered material. Every fear Jordan ever knew charged when she did not find the bullet proof vest he should have been wearing. Feelings, running deep inside, so terrifying, and painful, caused Jordan's fists to flail Jake's chest her fingers tearing cloth as she shook him. He could not die, not now, not ever, not before she told him, he was her hero, how full her heart felt, word's remarkable anger shoved aside. "Damn you, Morgan.

Where is your vest, you, stupid fool, you, idiot. Don't do this, don't do this to me, you can't leave me now. It should have been me. Why wasn't it me?" Shocked numb, her heart, and mind completely stripped, she cursed heaven, and earth for surviving the petrifying battle, still, tears begging for freedom never came.

Billy watched the scene, revolted by his own weakness, consumed with feelings of remorse, and self-contempt staining everything he saw, and heard. Alarm bells rang in his brain, fear knifed through him. Somehow, he had to banish the panic clawing inside, there was so much to come to terms with, why Jake? Why did he allow this to happen? Who was the woman in rags? Why were they dressed alike? Why did Jake care about someone so appalling? Hell had broken through the center of the earth, and was spilling over before his eyes.

When Billy attempted to pull Jordan off Jake, she turned on him, screaming, kicking, biting, scratching, and punching until Jake's garbled voice halted her. "Watch out, Billy, she is a tiger, trust me, it is easier to surrender. She is better than both of us." Lips curled into a half smile, thinned, he grimaced, and as a dark shadow fell across his face, he whispered, "I love you, Jordan."

Jordan's back came sharply against the casing of the door hands quickly covering her face hiding the disbelief registering there. No one but her mother ever said those words to her. Jake was crazy, surely, he was dying. Why would he say something so ridiculous? How could he love someone like her, why? The sensation of moisture on her face convinced her, the tears screaming for escape had finally come red tears, the sight of which forced her glance to the front of her clothes, then to the floor where Jake's gun lay. Within seconds her mind, rewound, and replayed the events she had pulled the trigger; and killed the only man she ever loved. Turning hurt filled eyes on Billy, Jake's words shrieked in her mind. "Damn you, Jordan, you will be the death of me long before my fucking cigarettes." Plucking Jake's gun from the floor, she held it to her head, and fired. In the far off distance, she, heard the most horrible scream, felt her body hit the floor, then more voices, and flashes of light. God had granted her wish, at last, she was dead.

No one at the scene was, aware of the new dawn, the sky aglow with streaks of pink's, and gold, the sharp edge of night disappearing behind the peaks of the city.

Chapter 22

The entire hospital knew the instant Jake ultimately penetrated a drugged state, the residue inadequately repressing a detestable mood. Jake repeatedly ripping the paraphernalia from his arms required undivided attention from concerned doctors, confrontations ending with Jake's boisterous demands for a phone, and newspapers. Unbelievably, one patient out of an entire floor succeeded in creating complete chaos.

No one knew, at the core of Jake's anger was an insatiable desire to see Jordan to be reassured she was safe. Even more oppressive was the compulsion to find out if she heard him say he loved her. A hand holding the newspaper, revealing the headlines, angrily slapped it onto the hospital tray.

> MORGAN BARELY ESCAPES DEATH IN
> SHOOT OUT
> CHICAGO'S HERO STRIKES AGAIN
> SIX DEAD, TWO DEA OFFICERS WOUNDED
> MORGAN SAVES LIFE OF MYSTERY WOMAN

Jake's worst nightmares charged in the form of colored photos' of Jordan, and himself as paramedics carried them on stretchers to the ambulance, one in particular depicting a close up of Jordan's face wiped clean. During the past few days, the media regurgitated her as a headline, at night, a sound bite with film at 10:00 p.m. Thanks to them, Scorpios' suspicions would be aroused he would wonder why Morgan risked his life to save a courier. A brilliant man, it would not be long before he placed Jordan at two locales during a raid. Her innocence would not matter Scorpio would suspect her of being an undercover agent. He would order a hit on her, and offer an obscene amount of money to insure its success.

For the fifth time, snatching a bandage from his arm, Jake jerked the needle from the vein. Though he pressed the buzzer to summon a nurse, deciding not to wait bare feet smacked the floor determined strides bringing him to the closet. Before assistance arrived, he was dressed, and across the threshold.

"Sir, you cannot leave. You are not well enough."

"The hell I'm not watch me," Jake spat, a swish of his arm shoving the petite nurse aside.

"You must sign a release form before being discharged, Mr. Morgan," she said shakily, watching helplessly as he disappeared into the elevator.

Outside the hospital entrance, Jake boldly entered a taxi summoned by another customer. Everyone in Chicago knew Morgan, the taxi driver no exception. Feeling honored to be of service to Chicago's very own hero, he asked no questions when Jake snarled an address.

Margaret was thankful Jordan's attempt at suicide had failed, the bullet grazing her skull, lodging instead in the wall behind her. For the third day in a row, she tugged Jordan out of bed, as though a limp rag doll, washed, and dressed her, before positioning her in a chair in the living room in the mellow sunlight. Again, she refused to eat or drink what little nourishment

Margaret managed to force down, she regurgitated minutes later. For seventy-two hours, Jordan's emotionless features remained unchanged, the lack of sleep, the reason her eyes resembled glass marbles fixed straight forward. The doctor's prognosis was far from encouraging, there was nothing more he could do, they should place her in a rehabilitation center.

In the recovery room, as soon as Jake opened his eyes, he pleaded with Margaret to look after Jordan she was to take her to his apartment, keep her safe. Margaret never questioned why Jake thought he had to ask, and never told him Billy had already done so.

Not knowing exactly how to explain Jordan's presence to Billy, Margaret called upon the first lie reluctantly coming to mind. Jordan was Jake's cousin from Michigan visiting for the summer. She was in training for undercover work. A novice at deception, it was there in Billy's features, she had not been convincing. Now, troubling Margaret most was what shown in Billy's eyes whenever he looked at Jordan. He was smitten, all right. Despairingly, her plans backfired.

How could she blame Billy? Framing Jordan's sweet face was multicolor hues of shiny pale gold, her clothing fit perfectly now, faded jeans defining shapely legs with a pink tank top exposing creamy skin, and other enticing attributes. Barring her sorrowful visage, Jordan resembled a porcelain doll whose creator perfected a masterpiece.

For three days, the only encouraging factor of Jordan's condition was something seemed to click each time Billy touched her hand. Inevitably, she withdrew it quickly, her reaction stunning him. It was obvious he was blaming himself for the catastrophe. Despite Billy sitting for hours explaining over again Jake had survived, Jordan never batted an eyelash. The bullet entering Jake's back fracturing a rib miraculously missed vital organs, complete recovery was expected, Billy patiently repeated. Ballistic tests proved the bullet did not come from Jake's weapon, futile explanations ignored as though Jordan were deaf, and blind.

The startling metallic sound of a key in the door snatched Margaret from worrisome pondering. Watching the hinged wood slowly creak open steadily escalated her heartbeat. Instinctively, her hand sought Jake's gun. Drawing his, Billy positioned himself between Margaret, and the intruder. Shock instantly brought Margaret to her feet. "Oh, Jake, you should not have dear Lord." There was no misinterpreting the pain contorting Jake's face, nor the red patch of blood on his shirt. Slumping into Billy's arms, Jake barely made it to the couch before passing out.

An hour later, Jake awoke to Margaret's soothing words and cool fingers on his forehead. Through a blur, he recognized Billy frantically pacing in the background. Struck with a stabbing pain, Jake's hand explored the clean, dry bandage before moving to caress Margaret's in unspoken thanks. It was not until he tilted his head, that Jordan came into view relief dousing him somewhat draining the tension responsible for crunched features, a short respite before terror registered. Jordan's obvious state scared the hell out of him, more so than what he had yet to face. Completely oblivious to, everyone around him, his own suffering, he could no longer fight the oppressive urge to hold Jordan in his arms.

The instant Jake attempted to stand, Billy rushed to his assistance. Feeling weak, and dizzy, forcing himself upright, he slowly approached Jordan. Coming to his knees, supporting his weight on the chair arm he placed his hand close to Jordan's yet, not touching. When Jake began to speak, his words brought joyful tears to Margaret's eyes, and shattered what little remained of Billy's wits. "Jordan, it's me, Jake I am alive. You should know by now, I would not leave you I could not leave you, not when I promised to protect you, and keep you safe. I will always be here for you. Thanks to you, I am standing on solid ground and know I have it in me to keep all my promises. Jordan, look at me, do not block me out like everyone else. I will not let you crawl inside that hole. It is over, Jordan I am no longer going after Scorpio."

There was no need; Jake knew the identity of Scorpios' spy. Waiting for the investigators report was not necessary, the reality brutally stabbing him between the shoulder blades. He had grown to like Billy, no, it was more than that, he loved Billy as he would a brother, as he did John. Disregarding his vows, he allowed Billy to burrow into his life now, not only would he pay the price for his error, but also, so would Jordan. However, he could not think of that now snatching Jordan before she entered that place known for rarely giving up its trophy's was imperative. "I have done all I can do," Jake, continued, "It is someone else's turn. I am tired. I am quitting the force. Someday there will be a time for us, somewhere, somehow besides, you cannot leave without taking me with you. I cannot go on without you, Jordan please, just trust me one last time take my hand, and we will go together to find that day, that time, that place." Jakes head finding his hands rocked back, and forth though it came as a whisper, everyone heard every word. "I need you Jordan. I love you."

As the tenderness in his voice slipped around her guard, Jordan's mind tried desperately to return to the real world. For so long she had been running through a maze of darkness frantically searching for someone to save her, Jake was the only light on the other side of the door, she had to find him. She could hear his voice smell him and yet feeling excessively weak and tired made each door more difficult to open. There was one more, just one more God, help her she had to find the strength. Lost in the world trying to claim her, in a dark narrow hallway lined with doors she opened one after another only to run once more. Behind each a, different monster, her father, other men, her dead mother, dead friend's, Jake's blood drenched body lying on a stretcher. Then, a man with no face at all whose unmistakable cologne made her head throb and, a woman, laughing - Brenda. Slamming each door, Jordan ran, and ran, as the hands reaching through tiny crevices clawed at her, tearing her hair, her clothing lapping at her heels, the echoing laughter bludgeoning her ears.

She was so tired, very, very tired exhaustion making her body ache. Her mind was banging against her skull screaming for rest. Lying at her feet, she could see her heart cut into a trillion pieces spurting blood. She wanted to stop, longed to sleep forever, and, had it not been for one last door, she would have. Eyes closed, she stretched her fingers toward the knob despite knowing she could not withstand another disappointment. Sluggish senses told her the knob was not cold, or hard, but soft, and warm there were fingers then a thumb. Beseeching her eyes not to look at the final atrocity, that would surely immerse her into the deepest sleep, they spurned her. Once more, she was deluded the revelation was not real, it could not be. She heard words pealing in her ears, promises of a better day, a new life, of love. Was Jake alive did he really say he would quit, and forget Scorpio?

Catapulted on a journey of everlasting obscurity, a force elevated her hand; trembling fingers traced an eyebrow, a nose, and eyelashes. She felt a, cheek, chin. Lips were planting kisses on each of her fingertips. A finger erasing the tear escaping from the corner of her eye tore away the steel bars to eternity's fortress. Jake's arms sliding around Jordan's narrow waist tugged her gently toward him. Hers flew around his neck. Faces buried in each other's neck the dam holding back Jordan's tears broke shattering the past into particles, sweeping up the pieces of her heart now surfing on a wave of joy. In Jake's arms, the only place she felt safe, Jordan sobbed wretchedly, broken little wails stabbing him like a knife digging at clay.

Unable to repress the joy exploding, barbed yet sweet, a gush gurgled up past her lips with a small yelp of sound, the hoarseness startling as she kissed Jake's cheek. Another escaped, then, another until she recognized the sound as laughter. Her head seemed to be twirling around, and around, as laughter continued, the reaction causing the world to whiz past as if spinning out of orbit while Jake held her until his arms ached. They did not hear the sounds of, Margaret's sobbing, and blowing her nose into tissues. So swelled with emotions was the room no one heard Billy leave, except Jake.

Chapter 23

Permeating Jake's apartment was emotion Billy never experienced before. Contrition turned him from the scene; his mind, doing mental gymnastics, assailing him with fresh doubts, caused anguish to flash high. Never again could he look into the eyes of the one person he respected, and loved, the one he betrayed. Glaring Emerald eyes told Billy Jake knew.

Whom did Jake think he was kidding? Had he come to know him better than Jake knew himself? The show down would surely come Jake had no choice but to expose him. He could not expect mercy did not deserve it. Having deceived his best friend, he complicated matters by jeopardizing the life of an innocent woman someone Jake loved.

If he had not followed his instructions to investigate Jordan, maybe there would have been a chance. A treasonous act committed the day following the raid. So filled was he with a powerful need to find out why his hero went against his own steadfast rules, by risking his life to save a courier, an enchanter in disguise, whose pictures captivated him.

When his investigation failed to uncover the slightest detail, as though Jordan never existed, as though someone purposely erased her past his suspicions worsened. The only alternative was to break into Jake's office. There he unearthed the unexpected, all in one neat little package, Jordan's past, Jakes' plans' for a major raid, evidence against drug couriers, and shockingly the results of the investigations of fellow DEA enforcers, an envelope filled with evidence now hidden safely in his apartment. Billy's present emotional state induced flash backs as to how relieved he was when no condemning information pertaining to himself was found in the envelope. If Jake suspected him, he found nothing conclusive, thanks to Scorpio. Born no fool, finding the evidence had been too easy, as though that was Jake's intentions.

Considering Jake placed himself in jeopardy in the name of love, how could he deliver the information to Scorpio? The kind of love Billy, forgot existed, envied, and only knew from his mother. Gagging on lumps of regret, his sleeve swished across damp lashes. As if dice tossed upon a gambling table, thoughts of his mother, Scorpio, Jake, and Jordan spun in Billy's head. In split seconds, as if the dice hit, bounced, spun, rolled, and abruptly slammed against his heart, he decided his destiny. Without counting the black dots, Billy made his choice knowing Jake would not stand in his way.

Orbiting flashes of red reflected off the roof of Billy's car, the sirens' shrillness nothing compared to the alarm ringing in his chest. Breaking every traffic law, he pursued his fate.

As if savoring the torture, it took an unbearable length of time for the elevator of his apartment complex to reach the fifteenth floor each occupant's eyes writing an indelible message across his forehead, "TRAITOR" making the walls close in. Like the slime he was, squeezing through the crack in the elevator door, he vaulted so anxious was he to retrieve the evidence Scorpio would seek in compensation for losing six men.

Darting down the hall, he began fumbling for his keys. Once inside he closed the door, and secured the lock. Eager for temporary refuge, leaning against the cold steel, he released a sigh filled with relief. Though everything appeared normal, contaminated air told him his luck had run out.

Billy moved to the bedroom, every part of him aware, alert, eyes wildly scanning his domain making certain every detail remained unchanged. Just as he crossed the threshold, something horrible cloaked him. Struggling for the slightest breath, he brushed wildly at trepidations sweat slipping torturously down his face. Despite the illumination from outside, he felt as though he perforated the blackest cloud of doom. Body swishing this way, and that, one hand coming behind his back searched for the weapon perpetually holstered there. Claiming it, he whirled around fully prepared to challenge the smothering waves of terror making his heart bang against his lungs so forcefully he gasped for air. In the mirror, Scorpio's image made disgust's grip brutal. At once eyelids went rampant, like the wipers of a car in a driving storm, attempting to eliminate the confronting stigma. He should have known the futility, forever etched in every mirror encountered; there would always be the very image of the man he despised.

Cold fingers raised deadly hard steel to trembling lips willingly separating to allow the weapon access. For a breath of a second, acceptance shaded his features. The only thing halting him from pulling the trigger was an invisible current wafting through the open patio door, puffs moving thin curtains, and dancing across the room. A familiar pungency followed turning the air rancid, and making him desperate to release the lurking geyser of bile as it drifted up the shaft of his nose, and penetrated the mind balking at life. Long, dread filled strides brought him to the dresser where the hinged top allowed access to a fake drawer only he knew existed. Finding it empty meant one thing.

Day light sprinted for cover as darkness crept forward. The sky was not nearly as black as the blood gorging veins so viciously they throbbed from pain. In a trance like state, moving to the patio, he glanced below at the cars innocently moving about as if insects with glowing antennas. Listening to the rhapsody of the city, his hands clutching the railing prevented the cowardice within from hurling his body over. Long agonizing moments passed before his eyes leveled at what he knew was there.

Across the street, on a patio directly opposite his, with light from the apartment outlining his body, as though he were God, Billy glared at a man in a white tuxedo whose eyes brazenly challenged his. Billy could almost hear his father's evil laughter, see the flash of white, vixen sharp, teeth, and feel his nails puncture the skin around his neck. On the other hand, was it Billy's nails penetrating his palms as he clenched his fists to hold back a fierce need to kill? Billy's laughter spiraled as he imagined spilling Scorpios' venomous blood, as he imagined his razor sharp teeth severing the umbilical cord linking him to the devil.

Ever so slowly, Billy counted the black dots on the imaginary dice rolling in his head, five, six, and seven.

Chapter 24

Jake moved Jordan to the couch where she lay limp in his arms, an occasional hiccup shaking her. Love seemed to be a mediocre word for what he was feeling, just as he knew she did too. The strangeness masking even the ordinary words they whispered as if their speech had learned a language of its own.

Mumbling prayers of thanks, Margaret scurried about Jake's kitchen preparing whatever she could find to feed the bewitched lovebirds. Quaking at the mere thought of how close she came to losing them, she permitted no time for frightful thoughts to wander. "Them," she reflected, a smile wrinkling her cheeks when she considered how much space Jordan now occupied in her heart. Never having a daughter, she always wondered what she missed apparently God answered more than one prayer.

Preparing the meal, she pondered her remaining years. A survivor of life's tribulations, she knew how losing a loved one could rip seams in one's soul. Dear God, she could not survive another tear. She would have no reason to live if anything happened to Jake or Jordan. Just the thought of what it would do to either of them if they lost each other after just discovering love's magic, made her ill. They were so young with a whole lifetime ahead.

Margaret knew Jake lied to Jordan, he would not stop now; unfortunately, Jordan was as bull headed as he. Two people she loved were hell bent on saving the other. If given the slightest opportunity Scorpio would destroy them. Scrambling eggs busied her hands, scheming to make sure he would not, busied her mind.

It took considerable coaxing to get the couple into the kitchen where placed in front of them were heaping portions of scrambled eggs, toast, and bacon along with tall glasses of orange juice, and milk. Laying her apron on the counter, Margaret sat watching them eat.

One would have to be blind to miss their magnetic eyes. Though their hands never touched, nor words spoken, she felt the fervor of passions' electrical storm foaming the oceans of gold, and emerald, to a boiling point. With their minds so completely immersed in each other, they were drowning in the words they wished to say. Amazingly, each time their lids draped, and slowly lifted again; an invisible current decoded it all. When Jordan dropped her napkin, and Jake instinctively bent to retrieve it, as their hands met the most stunning smile she ever saw made Jordan's translucent skin shine with the rush of joy. At that moment, Jake seemed to have forgotten everything about everything, his countenance transmitting a song as old as time.

Watching them, Margaret could not help but recall when they were far from friends, and marveled how they changed, like a Willow tree swaying gently to the breath of love. Releasing a sigh, dabbing at a tear creeping out of nowhere, she pondered their love story, the ending of which she would never know unless she left them alone. With fingers crossed, she returned to her apartment muttering incessant prayers.

Concerned over how Jake's face turned ashen, how his eyelids drooped wearily, how his forehead crinkled signaling pain, Jordan insisted he lay on the couch while she straightened the kitchen. Despite rushing through the chores, upon returning, her prince slept. It was best, she concluded considering his love for her had shown so bright she realized more than ever her ability to love him equally had shriveled, and left her dry. Yet, she did not want to go to the bedroom alone to sleep in his bed without him in the chair nearby. She could not wake him when the passion, and need in his eyes said he wanted her as any man who loved a woman would. Considering all that took place, things would not, could not, be the same between them ever again. That unspeakable act could not happen she was soiled beyond any humans' ability to forgive. No matter how much Jake believed he loved her; when he found out how damaged she was, he would always wonder, always expect answers she did not even know. Those emerald eyes, that once shined so brilliantly with adoration for her, clouded over with disappointment, and disgust, would be unbearable.

Besides, the day, the time, the place for them would never come to be. She was not stupid, Jake was a lousy liar he would not stop now, the reality a blinding bright light. Though she did not quite understand why he hated Scorpio enough to risk his life to bring him to justice, she did understand hatred, how it thrived on revenge. The man who wanted to take Jake from her would not be successful, she would see to that.

Although she did not see the newspapers, Jordan remembered bursts of light from camera's, and Billy, it was in his eyes, the way they gleamed, that said he was untrustworthy. How he fit into the labyrinth she was yet to learn, but instincts told her he did. Knowing Scorpio, he would come to claim revenge. Well she would save him the time, and bother.

181

Opening Jake's dresser drawer, Jordan withdrew the shirt she wore before, it would help her feel close to him one last time. Help ease the aching pain telling her just when she thought there was a chance for them she could not latch on to the dream. Jake, she mused, while slipping into his shirt her nakedness against cotton so normal now she even chanced a look in the mirror a time or two wondering what there was about her that brought light into Jake's eyes.

Nestled inside she smelled him, felt his arms around her, his sweet lips, and heard his words temporarily convincing her anything was possible. Crawling into his bed, hugging his shirt as tightly as she desperately wanted to hug him, she made plans to kill Scorpio.

Chapter 25

Brazenly stalking, the man without a face caused pearls of moisture to form on Jordan's forehead, dampening strands of hair leaving impressions on the pillowcase. A hand, hidden behind her, clammy from fear, grasped a gun vibrating to the tune of her frantic breathing. Eyes glued on Jake, though cautiously approaching her target, the speed of her feet scraping sheets increased. Scorpio's traitorous eyes, like mirrors, exposed Jake's presence, her fear for him sufficient distraction for Scorpio to pluck the weapon from stiff fingers, raising the gun, he aimed and fired. "No, Jake," the words scrambling from the constricted walls of her throat as she ripped away the covers feeling as heavy as steel weighing her down. Feet under her now, she sprinted, bravely positioning herself in the line of fire just as gunfire ruptured the silence. A burning pain shot through her interfering with her equilibrium.

Amazingly, before her body hit the floor, powerful arms scooping her up laid her gently upon soft padding. Sitting alongside her, holding, rocking her, was someone speaking comforting words against her battle-lined forehead that ultimately penetrated the fog. It was Jake. Both survived, but only if the dream kept her eyelids sealed if they opened Jake would vaporize a loss that would make her wither, and die. Things could not end between them when, there was so much left undone, more importantly left unsaid.

Allowing Jake's comforting, feather like, kisses, slender arms circled his neck pulling him with her as she eased back upon the pillow. There were agonizing moments of hesitation before he tried to move away a time when her parting lips, coercing him to linger, deepened the kiss. He gasped. Feeling his heart pounding against her bare breasts told her she neglected to button the shirt.

Having mastered pretense, before leaving to fulfill her destiny, she would try to grant Jake what he desperately wanted. Never had she known a man, so full of desire, to be so unwilling to take, despite the heat burning through his clothing. Determined fingers threading through his hair, tracing his scalp, made him shiver. Moving to the nap of his neck pressing him closer prolonged the kiss, and brought forth a scalded groan still he continued to deny his tongue the pleasures it sought. Until, masterfully, Jordan's took the liberty of persuading his to cross the threshold of ecstasy, a time when the tender, manipulative, pads of her hand's tracing the naked plains of his shoulders, kneaded the tension from knotted muscles before coming to rest on moist bandages. Fearful, she had hurt him she hesitated.

Jake's whispers found her ear. "It doesn't hurt. Nothing hurts any more. There is no room for pain since I have known you. You have opened my eyes to the bright light shining down from the heavens."

Jordan knew better a part of him was hurting that only she could mollify. With his arms around her, gently holding her, his hands continued to abstain until she took them within hers and began encouraging him to take pleasure. "Take me through the night, Jake; make all the shadows go away, make everything all right." Trepidation squeezed her eyelids into tight creases, behind the veil she called up pictures of Jake's loving face to give her strength for what was yet to come.

Using great caution, Jake tenderly began satisfying his hunger, eyes lingering on each morsel, fingers, stroking her neck, her shoulder on the way to her breasts. His touch sent sensations through her that collected, and multiplied, within her core. Beginning at the cord beneath her ear, his lips flowed on to curves, and hollows with ease, and sureness. In response, her breasts swelled to fill the palms of his hands encouraging his thumbs to draw lazy circles around rosy peaks skillfully molding them into hard erotic buttons, shocking tortures making her gasp as his mouth claimed the summit in need of exploration.

Unbelievably, his gentle efforts sprang Jordan's body to life, made her breast's ache, and hips press hard against the length of his thighs. Struggling to come to terms with a latent sensuality she did not know existed, she felt sick, faint, and, stripped of defenses. One gigantic, coiled, knot of need swelled her stomach. Never did she experience such a multitude of riotous, bizarre, sensations dancing through her, body that made her want more. Suddenly, it did not matter that it might be painful it would hurt more if Jake refused. There was no other gift she could give, no other way to thank him for, sweeping her from the gutter, for breathing life back into her, no other way to say goodbye. Besides, to her utter amazement, she could not still the body wanting to move with such urgency too choked up she was with feelings growing within her heart making her whimper low in her throat. Despite making her feel weightless, as though a magic wand was, whirling her bloodstream, awakening senses, making them bubble with heady shock, and wonder Jake continued to withhold what she now desperately needed until seductively her body began beseeching him to mollify some nameless craving. Coaxing him over her she did not know what made her legs part, so certain was she, she would die from the pain. It was Jake's, hands cradling her head, thumbs rouging her cheeks, his worshiping words erasing all traces of doubt.

In her eyes, seeing shadows of old pain, and uncertainty with a voice like black velvet, "Are you sure? If not, tell me, and I will stop. We have our whole lives to mend wounds. I can wait forever if I have to. I will never tire of loving you because I can make you mine anytime night or day all I have to do is dream." Butterfly kisses found her face whispers kissed her skin, "But if you let me, I promise to show you what happiness is and prove the extent of your love for me, and mine for you," heartfelt expressions easing her marginally.

Though she could feel the level of energy in and around him increase, she guided him in answer believing she would parish if he refused. Dizzy with pleasure, she never imagined a man, so rugged, so strong, so virile, could be so patient, and gentle the anticipated pain instantly replaced by pleasurable sensations making tears rise effortlessly riding on the crest of her emotions. What was there about Jake that always made her eyes run over? Her answer came when their cheeks met, and she felt his tears mingle with hers. Calling upon life's deed's, Jordan searched for what she had done worthy enough to find a man who was as vulnerable to life's experiences as she thought only she could be.

Surprise engulfed her when Jake stopped, and her hips began to stir creating foreign thrills that shot through her, sweet currents of warmth, as though they were cleansing her within. Unbelievably her body was encouraging his to match every move. Terrified his need for her would swallow her whole, when he gently began matching her efforts, Jordan realized Jake in his own compassionate way was keeping his promises the control of his body proving there was time for them to forgive, and forget. Holding her breath, hanging on for dear life suddenly she prayed he would not stop taking her to a place, somewhere she had never been, and somewhere they could only go together. How sad, she reflected, that he would never know that he was her first that in her mind she was a virgin after all, to the true sensations of making love because she wanted to, needed to, because she loved the person crawling inside her more than life itself. Someone who was leaving her breathless while bringing to life the dead woman inside. Unexpectedly, her whole body became one consuming heartbeat, as if, the fingers igniting the fire had become threads of excitement weaving through her heart taking up stitches in a fatal tear.

There was a tightening of her core as if unwilling to re-lease the love relieving the tension holding her in its grip the reality, more than her heart could bear, catapulting her with such force, such intensity; she screamed, and stiffened from fright, from wonder, from an ecstasy caused by fusing flesh. Wanting him so much, her nails bit into Jake's buttocks forcing him deeper, her response catapulting him over the edge, and bringing the urgency of his need to a crest releasing a spiritual cleansing making tremors cascade down his back. Wondrous was the sound of, his gasps reaching the pitch of hers, his breath catching as if he also was hanging on for dear life arms constricting around her trying to bring them back from the glorious place they rocketed to together. "Breathe Jordan, breathe for both of us, for I can never breathe again without you," his voice like sun warmed Carmel. As her stomach knotted with residual anxiety, she wondered how she would ever tell him he, not only filled the emptiness of her body, but drowned her heart as well, irrigated that smidgen of love she believed had shriveled, and died making it grow beyond the capacity of her very being.

Pure foolishness made Jake pepper Jordan's face with happy kisses. Rolling from her, hauling her to him, the aftermath of love became effervescent sounds of joyful giggles, and laughter. Wrapped in an embrace, while the quietness pressed in on her, Jordan struggled to fight off the immensity of the implications of their union. All that mattered was, she discovered happiness, and she was in love for the first and last time, the kind that if it had wings could fly her to the moon. Wings she prayed were strong enough to take her where she had to go.

Jake held Jordan close, his arms never before filled with so much a woman. The emotional price she paid to give the pleasures his body demanded he could only imagine the forbearance it took to set aside the onslaught of her past. Though he wanted to love her again, and again, he could not so uncertain was he she did not refuse because she, truly wanted him, or feared what he might do if she did. Wondering made his insides ache beyond any pain ever experienced. Fury began burning like hot coals, if only he could rip the hearts out of the men, who touched her; hurt her, a revenge that would do little to quench his thirst for blood.

For a long time he had been searching for a Sunday kind of love, one that lasted beyond Saturday night. There were no words to explain how he had given up on love until tonight. Before, when he believed he found it, when he kissed, and made love to the best, now they seemed nothing in comparison. How could he explain to Jordan she was, every woman in the world to him, his fantasy, his reality, everything decent, and fair, everything he would ever need the purest thing he had ever known. With tears poking at his eyes, he wondered if he would ever know her love again, for he was listening to her heart beating and, when he listened hard, he heard the sounds of leaving.

Rudely invading rosy thoughts was the devastation he felt the night he learned about Brenda, and Scorpio. Brenda, his feelings for her a moment in time compared to those for Jordan filling him so full, they became liquid seeking refuge from the corners of his eyes. Clinging tightly to the future, Jake stared at the ceiling mulling over something   Margaret once said, "Destiny, when it arrives, will bring all your dreams to you. Have faith, believe in magic, and nothing will stand in your way." Was Jordan his destiny, his magic, could she make his dreams come true? Jamming eyelids closed, sucking in his lips; Jake managed to keep the pain wrenching him from becoming audible. Right now, he had only one purpose, to kill Scorpio before he killed Jordan then she could go on with her life the best way she knew how. If she were his magic, possibly holding her, loving her, gave him some of her courage, enough to accomplish his goal.

Jordan stirred in Jake's arms as though hearing his thoughts. Embedding to memory her every feature, the moonlight silvering the room exposed a sweet face aglow from the aftermath of love. Tomorrow he would, take Jordan to retrieve the airline ticket, and money then, make sure she was safely out of harm's way before going after Scorpio.

When Jake reached his thumb out to smooth over Jordan's lower lip, though another sharp pain almost doubled him over, he did not move. He could not disturb her, and, while his thumb continued exploring her mouth, his other hand sought the bandages now soaked with blood. Afraid Jordan might see the telltale signs; he pulled the sheet over him. Never before did he felt so tired, every muscle, and bone screaming with exhaustion, yet, he did not dare close his eyes staying alert was imperative, until she slept, then he would leave, only then.

The euphoria dousing Jordan almost pushed her beyond coherent thought, almost. Deep within a trapped breath was growing in her midriff. She prayed her pretense of sleep was convincing while struggling with the delicious tingling heat spreading, threatening to expose the now tiny pants of breath. Jake was running his thumb across her lower lip, tracing her mouth all the way around, and around making her lips tingle.

Masterfully fighting off languorous feelings, Jordan waited for his breathing to altar. Splaying her hand across his broad, furry chest, she felt a steady, slow rise, and fall. Warily eyes cracking open, ever so slightly, examined his now closed, an inspection that if it had continued on to his torso, would have exposed life-draining blood seeping through the sheet.

Slipping from the bed, she quickly dressed. Painstakingly, pressing her hand between the mattress, and box spring she retrieved the key, and envelope.

Holding them to her breast, she glanced at Jake's face, a sight as though a lighted match had ignited her soul. Yes, she was doing the right thing.

Chapter 26

Crowns of imposing edifices' piercing the sky gleamed from the sun, just waking up stretching, and yawning, displaying its rainbow shades. In the wee hours of morning, rain had purified the sedated metropolis the now inky streets taking on life in diverse dimensions of motorized conveyances their vapors, and shrill racket desecrating the atmosphere.

Toasters popped, and coffee pots puffed, filling kitchens with a bouquet of fragrances. Obnoxious alarms awoke the hordes of humanity soon to litter the sidewalks, stores, office buildings, and parks.

A rejuvenating breeze stirring lush leaves coaxed dew-drops to sprinkle the ground below, and awoke birds who chirped their greetings. Flowers raised their heads toward the promise of a brilliant day as if thanking the heavens for nature's nectar. Lush lawns, playgrounds of sand, along with contorted workings of steel stood proud awaiting the squealing sound of children celebrating summer. For many a typical day consumed by boring routines, for others, a few hours' reprieve from the shadows of evening that, once again would haunt them, and lower their odds of surviving the sickle of death.

For eight individuals today would be one of resolution, and restitution. Hours quickly depleted by, reviewing the past, glimpsing the future, and making choices that could mean the loss of their life or that of a loved one. Every, second, minute, and hour, diminished desperately attempting to salvage a portion of their life aimlessly squandered. Today, their decisions, efforts, and spoken words, would affect the aftermath.

Their conscience was on trial. Upon reviewing all the evidence, contemplating, and confronting it, the verdict would be unrelenting. Hidden away in their own self-inflicted incarceration, with no outside influence, in a whisper of a second, with their heart as the jury, they would make their final choice.

Something awful fluttering around in her head, bludgeoning her mind startled Margaret awake. As if to keep her inner-self-contained, she clutched the blanket to her breast, and began interrogating her intuition. What was the dreadful feeling telling her, what did she do, or forget to do? Despite the warm morning air sweeping through the room, she shivered. Instantly, her plump toes poked into fluffy slippers, her arms plunged through terry cloth sleeves of her bathrobe.

Hastily arriving in the kitchen, her eyes, flicking back, and forth, said she did not know why she chose that room. All she knew, her lungs were shouting for air bringing her hands against the stomach expanding with something icy exploding, and distending her chest. For no rational reason, she glanced at the towel rack. Her apron was gone.

It took both trembling hands to maneuver her key into Jake's door. As quiet as a mouse, she padded into the kitchen. Though somewhat relieved to find her apron on the counter, she could not dispel the alarm clamoring against her skull. Hesitantly, she reached to snatch the cottony material, hoping, and praying she was wrong. As her worst premonition came true, ten fingers twisted the softness into tight wads. Jake's gun was missing. "Dear God," lurched from her mouth as a squeal. Before reaching Jakes bedroom, a horrifying spark of reality told her Jordan would not be there.

Seven miles in the air a seven fifty seven destined for the East coast left a trail of vapors crowning the mountains. An average looking man, casually dressed, lounged in a seat, his fingers drumming nervously on his knees. To his mortification, a thunderstorm delayed his flight. He was eager to return to, claim a sizable check, and witness the gratification on his friends face when revealing the results of his accomplished task. Knowing that once he informed his colleague the disillusionment would be too heavy to digest, the reason for the irrefutable verification, sitting next to him, and documentation safely within the briefcase beneath his feet.

A wall-sized television hissing relentlessly, lights still glowing on the face of a DVD recorder, erotic pictures strewn on the coffee table alongside several video cases of pornography all evidence of what took place during the middle of the night. Scattered on the floor was, Jake's plans for sweeping Scorpios' places of distribution, including photos' of hired henchmen, and their lengthy records. Torn pieces of a red sequined dress draped a lampshade, a chair and portions of the carpet, high heels, a garter belt, and black silk panties lay on a library table behind the sofa. Twisted nylon stockings draped from the arms of a wooden chair. Beneath diffused light, the blade of a knife gleamed. A level of exhilaration from, alcohol, drugs, and the culmination of sexual fantasies had summoned the realms of insanity. Sitting nude in a chair, a maniacal smile pasted Scorpios' face.

Billy's torso was slumped over his desk, a pen in one hand, a gun in the other. A white tuxedo spread neatly on the bed. On the floor black polished shoes, in a corner, two suitcases, and strewn on the carpet, balls of crumbled paper. Taking the entire evening to compose, two letters' were propped against his mother's photo, one addressed to Jake, the other, McMaster's. In front of them reflections of light drew attention to a badge. What appeared to be another letter was partially visible beneath the weight of Billy's chest, a composition of conscience.

Dear Mother,

By the time, you receive this . . .

Wearing a silk bathrobe, Marla sat at her dressing table, her fingers filled with tissues dabbing at blood seeping from the corner of her mouth, while others attempted to straighten snarled curls. The lights circumscribing the mirror corroborated what she already suspected as a palm smoothed over a shoulder bearing imprints of fingers already turning into bruises. Her meager effort to scoop cold cream to remove smudged makeup alerted her senses to the multitude of muscles trumpeting pain, and brought her attention to wrist burns caused by nylons tied to a chair. Scrutinizing the results of the evening, she shivered, and shook uncontrollably.

Rendering the sympathetic touch she craved, in slow motion the cushions of four fingers, smoothed over blank features, wiping away remains of moisture turning the whites of her eyes into a sea of red. Lowering her gaze to the capsule on the vanity top, she contemplated the contemptible injustice Scorpio demanded she perform. Elbows seeking stability allowed her face to fall into the welcoming oblivion of her hands.

Fists tightly balled, his obsession for Marla radically out of control, Butch peered through the cracked door inspecting her while his heart wildly tapped out messages to his brain. Hostility twisted his features. After spending the evening with Scorpio, as he viewed videos of a Jordan Montgomery, and abused Marla, Butch came to realize how proudly Scorpio wore his mantle of debauchery. Forced to watch Scorpios' warped methods of relieving his sadistic lust for another woman out on Marla severed the invisible bond between his master, and himself. Butch despised his cowardice for not slaughtering Scorpio then a desire thwarted by the knife Scorpio held against Marla's throat. As intended, Scorpio's definitive blow made its mark. Never again would Scorpio touch Marla or any other woman. It mattered little that the color of his skin would prevent him from winning Marla's affections. Now loathing the man he once admired, Butch wanted him dead.

The vibrating jets circulating warm water around Jordan's body did not succeed in relieving the tensions building within, nor did the liquid once filling the Waterford crystal goblet on the marble basin. Reliving her one night of euphoria with Jake, the fragrant bubbles, mushrooming creatively, spilling over the edges of the tub, sought new dimensions. Beside her, on a glass, and brass-serving cart, a half-empty bottle of an insanely expensive wine, and delicacies on fine bone china, that remained untouched.

Littering exorbitant carpeting and European antique furniture were thousands of dollars previously hurled into the air. Closet doors sprung wide proudly displayed its unnatural vacancy, except for the gold, satin, floor length gown, and matching sling-back heels. Visible from an opened sequined purse, tossed on the bed, was an airline ticket, the nozzle of a gun, and a special delivery receipt stub.

Discovering Jake in his bed unconscious from the loss of blood, Margaret summoned the doctor. Leaving the physician to tend to him, she quickly returned to her apartment to dress. Before she finished, the doorbell rang. Expecting the ambulance she summoned, she hastily opened it surprised to find a Special Delivery courier.

Despite the ambulance waiting outside, belligerently dis-regarding doctors' orders, Jake was up, and dressed by the time Margaret returned to his apartment. Breathless, she shoved the package just delivered into his hands. As Jake's trembling fingers clung to a note, the box containing forty thousand dollars crashed to the floor. The message he was trying to decipher, like shards of glass tearing at his heart, and filming his eyes.

Jake,

I know neither of us wanted this to end badly, but we are smart enough to know in order for things to end, it usually does.

In your own words, a bargain is a bargain, so I took the airline ticket, and the ten thousand dollars that were rightfully mine. The remainder of the money belongs to you. By the time you receive the package no one will be able to find me.

It would be best to give our lives up to fate. Maybe in another life, another time, somewhere, things would have worked out. Right now, all I ask is a moment in time to be all I can be.

You see I have discovered life is nothing more than one gigantic hole some people fall in, and fill it with light so that others can find their way out. That is you, Morgan. My life has so many holes if you stacked them together you would fall in forever. Problem was I did not know I was lost, that I was waiting for someone to turn my life around, until you found me.

If our eyes never touch again, always remember what we shared was an incomparable gift. You kept your promises by proving to me my love for you, and yours for me. In my cold, desolate world, I did not know sunshine existed until you shined on my shoulders.

Say goodbye to Margaret for me, and thank her. Tell her I love her with a hug, and kiss. She is, without a doubt, "Mary" herself. Please listen to what she tells you Morgan, she loves you so much.

Remember when you told me you now had it in you to keep all your promises, well; I know in my heart that you would have done your best. I pray your heart can forgive me, and grant me a few more. Give up those damn cigarettes, cut your hair, and fall in love again, be happy, and when you meet all the Scorpios your life is destined to destroy, wear your vest, please, Jake, please.

Jordan

Jake would have believed Jordan was safely out of the way, as he intended. That she went in search of a new life if Margaret had not confessed Jordan rummaged through his trunk, and stole his gun. Anxiety, and anguish colliding, scalded his throat, his skin, and gushed in liquid from his eyes.

Chapter 27

Black velvet was the night, dotted with sequins brought to life by the moon's kiss. The metropolis' was dressed to kill. Record breaking temperatures radiated off sun-scorched structures, pungent smells of asphalt mingled with echoes of the familiar songs of twilight; tires, horns, sirens, squealing brakes . . . gunfire. As the majority of the masses snuggled, falsely secure, wrapped in the arms of their dwellings, others went in search of the promises of the night.

Moonlight glimmered on a lustrous white limo parked in front of the fashionable Parakeet Club, inside; gloved fingers were nervously twisting the gold chain of a sequined purse around, and around. Hidden behind tinted windows, Jordan searched for the once so easily summoned switch capable of shutting out a mass of sensations troubling her mind, toying with every muscle, and every speck of skin. To her dismay, the proficiency no longer existed.

The love she found considerably melted a hardened core leaving in its wake new and wondrous consciousness lining her interior with sugar. Fear of losing Jake brought tightness to her chest threatening disaster, for his sake, recovery was necessary to re-enforce what little courage remained. Somehow, someway, she had to stitch together unraveling nerves, and extract from memory a smidgen of the strength, and bravery Jake exhibited.

Filling the day with lifelong dreams, she wandered aimlessly through exclusive stores, wallowed in penthouse luxury, and sampled the finest gourmet foods nevertheless, long before the evening tide chased the sun away Jordan came to understand the hollowness of such extravagances. Now enveloped by plush leather the truths were even clearer. What she truly wanted she would never experience again, Margaret's company, her delicious meals, her friendship, the comfort, and security of Jake's meager apartment, his arms, his kiss, his love. Unimaginable as it seemed, the final day of her life had been more miserable than all the others were.

Swiftly, as if a shade stretched beyond its capabilities snapping, and rolling in defiance, Jordan stuffed self-pity into the deepest crevice of her mind. Before her, displayed on the façade of the building, staring back were posters of Brenda Star the club's featured singer, images turning her to stone, and abruptly reminding her of her mission. Scrutinizing the billboards, she came to admit the captivating creature was indeed breathtaking the reality erupting a beastly jealousy honing teeth, and lengthening the nails feeling as though they would pierce the fine material of her gloves.

God how she despised the Brenda's of the world who, flagrantly paraded their womanly wares, pretended a false fragility using it as a weapon to solicit the male ego. She would have thought Jake, of all people, had more sense than to fall for such deception then, again, she had to admit when it came to matters of the heart all barriers were easily disintegrated.

If Margaret spoke the truth, that all of Jake's problems began at this club, how fitting they end here as well, Jordan reflected. Though uncertain as to how the evening would end instinct told her the two people she had come to hate were waiting inside.

Entering through the burnish swishing doors, spellbound by a spectacle beyond imagination, she was unaware of a door attendant, dressed in a tuxedo, whisking her cape from her shoulders. Beautiful people were everywhere drinks in hand, laughing, conversing, and dancing, men in white and black tuxedos', women in an array of glamorous, glittering gowns.

The subdued light fixtures fanning upward, and the black and white portraits of Bogart, and Bacall hung artistically on ivory walls, were the only draping on otherwise sterile partitions. Black tablecloths and red napkins twisted in decorative shapes, along with a single red rose, and flickering white candle, dressed each circular table. Providing privacy, white wicker high back chairs added their charm to the scene. Crimson velvet sprawled over areas unoccupied by the ebony dance floor shining so brilliantly it shimmered like water. Black glass topped a bar; curving like a reptile, while white padded edging offered comfort for elbows of those choosing to sit on matching seats supported by tubular chrome. A mirrored wall behind the bar provided an overview of the club calling particular attention to the orchestra, and the female performing under hues of multicolor lights. Not only was Brenda gorgeous, her voice was alluring as well. At once, Jordan felt like the ugliest of ducklings.

Staring overly long at the couples swirling around the dance floor, beneath a mirrored ball hanging from the ceiling sending dots splashing everywhere, she felt faint. She probably would have if not for men, whose eyes had zeroed in, as though binoculars, making their customary repugnant perusal. Defying the urge to run, head held high, posture perfect, a picture of grace, and beauty, giving no clue to the emptiness inside, Jordan searched for the man she would recognize anywhere.

Just as she inhaled a deep breath to enable keen senses to detect his presence, a man across the room stood, before the odor of his cologne reached her, the way he moved, his face, his eyes, Jordan knew she found the enemy. Scorpio's demeanor, filling the room with a crackling force, reminded her he was nothing more than a parasite who thrived on devouring people. It took long seconds to clear the hovering miasma caused by the anticipation of their meeting each second forcing her heart to drum in mute trepidation.

When Scorpio stood tall, an arm's length away, his hand plucking hers, his mouth whispering her name, Jordan might not have heard for all the reaction she gave. However, as her body vibrated recklessly inside, the unwavering eyes staring through him warned Scorpio the, elegant, fragile, woman standing before him came tonight with lethal intent on her mind. When his hand swallowed hers, despite the hate-filled words wobbling on her tongue, and the pulse beating wildly beneath her skin, she managed to cage them by closing the bars of tightly clenched teeth.

Surveying Jordan, it was as though the heat wave of the day had sifted through Scorpio her cool, and refreshing, presence rewarding his instincts. Eyes' devouring hers allowed his mind to wander to the videos of a young girl that now seemed nothing compared to the goddess before him a temptress who sent a sizzling message alerting him to the pleasures yet to be discovered. It did not matter Jordan's once long, wavy, pale blonde hair was now short, it was her, sculpted features, and sweetly rounded chin her tempting full lips, lush lips, infinitely kissable, that not a trace of lipstick could improve, sending immeasurable tremors penetrating his bones. Imagining how they would taste made his mouth water. Never before had he known a woman who's natural beauty out shined the brightest jewel that surely they would have looked dull in comparison.

Jordan's, gold, satin, and spaghetti strap gown appeared as though painted on, the brush calling particular attention to a lean rib cage, and sharply curved waist. Its designer had taken great pains to expose a liberal portion of flawless, porcelain, skin glowing with a pink sheen. Heaving generous, full breasts pleading for attention were pitching erected nipples against the material.

Despite her beauty, it was not until within firing range of her magnificent tiger eyes, radiating bolts of hatred, and disgust, that Scorpio became irreversibly bewitched. Jordan was indeed an enchantress taught well the supple movements of the body, the eyes, and the mouth, that enticed the male species. She would be a prize kept under lock, and key for his amusement. The way his body was reacting to, the mere sight of her, the touch of her gloved fingers, he knew it would be a long, long time before tiring of her gifts.

Wearing an insolent grin, his voice reeking with confidence, Scorpio spoke, "Well, well, my dear Jordan, this is indeed a pleasant surprise."

Eyes fixed, face void of emotion, Jordan's whip like tongue lashed across his face lacerating it to the bone. "Let's eliminate the bull shit, and cut to the business at hand. I believe we are sitting over there." Tugging her hand free, she sauntered in the direction of his table.

Staring after her, lost in the sway of her body, the creases of her buttocks evident beneath shifting material, Scorpio was struggling to come to terms with finally meeting a true competitor for his games the thought alone sending scalding spasms to his loins.

There was not a woman in the world that would not drool over Scorpio, the briefest thought making Jordan gag. With bronzed skin, black hair, and ice blue eyes, capable of drawing the attention, and envy of even the male gender, Scorpio was extraordinarily handsome. The smell of his cologne, mind numbing, along with his tuxedo, stark white, fitted to a washboard torso like a glove. Tonight, however, he was the enemy, and without the slightest feeling of remorse, she would send him to hell.

Reaching to assist Jordan with her chair, a stiff posture accented by a razor-edged glare demanded he reconsider, and while he stared in awe of her bravery, she, positioned herself confidently, drew the chair forward, and placed her purse on her lap.

Seated beside her, a slight movement of Scorpios' eyes summoned a waiter who poured wine. Lifting a crystal stemmed flute of ruby liquid to his sinister lips, Scorpio spoke. "Tonight should prove to be very entertaining, don't you agree, my love?"

Jordan's fingers itched to slap him. Visibly bristling, with a sweep of her eyelids, gold challenged blue, her reply clipped, and as sharp as shark's teeth. "I am not your "love" and never will be."

Though her bile wrenching confidence exposed Scorpio's pearl white teeth, he rallied, "Well now, my darling, I would not be too sure, the evening is still young, and we have only just begun." His, feminine, manicured hand wandering to her lap, halted abruptly when encountering a cold steel cylinder trained at his waist.

Sneering contemptuously, Jordan's expression turned stubbornly belligerent, her countenance giving every indication of a woman about to lose her temper. "If the thought of ever touching me again becomes as much as a glimmer in your eyes, you will be wearing a hole where your heart now beats."

There was no mistaking Jordan's murderous stare, the deadly purpose emanating from gold orbs turning them large, and bright with repulsion. A smart man, Scorpio knew she meant what she said. With thoughts of crushing Jordan's spirit thrilling him beyond reason, he reluctantly relented.

Laughing without humor faded his grin into a thin, firm line. Flashing across his face was a warning fearsome enough to make a rattlesnake reconsider. Still, to his disappointment, the look of intimidation failed to bring a trace of fear to Jordan's features. "You will not get out of here alive," he taunted.

Jordan's frosty reply shot slivers of surprise up his spine. "I do not intend to."

Abruptly, Jordan's glare pinned a figure entering from the rear of the club each advancing step making her elegant brows collide, her gaze become wild, and fanatic. Silently, she commanded her hand to halt that otherwise would have flown to her mouth to trap a gasp of surprise. In her heart, she wanted to disbelieve what she now knew to be true. There was no mistaking the similarities, black hair slicked back, ice blue eyes, and dark skin except for age, dressed in identical formal attire, exceptionally well groomed Billy was Scorpios' double. Instantaneously, an understanding flowed through her as to what there was about Billy all along that was untrustworthy. She could not help but wonder how crushed Jake would feel upon learning the truth.

"Sit next to me, my son I have an interesting party planned for this evening." So filled was he with a wealth of satisfaction that the word "son" summoned the reaction he had been unable to, Scorpio never once took his eyes off Jordan's melting features.

Deciphering Jordan's narrowed eye's, spitting venom, and screaming questions, feeling her intent of murder sift through him, Billy complied despising himself for bringing that look to breathtaking features.

Filtering out the music filling the background, Jordan heard only silence bred from deceit. It was not until a woman stood beside Scorpio, that her eyes' became daggers directed toward enemy number three.

With a smile full of amusement, Scorpio gloated, "Marla! I don't believe introductions are necessary, do you?"

Marla's eyes fell short of Jordan's glare.

Understanding flowed through Jordan Brenda was Marla's stage name.

As if a mechanical robot Marla positioned herself in a chair on the other side of Jordan there was no need for her to speak the frothing inside Marla was emanating through every pore.

With a lift of Scorpios' pointer finger, Jordan instantly recognized the black man reaching his side in a matter of seconds. "Take a seat, Butch I would not want you to miss the party." Looking uneasy doing so, Butch now sat beside Marla.

Hawkish eyes' darted around the table authoritatively. "My, my, my, aren't we one happy family," spoken through a wide smile exposing venom tainted teeth. "Only one person is missing, the most important game piece of all." Obviously relishing wielding his lance, Scorpio turned his attentions to Jordan. "Now, my little cherub, it should not be too much longer, while we wait, let's toast the master of drug enforcement."

"He will not be coming," Jordan confidently spat through meshed teeth. "He does not know I am here. Any game played tonight will be between you, and me."

Scorpios' gaze dropped to well-rounded breasts in the candlelight, Jordan was soft and creamy looking, edible like the most tempting of deserts. Eyes leveling with hers, appearing liquid gold, and surprisingly intimidating, dove to luxurious cherry lips. The heat massaging his groin told him tonight no menu would be required. "I am sure you are quite mistaken, Jordan you see, if you were mine, I would not allow you out of my site for one second. Knowing Morgan, trust me, little one, he will be here. Marla, my love, I believe you have a special additive for our honored guests drink."

As jealousy gave a little punch to her heart, Marla's glance flicked to Jordan's then to her purse on the table. Scorpio's glare, boring through her, collapsing her defiance, forced trembling hands to retrieve, and clutch the handbag. Melting from Scorpio's heated stare, fingers hesitantly withdrew, and held a capsule. Like a tennis ball, Marla's pleading eyes bounced from Billy to Butch hoping one of them would intervene. With disgust, and disappointment realigning her features, obediently Marla dropped the capsule into Jordan's glass.

Releasing a savage laugh, Scorpio returned his attentions to Jordan. "Now the game has begun, sweet thing. You see I will not have to touch your precious Morgan you are going to kill him. I have a feeling Mr. DEA is just a trifle smitten by you, and you, well, maybe, just maybe, you feel the same therefore, whether or not he walks out of here alive is up to you.

Choice number one, if you agree to come with me, I will leave Chicago and Morgan in one piece." Reaching under the table, tugging on a package taped beneath, with a thump, he placed the sizable parcel in the center of the table. "As an incentive to make the appropriate decision, inside this envelope is riveting information pertaining to a young girl that would be of great interest to Morgan.

Choice number two, you can give your lover this informative package yourself, or I can." Scorpio chuckled, then continued, "Either way I will get to watch him die."

Like the best of poker players Scorpio was bluffing, he knew "love struck" Morgan would keep his investigation of Jordan a secret from everyone, especially her. The thought of his own cunning swelled his chest, like that of a pigeon's, as he watched Jordan shrivel in agony, how she turned ashen halfway through his speech to sickly-looking at the end her agitation soothing his temper like nothing else could.

As Jordan's past stood out in memory with unnatural sharpness, the room spun like a top. Lapping flames exploding from her neck set her hair on fire. The pieces of her heart Jake stitched back in place ripped open, and propelled into oblivion. Inwardly, like a leaf in a hurricane, she felt herself shake from the hatred, and frustrated helplessness caused by Scorpios' patronizing amusement. She wanted to, scream, claw his heart from his body, and vomit in his face the bile pitching into her throat. Instead, in useless supplication, her eyes found, Billy, Marla, and Butch, before flicking back to Scorpio.

Jake could not find out about her past. If he did, no one would have to kill her, she would do it herself. As the finger on the hand holding the gun trained on Scorpio tightened, another found, and pressed, that misplaced button capable of catapulting emotions, and sensations to the familiar side of darkness.

Teeth mashing, Billy forced himself to stay in his chair though he desperately wanted to, erase the torture conquering Jordan's confident countenance, and cleanse away the poisoned screams she barely managed to imprison. Wide eyes' turned the palest blue as he shot a disparaging glance toward Marla, and Butch wondering if they would remain loyal, considering they learned to disregard the atrocities Scorpio employed. They too had joined the ranks of many others too weak to survive his wrath, himself included.

As if spinning a roulette wheel, Scorpio continued to strip Jordan of her rebelliousness. "Of course, my precious, you could pull the trigger of the gun in your lap but then one of my marksmen would have to shoot the man entering the club behind you."

Every ones' attention found a starkly masculine clean-shaven face, Jakes hair meticulously cut, and styled, the snappy white tuxedo revealing a sinewy musculature like a second skin. Blatantly there was handsomeness impossible to ignore. Jake's reputation, endorsed by his countenance, the embodiment of arrogance, and poise and his slow, easy movements spoke of a self-confidence forged by experience. Square shouldered, and erect, simply strolling through the club commanded everyone's admiration oh, not from his appearance alone they sensed, the ruthlessness in his eyes, the violence, making him capable of anything.

Jake's entrance further aided in concealing three people, entering long before Jordan, seated unseen by either Billy or Scorpio. Positioned behind the enemy, the high back chairs facilitated their camouflage. Despite their efforts, unable to locate Jake, what they knew remained their secret.

The sight of Jake robbed Marla's breath making her thankful she was sitting. Completely unstable, she felt her heart leap like a bird exploding from a cage, flaring, soaring, and swooping. Nervous fingers locked. It had been a long time since she saw the elegant, magnanimous Jake who was, too good looking, too assured, too male, too much the goddamn hero. Slowly, shriveling inside, her black dress seemed to be consuming her. The way she had, mistreated him, torn his world apart, ate at her far too long, the memories staining her body from inside. Realization hit full force; he was the only man she truly loved.

Watching him stroll toward the table, she knew why he came, to claim the woman he loved. It would not be her. Like an awful blow to the heart, Marla suddenly understood that if Jake truly loved her he would have snatched her from Scorpio long before now, tough to admit, the feelings filling her, she had coming.

Jake's eyes, filled with the sunshine of love, were only for Jordan a look every woman in the world would give up everything for, Marla believed, if this magnificent man would only look once at them the same way.

Suddenly, realizing the summer sun never truly rose on their love, the chill of reality made her draw in a breath to coax a heart barely functioning back into place.

Plucking her thoughts from the clouds, Jordan tried to still the alarms blasting her ears. Wearing a smile looking as though she had a lip full of Novocain, she stared at Jake, loving him, and fearing for him, her heartbeats clattering like a pair of castanets. The fine bone hand fingering the gun on her lap shook uncontrollably. Surrounded by, and absorbed in Jake, for a brief moment she became lost in the realization she loved the crazy fool. He was, gorgeous, completely edible. Admittedly, attuned to him she was, with undeniable sensitivity, and precision the knowledge of what they shared temporary isolation from the real horror pending. She could not blink, move, or breathe Jake would have to do it for her. All she envisioned was how his splendid features would shrivel in pain once he learned the truth about her past how the pain might return him to the gutter. All he saw was a picture perfect portrait he painted of her. Grating her teeth in frustration, "Why now," she wailed inwardly, when happiness was so close. Maybe there was a God after all, and he was just waiting for this moment to punish her when it would hurt the most. How could she believe in heaven when she had only known hell? Even if sentenced to hell tonight, how could it be worse than what she already endured when in truth she could teach the Devil himself a little about suffering?

As she gazed at Jake, Butch, saw the blush of love come to Marla's face, felt the vibrations of her heart pulsating, heard her silent cries. He would give everything if she felt the same toward him feelings that, tonight were inconsequential. What mattered most was protecting her from Scorpio. Invading danger was, steadily advancing, thickening the air, growing hot, and suffocating.

Billy detected the familiar message in Jake's eyes pleading with Jordan not to move both knowing in a matter of a split second death could claim her. Sluggishly, Billy's hand slipped into his pocket, quivering fingers locking on a gun steadying staggering thoughts.

Concealed in a wicker chair; one of the three entering previously, Margaret's chins were wobbling as she tried to stay her emotions. Pudgy hands clutching, and twisting a handkerchief, one minute, now retrieved from her purse John's gun placing it on the table beneath a napkin, actions drawing a shocked reception from the other members of her party. Knowing the odds were not favorable for Jake, if it was the last thing she did, she would even them a little. Jake's expertise would handle Scorpio and she would settle the score with Billy.

Two years ago, when her son died of a suspicious over-dose, there was no doubt in her mind Scorpio was responsible. Now she knew who carried out the mandate. Well, he may have gotten her son; Margaret fumed, while the scriptures of the bible tug-of-warred in her ears, "An eye for an eye. Vengeance is mine sayeth the Lord," however tonight Scorpio was not going to claim Jake or Jordan her assurance greatly re-enforced when the other two in her party, one on each side of her, withdrew their weapons.

Each step forward, Jordan could almost see it happening, the change in Jake, the ruthlessness, the violence, coming to the surface, taking control. She felt his scrutiny, his caution and, wondered what there was about her that always managed to prick at the demons inside him. So intense were the spotlights of his eyes, her hand inching upward crept across the tablecloth, like a spider escaping a predator, seeking a cowardly escape in the poisoned wine.

Out of the corner of her eye, when Marla saw Jordan's hand move toward the glass, her fingers began gathering the edges of the tablecloth. Once Jake learned she was responsible for John's death, her life would be worthless. She could never endure the wrath of the man who, once held her in his arms, loved her. Nor could someone like her, accustomed to pampered indolence, serve time in prison. By ending her life tonight, at least she would go out in a blaze of glory. What better gift could she give the man she loved than to save the life of the one he loved?

Butch noticed Scorpios' eyes track Jordan, and Marla's moves. Unknown to everyone, his orders were to plant a gun beneath the table where Scorpio sat. Without batting an eyelash, Scorpio would kill Marla for the mere thought of betrayal. She should have known he would handle the situation; damn her for not trusting him she must know by now how much he loved her.

Reaching the table Jake's eye's fixed on Jordan's, shadowy caves of gold burning bright with orange flames scorching him. For a moment, he challenged her rebellion, so angry was he she put herself in eminent danger, his look enough to make a crazed animal cower nonetheless, her baleful glare continued. Like a whisper, faint, and far away, the desire she stirred by simply existing toying with him was startling. The fact he could even think of that now was a threat, a hazard.

Jordan's dress and the body exploding from it were inconsequential it was her divine soul straining Jake's heart dripping blood. She was, and always would be, everything to him. Aimed only at him, the sparks spitting from her eyes he knew ignited from fear for his safety. The barest smile tilted the corners of his mouth from knowing she loved him so. Never had he known love, so true, so pure, no sacrifice was too great, no pain too horrible to endure, until tonight when he saw the love for him in her eyes, a love positioned on a launching pad destined for disaster.

Sitting like a living portrait, the tiny movement of Jordan's hand toward the glass-triggered memories of long ago. Heartache returned Jake to the night of John's death when John drank heavily, and danced with Brenda. Though John had been drug free for some time, he had been showing signs of increased depression, and agitation. When John, and Brenda, returned to the table, he tried convincing John to take a taxi home. To his dismay, John insisted on one more drink. Horrified by the reflection like the flashing lights at an intersection, Jake's attention jerked back to Jordan's glass. Suddenly, he remembered how anxious Brenda was to appease John's wish. At that time, he did not believe the woman he loved was capable of murder. Now, he was certain. He could not take that chance again, not with Jordan, and while he prayed for a miracle, terror enveloped him wondering if she had already taken a drink.

The closer Jake got the more tense Jordan grew, like a cat on a hot stove, skittish, and jumpy. Obsessed with the package, her heart hammering so loudly would surely give her away. Heartbeats that stopped the moment emerald eye's, pure as truth, fixed her with a compelling stare, one reaching out for her making sweet-talks superfluous.

"Jake," she sighed wistfully.

The anguish the word related like lightning bolts, entering the top of Jake's head, arcing off bone, flesh, and muscle, working its way slowly through his mid-section. Jordan was teetering on a fraying tight rope stretched taut linking life, and death. One wrong move, one wrong word, and it would snap. "Have I told you lately how much I love you?"

Long moments passed before Jordan could choke out a single word, tension quivering in her voice, "Still?"

"Always," Jack's voice cracked from the weight of the word the tentative smile, so quick as to be almost nonexistent, flashing across her features making him wonder if he imagined it.

Eyes were riveted on the pair who seemed impervious to the rest of the world, their very immobility attracting attention. They were gazing at each other as if the few feet separating them were a complex maze they were desperately struggling to get through.

Deepening the spell, Jake continued, "Do you know that if anyone ever wrote my life story, you would be the best thing that ever happened to me?"

Moisture made Jordan's eyes sparkle. Blinking rapidly they strayed to the package, then to the goblet. Her face crumbled. How was that possible when he knew nothing about her, she screamed inside, if he knew, he would have never come after her. Shame entering her toes worked its way through her turning the roots of her hair red.

Comprehending what Jordan's eyes sought, though panic seized him, Jake's words remained as soft as a feather. "You are my one in a million chance of a life time. Life made a concession, and gave me a stroke of luck, and that is you. I have never known love. . ." When Jordan's glance shifted to Marla, then back to him, he continued, "I mean real love, until you. I am not going to lose you, not now, not ever. You are a fire I cannot put out. Look at me, look into my eyes can't you see you have always been there, and always will be." All Jordan saw was a sinking soul trying to change the tide.

Although I find this scene quite pathetic, and touching, I am afraid you are a little too late, Morgan then again, you always are. You do not seem to have much luck with people you love, do you? You see Jordan, and I, are engaged in a game that should prove quite amusing in the end."

Scorpio's fingers lightly brushing Jordan's flushed cheek was like a bullet piercing painfully. Recoiling, Jordan sharply cut her eyes toward him, and had they been a cobra's tongue they would have struck him dead.

Eyes telegraphing despair swished back to Jake so frightened was Jordan he would lose the control he was struggling with, a control he never mastered. She saw the bright flames shooting color across his face, and then watched him become, soulless, conscienceless, and fearless, as intense simmering anger contorted otherwise handsome features.

Transparent was Jake's skin when it came to Jordan. Wood catching on fire his glare directed at Scorpio erased his arrogant smile. Knuckles bleached of color, teeth bared Jake snarled, "Tonight you will find out life is not a neat little package you can hold in your palm, and crush. In every game, the winner takes all tonight you lose. Jordan is one woman you will never have. Your complete lack of scruples and compassion for human lives ends here. You have seen your last sunrise, Scorpio right here, right now, your ass is mine."

Wearing a garish grin, Scorpio retaliated, "My, aren't you the epitome of confidence. It took you long enough to piece things together. Kind of slow, wouldn't you say, for someone as celebrated as yourself?"

Jordan was certain Jake would leap across the table to choke the life from Scorpio, in his glare, a neon sign flashing MURDER. Then in an instant, eyes', sparkling with renewed clarity, as if suddenly gaining vision, danced back to hers touching her heart.

"It takes' someone very special to teach a dead end street is just a place to turn around that rock bottom is good solid ground that when you are down to nothing, you have nothing left to lose. Now, the only way is up. By standing outside the fire, life is merely survived not tried. Tonight it is time to dance within its flame."

Though Jake's outward appearance had changed drastically from when Billy first met him, inside, he remained the man who earned not only his, but also the city of Chicago's, adoration, and respect. A man who stood up for all the Jane and John Doe's in the world too weak to fight their own battles someone who, dared to defy the odds, wielded his sword for truth, and justice. Jake's intentions were clear, Billy knew, as sure as there was air to breathe, his hero would not back down. Brazenly, he stood with, no weapon for protection, just pure guts, as if believing justice would shield him from evil. Billy knew better, Jake did not stand a chance in hell of getting out of this one alive.

Unwittingly worrying at her bottom lip, Marla sat smitten by Jake's loving words to Jordan sending tiny shivers through her exposing a hidden raw spot of unhealed pain. Witnessing enemy's draw invisible weapons, a cold feeling of apprehension touched her spine, a jagged icicle of fear. If she were to gamble tonight, the stakes were against Jake. Thinking of him lying dead at her feet made her, want to cover her face, run, and hide, scream at the top of her lungs wisely, she never faltered.

When Jake's eye's pinned Scorpio's, out of the corner, he saw Billy, and began cursing himself for being so foolish trusting him was stupid, believing in him, growing to care for a person whose veins flowed with the same icy blood as his worst enemy. For the first time seeing them together, if not for age, they could be twins and he wondered why he had not noticed the similarities before, why he had been so blind, what were the odds? Right this second, he wondered if Billy's blood was tainted with enough of Scorpios' poison to make him as deadly. For a split second Jake's mind wandered to the night of the raid when, if not for Billy's backup, this nightmare would have ended. Could he trust Billy one more time? Did he have a choice?

Those of a psychopath, Scorpios' features showed bright with the lack of human care, human frailties, or vulnerabilities. Blackest sludge colored over ice blue eyes filling them with cold determination that spoke of smoldering, powerful anger. Still, his voice held no trace of the hatred eating like piranha's at his insides. "I believe you have met my son," then with a laugh full of tyranny, Scorpio persisted twisting the knife. "In fact, you groomed him to be as good as "Chicago's Mighty Hero."

With an audible click, Jake's glance struck Billy then, re-turned to Scorpio, his reply severing Billy's jugular vein. "I consider him one of the best."

Scorpio turned his attention to Billy, "Quite a compliment, wouldn't you say, my son?"

Blood gushing from an invisible laceration made it impossible for Billy to speak, so full was he of humiliation, and remorse.

Speaking with a good amount of rage, "Though, I must admit I admire your arrogance, and guts, the odds are not in your favor, Morgan. You have my finest bodyguard on one side, my son on the other, several men spread around the club itching for a signal to put a bullet through your head, and me in front of you. It would make my day if tomorrow's headlines read one of your own was responsible for your extermination. His attention spun to Billy, "If Morgan even as much as flinches, son, kill him."

Jake could visibly see Jordan shaking. An admirable effort at remaining calm and collected seeping from her filled her eye's with bleak infinite hopelessness. Grief transmitting from her features tightened Jake's nerves, so frightened was he of what she might do next. When her hand gripped the stem of her goblet, fear sent icy spears through his chest, gorging his guts, corkscrewing around his heart, and constricting it into a tight sphere of pain. If he made the slightest move all hell would break loose, there was no way Jordan could escape the gunfire, no way.

Steadying his voice, having all it could do to break through trepidations iron curtain, Jake made a last ditch attempt to chip through the invisible fortress Jordan built around herself. "Jordan, you have to believe our love is magic, nothing or no one can stand in our way. When we get through this, we will go find that place in time I promised you. Look at me see only me haven't I kept all my promises?"

Jordan felt like liquid, nothing more than a puddle of tears. Jake was maniacal to believe there was a chance in hell they would survive tonight. A foolish romantic, beating her fists against his chest, pleading, and begging, would be useless. She could tell him she, hated him, did not want him, did not love him, words that could never form on lips still burning from the memory of his.

"You do not know anything about me, Jake, if you did…" control cracked, the pain pulsating inside winding her so badly she could no longer protest. When Jordan raised the glass to her lips, though Jake knew it was not as simple as snatching her out of harm's way, he could not give up. Then again, how could he bring himself to confess he already knew the contents of the package? If they survived tonight, she would hate him for deceiving her she would leave him, and if she did, Scorpio might as well shoot him through the heart. As debilitating terror lurked, a cold feeling of fate settled in his gut.

Through the snarled net of his thoughts, Jake managed to summon words that for an instant seemed to freshen the stale, putrid, air hovering like a dense fog overhead. Eyes appearing as if they knew the darkness of her soul, he said, "I don't know much, but I do know I love you, and that is all I need to know all there is to know. When a person truly loves someone their love will see them through hurtful things said, and done, not because they forget, but because they love enough to forgive. Do not snatch the very breath from me; rip my heart from my chest for without you, I will have no soul."

The second hand on every timepiece in the room stopped as if waiting for father time to make a decision. Despite, flexing muscles, nerves screaming with pain, sweat soaking collars, the only sound heard was the swish of the sickle of death.

When the second hand moved, it was like a slow motion movie. Jordan stood her plea echoing off the walls bringing everyone to their feet. "Forgive me, Jake." Pressing the crystal glass against ruby lips, raising the gun, held limply in her hand, she aimed at Scorpios' head.

Leaping into midair, "No," Jake roared.

Jerking to her feet, Marla made a frantic attempt to knock the glass from Jordan's hand.

Snatching the gun from beneath the table, Scorpio fired.

Butch lurched in front of Marla.

Margaret stood, spun, and raised her gun.

Billy pulled a revolver from his pocket, and fired.

A member of Margaret's party scanned the room with his weapon. Without batting an eyelash, or the slightest thought of remorse, the other member of Margaret's party stood, aimed, and fired.

Shrieking innocent bystanders dove for cover, tables and chairs toppled, glass-shattered, silverware clanged flames from candles ignited whatever was in the way, rose petals tore from their stems, dresses, coats, and jackets ripped at the seams.

Doors of the club smashed against walls from the force of DEA agents' barging in. Sounding as though they were cannons, in rapid succession gun shots rang out splattering blood, tearing skin, ripping muscle, and shattering bone. Shrill screams of pain joined the pungent smell of gunpowder; eyes sprung wide became clouded, and vacant. Covered with blood, four people lay on the floor, one on the table. The slightest squeeze of a finger changed the course of the river of life.

Chapter 28

Glaring lights exposed the graphic hues of the repulsive scene. Dispersed throughout the structure, the countenance of the gathering affirmed the hysteria transpiring only moments ago. Testament to the certainty no one is quite as blind as victims of crime.

Of the gathering, some resembled petrified pieces of wood, their features lacking expression, others visibly shaking. Women were, weeping hysterically, sniffling into men's hankies covering their faces. Others were in the process of pulling themselves from under the tables providing protection, while paramedics made their rounds trying desperately to placate disgruntled clientele.

Portions of bodies gashed, and abraded, were beginning to swell, and discolor as the inflicted stanched the flow of blood with anything within reach. Expensive garments were ruined, hairdos in disarray, and jewelry scattered like worthless gravel among small smoldering fires. Glass crunched beneath shoes. Sirens screamed, and red lights flashed. Cameras', and video recorders, captured police officers reciting rights while securing handcuffs. In the midst, reporters made their rounds entering on IPads the varying renditions of shocked witnesses.

All of Chicago, and the rest of the world, would awaken, and as they consumed their morning meal, sipped caffeine, commuted to work, while moms' shushed their riotous children, newspapers, and broadcast systems of America would unravel the holocaust.

Again, Jake, and Jordan, would make front page headlines. Shaking their heads in disgust, clucking their tongues, and releasing sighs of relief, the citizens that did not go in search of the music of the night would deem themselves fortunate to have been safe within the refuge of their homes. Others, less fortunate, would forever remember the "Phantom of Death."

Psyche deranged from bereavement, tears splashing over cheeks, Butch mumbled undecipherable agony as he sat on the floor cradling, and rocking Marla's body, her elegant black dress scarlet, face ashen, her eye's vacant from death's grip.

Amazed McMasters stood wondering how, without firing a shot; he managed to prevent Scorpios' men from interfering, all now handcuffed by DEA agents.

Stunned by the suddenness of it all, Margaret neglected to release the safety on the gun she held. Instead of firing, it fell to the carpet the moment Jake, and Jordan, plummeted to the floor. Rushing to their aid, finding them motionless, and splattered with blood, she became hysterical. Knees, buckling, smacking the floor with a thud brought her between the two people she loved.

There was no time for deliberation paralyzed by shock, his white tuxedo, and hands splashed crimson, Billy tried to comprehend all that took place. Eyes flicked from his father's body slumped on the table, blood gushing from a bullet wound to his head, to Jake, Jordan, Marla, a smoking gun. Nothing else registered as the scene replayed, like a scratched record.

The instant Scorpio fired his gun Jake wrenched his body toward Jordan, the thrust of the bullet hurling him into her. Billy's ears still rang from the horrible sounds of Jake's groan, of Jordan's head cracking against the floor. Eyes jerking toward Scorpio he saw him turn his gun on Marla her facial features depicting pain, and anguish, her blood curdling scream, and Butch's grief sending icy fingers up his spine.

The worst was when, a split second before they widened with surprise, Scorpio's eyes met his, how his ludicrous smile turned somber, how he stretched his fingers toward him as he fell forward onto the table. Never again would he endure one of his father's cold stares all too frequently, dripping with criticism, conveying disappointment, and disgust. Now all Billy comprehended was the assembly of admirer's, and co-workers gathering around the motionless couple on the floor. The bedlam making it virtually impossible for paramedic's to push their way through the frantic crowd, too much precious time elapsing before they were able to reach the victims.

As if his eyes were a video camera whose angle had been widened, Billy took in the entire chaotic scene, random close-ups of, the crowd's faces smitten with soulful anguish, lips moving in silent prayer, arms blotting perspiration, and tears, women turning their faces into escorts' lapels. People staring whey-faced, and incredulously as the paramedic's yanked open their bags, frantically fumbling for vital apparatus.

Before their experienced hands could summon any kind of a miracle, a scream erupted. Jordan shot upward. While the ranks closed in around her with an incredible amount of strength, she shoved Margaret aside along with those trying to attend to her, and Jake. Perched on her knees beside Jake she could see no visible signs as to where the bullet entered, nonetheless, she knew, with awful certainty, Jake had been hit. Desperately searching for the wound that killed him made the scene more heart wrenching. Profanities spilled from her mouth. Fingers tore maddeningly at his clothing, so overpowering was the need to pluck the deadly bullet from him, to breathe life into him. Physically thwarting, and verbally cursing, everyone who attempted to help, she ripped open his jacket, and shredded his blood soaked shirt. Ranting, and raving, her fingers continued until finding what they sought. Hand splayed across the wound to his heart, the bullet did not penetrate because Jake kept another promise by wearing his vest. Facing heavenward, eyelids squeezed shut Jordan's body fell limply across his chest, her voice giving in to screaming vocal chords expelling her relief.

Seconds seemed like years before Jake's fingers, snatched her hair yanking her head back his weak voice immersing her in joy. "Jesus Christ, Jordan. When are you going to learn to trust me? Didn't I tell you I would keep all my promises?"

Jubilation instantly realigned the mass of faces staring at their hero. Echoes of riotous cheers, and laughter filled the room.

Raising her torso slightly, Jordan's fists scrubbed her moisture riddled face pink with glee before her arms, finding Jake's neck, practically choked him in a mad attempt to bring their lips together.

Before allowing the kiss, gripping her arms, Jake held her from him barking worriedly. "You didn't drink from that glass, did you?" When she shook her head no, he shrieked, "Dammit, Jordan, don't you ever criticize my smoking again. You are going to be the death of me yet." Her, sweet, full lips crushing his, cut off what she knew would be a lecture littered with expletives. Hauling her to him, they became a tender scene brightening the gloom, and erupting thunderous whoops, and hollers.

Only then did Billy's eyes converge on the person responsible for killing Scorpio. Hands cuffed, an officer on opposing sides, one holding a plastic bag containing a gun, despite years of separation, he recognized his mother. Staring blankly at each other, as elation continued to ring in the room, no one noticed the parcel on the table had disappeared. No one could have predicted what tomorrow's dawn held in store.

Chapter 29

On the dark side of eventide is a sphere between sunset, and sunrise, coaxing the dueling of dreams, and nightmares. Together they toy with our sub-conscience until we can no longer distinguish tangible from fabrication a realm when we are most vulnerable, when sleep evades us.

Adamantly refusing hospital care, after long deliberation, Jake agreed to have Philip drive them home, a dear friend, and detective who recently returned from the West Coast with Billy's mother. Not wanting Jordan out of his sight, arm in arm, Jake, and Jordan claimed the back seat. Margaret joined them still biting at what little remained of her fingernails. No one spoke throughout the journey home. Shock had taken its toll.

Overhead, moving swiftly, dark swelling clouds trumpeted a coming storm. Moments later steady drizzles of moisture pattered the roof. A mass of jagged splinters lit the sky as thunder jarred the vehicle, an intense storm becoming hammering rain. Windshield wipers swishing rapidly at the deluge could not hold the sheets of water at bay, a torrential cloudburst, making crystal clear the obstacles blocking the path of a bright sunny day.

Eyes flicking to the rear view mirror, Philip examined his cargo. Everyone was withdrawn within his or her own cocoon. He was mulling over the information in his briefcase he never had time to discuss with Jake besides, considering what transpired, Jake already knew. There would be plenty of time for the remainder of the story tomorrow.

A tornado was twisting within Jake, and Jordan, spiraling, drilling upwards stealing their minds, the staleness of the past funneling, and picking up ferocious speed, a force making the fierce storm outside, irrelevant. It did not matter how hard or fast their psyche ran the inferno of change was engulfing them, a labyrinth ten times worse than in the past. Before dawn, both needed to find answers. Locked in an embrace, there were no words to ease the granulating emotions. As sure as the moon fell dark, the sun would herald another day, by then, the mountain before them needed to be concurred.

Margaret was busy thanking God for saving the two people she loved, and asking that they might find the peace both deserved. Woman's instinct told her there was more to their story; it was stirring the air, and robbing oxygen. It was best she never know all the buried secrets she had to trust their love for one another would be strong enough to carry the burdens of the past.

While the stress from all that happened mingled with that yet to come they listlessly entered Jake's apartment. Jordan went directly to the bedroom to lie down for just a few minutes, she said, to ease the nauseating pounding in her head. Unable to trust her, Jake settled into his chair beside the bed.

Margaret invited Philip to get a few hours of rest in her spare bedroom.

Thinking of how close he came to losing her, suddenly, Jake could not see beyond Jordan's elegant dress. Her restless changing of positions offering splendid views of the curves beneath the thin, adhering fabric, each breath stretching the material taut, making all too visible the dark circles, the erected nipples. Shifting gold clung to a lean rip cage, stomach, and the juncture between her legs. He cursed the moon's intrusion keeping him wide-awake, the search light magnifying a strap that had slipped from a shoulder taking with it a portion of bodice exposing a generous amount of breast. He could overlook the bloodstains, they were his therefore it did not matter still, for a breath of a second, he wondered if death would be easier than knowing she would be out there, somewhere, and that he would spend the rest of his life searching, wanting.

Already singed by desire, the heat, and humidity of the night was antagonizing. The urge to, go to Jordan, cover her with his body; enjoy the gifts her body offered was unbearable. A driving mad kind of lust that could not be quenched before persuading her to stay, to marry him, to spend forever in his arms. Troubling him now was, finding the words, and the right moment to accomplish the formidable task. Sweating profusely, he decided a shower would help clear his mind.

Like a sleek feline, Jordan stretched, and yawned, the room aglow by the light of the moon. Sleep provided a false sense of peace, now awake, and her headache had eased, everything came charging forward. The possibility of staying wrung her heart. Just when there might be a tomorrow, yesterdays came to torment.

The sound of running water signaled Jake was in the shower. "Now," her mind screamed. "Go now!" Surely, someone found the package containing juicy details that would bring great delight to the gossiping world, at this very moment, the universe probably knew.

The worst part was she could handle what other people thought no one mattered except Jake. If he discovered her past, she would evaporate into oblivion, crazy thinking considering eventually he would find out anyway. The past always has a way of creeping up when you least expect, as if dirt swept under a carpet. The longer they were together, the harder it would be to keep secrets' then, how would she say goodbye? It was best to be truthful now Jake deserved to know, but, not yet, not tonight, she was not ready to leave, so oppressive was the need to lie beneath him just one more time. Maybe, if there were a God, he would find it in his heart to grant a miracle that would allow taking a part of Jake with her.

Quietly Jordan sneaked into the bathroom. Never before was she unable to take her eyes off a man. Stealing her breath was the commanding presence of Jake's body, visible through the thin shower curtain. Rigid muscles covering broad shoulders, tapered to a narrow waist continuing on to perfect buttocks, his build, tough and sinewy, and lean like a cowboy. Time exposed his soft core, yet his exterior remained a visual display of sheer male sexuality.

It only took a second for gold satin to wither to the floor. A wave of her hand moved the shower curtain aside. Though Jake's back was turned, she saw him tense, every part of him alert, and aware. There was no stopping the eager hands finding his wrists briefly before slithering upward over the contours of powerful arms. Beneath her touch, she felt him quake. Head rearing back, he took in quick breaths, reactions encouraging her to massage the tense muscles, rhythmical movements playing a torturous melody, down washboard sides, and around a firm waist. Moving upward her fingers lingered in the forest covering his chest, then continued to explore the plane of his stomach, her body inching closer, and closer until his hands drew her body tightly against his. The only thing between them now was the night, making her wish she could enter the darkness with him where she would be safe forever.

Lathered with soap, manly hands, found her forearms, his fingers warm, and tender stroking gently. Ear pressed to his back, Jordan heard the propulsion of his heart as lungs frantically gasped for air. Still, he did not move, so content was he as her lips kissed his back, here, there, everywhere. He smelled wonderful, the taste of him even better, and, she wondered if it was remembering him dressed in a tuxedo making her shudder, or memories of the treasures beneath. Every part of her wanted to move, even toes raising, and lowering her body in slow, easy motions allowing her breasts to brush his back, a spontaneous notion that soon brought her stomach, and hips against his firm buttocks. Before her fingers found, and clung to him, she knew he was aroused. Despite the groan swelling the occupied space, Jake did not allow her exploration to linger his desire so great, unable to survive much longer, he turned around. With so much love for her showing in his eyes, the water spray was nothing compared to the tears drowning her cheeks.

Holding her from him, eyes touring her body did the kissing. Hands smoothing back her hair cupped her face to tilt it up to him. With a gleam of carnal fire in his eyes, terrified his need for her would swallow him whole he whispered against her mouth. "Whenever I look at you my feet don't touch the ground. Your beauty steals my breath away. Tonight let's not talk about tomorrow or forever, step into my heart, and leave your cares behind," his voice, dark, and warm, husky, seductive.

His thoughts wrapped around her. Tingling ran from the top of her head to her toes. They were dangerous commodities, his eyes', his smile, his lips, the thumbs roughing her cheeks yet, nowhere near as dangerous as his talented mouth slowly floating over every speck of her face, until his lips found hers drawing them in, separating them to allow his tongue to seek its reward. All at once, her past became sand castles in the tide, slowly washing out to sea and the night felt new with endless possibilities. Freeing her face, his hands glided over her neck and shoulders before coming to rest on her breasts where they lingered. Soon, his expression turned hungry, he was frantic, his desperation evident, suddenly he pressed her against the wall, his body restless to seek satisfaction, his mouth refusing to relinquish hers, her arms tight around his neck, his hands worshiping everything they touched.

Desperate for breath, feeling at a complete loss for words, her lips began exploring his stomach that drew in quickly, while teeth nibbled lower. Jordan's surprise echoed within the confines as masculine hands came to her head, fingers raking through hair maintaining a gentle grip lifting her face to align with his. She had no memories of, how their bodies found the floor, how the towel came beneath her Jake never released her senses long enough, but never would she forget her own cries of pleasure as each drew their own climax to mesh with the other.

Despite pretending not to be aware of her presence, Jake heard Jordan enter the bathroom. He was having all he could do to keep from hauling her into the shower then, when she entered, he thought he would die if she touched him, surely, if she did not. Her fingers spreading delicious tingling heat, each touch like a match setting fire to everything in its path, were sensations searing his heart, and soul. She was, pushing him beyond coherent thought, filling him with euphoria becoming whimpers low in his throat one minute, and gigantic sounds launched into space the next.

He was unable to believe the vision beneath him until seeing the rising flush of blood on her throat, her breasts, their joining, and flesh fusing. Pressing deeper swept licking flames through him making him gasp from a wild intoxicating pleasure. There was no stopping the bursts of flashing rays set off in his brain, the tremors before the familiar rush of ecstasy claimed him. Ultimate splendor, Jordan was. This time he knew she no longer feared him. In her eyes, he saw the same kind of hunger in her, the same raw longing burning in her eyes. She loved him, wanted him. Still, each of her tiny movements spelled out an almost audible goodbye bringing with it a rush of reality, and a deep sadness. Desire died like a flame doused.

Hoping to dispel those emotions, he carried her quickly to the bed to prove again, how much he loved her and her him. It was her turn to be tortured, and while doing so, Jake reached that realm of insanity convincing him as long as they were joined she could not escape.

Now, while holding her tightly silently praying she would not hate him for deceiving her he would confess his knowledge of her past. The sane portion of him, still in tack, knew that unless they cleansed the past, there was no future. Each evening when returning home, he would always wonder if she would be there the day she was not, he would, wither, and die.

The stupid, foolish, and frightened, part of him, so madly in love, stole his conscience. He asked her to marry him, and allowed her to get away with a smile for an answer. Her whispered, "I love you," a jubilant trembling jangling his senses, and robbing his honorable thoughts. She actually laughed when he handcuffed her to him easily accepting his explanation that he was not going to take any chances of her getting away again. As her spiraling giggles became louder, and louder, he could actually see mischief dancing in her eyes when he explained he did not have the strength left to pluck her from danger again, at least for the remainder of the evening. Sadly enough, the truth was, he hoped to buy time to regroup the nerves that had mutinied.

Feeling at war with herself, Jordan's mind flashed from one image of him to the next, a Kaleidoscope of sight, and sound, and smell. While the forces of strength, and weakness shifted within pushing against one another, sobbing silently, so hard she thought she might turn herself inside out, she decided a goodbye note signed with her last name was the only answer. It would take Jake a while to investigate, and of course, he would, by then she would be somewhere, anywhere, she did not care nothing mattered anymore. She was not surprised when he handcuffed her. Knowing Jake, he would make sure she did not escape while he slept, the reason she placed the keys to the cuffs beneath her pillow before entering the bathroom. Knowing there was no unlearning his love, she waited patiently until Jake slept, and he did.

Chapter 30

Pungent carbon monoxide inundated the cab weaving between enemy lines. Horn blaring relentlessly, it charged toward its destination. Preoccupied, the lone passenger failed to hear the clanking early morning traffic intoxicating the putrid air with uproarious sounds. Soon she would become insignificant and bewildered by the everyday chaos plaguing O'Hare airport. In spite of the warmth made murky and nippy by the gloom possessing her spirit, the brilliance of the morning persisted radiating through smog-streaked windows highlighting the tears coursing down Jordan's porcelain skin.

Dream clouds dissipating brought Jake one hundred percent awake. Handcuffs, once securing his wrists, sailed across the room denting a wall. Every profanity imaginable assaulted his mouth. Damn, Jordan was the sneakiest woman he had ever known. What a rotten, underhanded thing to do, seduce him with womanly wiles; exhaust him, meanwhile planning to take advantage of his weakness. How was he ever going to live with her? How was he ever going to live without her? Right this minute, what he would not give to teach her a thing a two then again, he knew the moment their eyes touched his bones would turn to dust, and the lesson would begin, and end with kissing every inch of her.

Forged indignation assisted him in jerking on jeans, and a tee shirt. Like a grizzly long overdue for prey, he grumbled to the door wrenched it open and came against a wall of Margaret, and Philip. Clad in her terry robe, hair unruly about her face, out of breath, looking pale and distraught she handed him a piece of paper. Having seen Jordan enter a cab, to Jakes considerable relief, she jotted down the company name, and the number of the vehicle.

Angrily plucking the phone, Jake's finger just finished punching out the number when McMaster's arrived, in his hand, the package Jake asked him to search for at the Parakeet Club.

The day Jake received Jordan's parcel returning his money he hightailed to the office. Discovering the break in, he knew no one but Billy dared to touch the contents. His suspicions painfully confirmed meant Scorpio had everything. After informing McMaster's of the theft, and what he anticipated Jordan to do next, they collaborated on a plan. Before parting, he reassured Jake, no matter what happened, he would search for the package, and destroy the contents.

Jake stared blankly at the parcel now positioned on the coffee table in front of him, his hesitancy to open it painfully apparent. Knowing it was essential to find out if the package contained the missing material Jake wanted, McMaster's persisted. Against better judgment, Jake finally relented.

Moments later, shrinking further into the couch cushions, in quick succession his expression registered shock followed by sorrow. Before McMaster's placed a DVD in the recorder, Jake knew the female would not be Jordan. When his instincts were right, the protective padding of his hands hid his horror struck face.

Shattered were his intentions to convince Jordan he destroyed all evidence of her past. There was no saving her reputation now. The condemning proof could be anywhere, in the hands of anyone who might decide to ruin her at any time. Forever sentenced she would be to a life of, loneliness, and heartbreak, running from the cruelty of the world. Scorpio got the last laugh after all. Whoever said someone could not hold people's lives in their palms, and crush them. Even from the grave, Scorpio managed to rip hearts out, and obliterate futures.

Margaret was beside Jake, her arm around his trembling shoulders, palms smoothing back, and forth, her voice reassuring, "Jacob, listen to me, my son. When you love someone, as much as it hurts, sometimes you have to set them free. If they come back to you, you know their love is as true as yours is. If they do not, you never had it to begin with.

Jordan is a free spirit now because of you. You have transformed her into a strong, healthy person, both physically, and mentally. She is a brilliant woman whose determination will get her through. You have to let her go, and trust one day she will return."

Cell phone in hand, McMaster's added, "Just say the word, friend, and I will close the airport. I cannot hold the flights indefinitely, but long enough for you to get there."

Despising the weakness in him, that huge yellow streak covering his back, keeping him from confessing to Jordan when he had the chance, Jake looked from Margaret to Philip to McMaster's, dripping from his eyes fat puddles of tears, as he shook his head no.

While the taxi driver weaved through the traffic with the ease of experience and familiarity, Jordan reached into her purse to reexamine her tickets. Withdrawing them, she found the note, that in her haste, she neglected to place on Jake's pillow. "Oh, no," she groaned. "Stop the car! Please. Stop the car," she shrieked.

"Hey, lady, you are nuts if you think I can in all this traffic. Christ, we will get run over." The words no sooner left the driver's mouth then he daringly pulled into another lane of erratic traffic made hazardous by buses, and other taxis.

What should she do? Jake was awake by now, probably frantic wondering where she was, and why she left. She put him through too much already, he did not deserve what she was dishing out, but it was too late lacking the strength to say goodbye to his face she would have to stay. The pain he was going through now nothing compared to what he would experience when she finally told him the truth then she would have no choice but to leave for good. Determination squaring her shoulders, ordered her heart to beat anew. "Forget it," she blustered.

Bursting to his feet, Jake grabbed Margaret's hand. "Come with me. I need to make sure she is on the plane, I have to see for myself that she is all right, know that it is over."

McMaster's drove them, the patrol cars' lights flickering, siren whining, hoping they could reach the airport before Jordan's flight departed. Knowing O'Hare, on a daily basis, they often delayed flights; just maybe one would be Jordan's, McMaster's thought. A speck of doubt made him increase the odds by calling the airport to apprise them of Jordan's full name. Minutes later an official confirmed her flight number, and time of departure, at least now, his friend had a chance.

Jordan had her seat assignment one meager piece of luggage was tagged, and on the loading ramp. You would think someone as insignificant as she would become lost in such a network of commotion. She was never lucky.

Walking listlessly through the confusion, sensing eyes following her she turned, sometimes they looked away sometimes they did not. Women's hands shielded their mouths while they spoke to a person beside them. Men smiled appreciatively, respectfully. Teenagers, wearing headsets, frantically waved as if to gain her attention, and, as she came closer to her departure station, the resonance of the conversations grew enabling her to hear bits, and pieces.

"It's her. I know it's her."

"Isn't that Morgan's girlfriend?"

"Wasn't her picture on the front page this morning?"

"She's the heroine who stopped Scorpio."

"Where's Morgan?"

"He must be here."

As though she was honey, like a swarm of bees, Jordan became enveloped by people shaking her hand, asking for autographs, and telling her how much they admired her bravery. They asked where she was going, how long she would be gone, why she was leaving, where Jake was, if they were getting married, if she loved him.

Baffled, and flabbergasted, color rose rapidly to Jordan's cheeks, warmth ballooning in her chest from the wild pulsations bouncing her heart crazily. Unbelievably she was returning the handshakes, signing newspapers, pads, books, and scraps of paper shoved under a pen coming from nowhere.

Pandemonium broke out. Perplexed, and anxious, security officers converging on the scene were helpless in controlling the surging crowd. No one heard the final boarding announcement, no one saw four people approaching from behind.

In order for anyone to hear over the humming crowd, after announcing the final boarding for the third time, the airline attendant resorted to shouting. Jordan was relieved; she needed to get away from the roaring crowd, from Chicago, from Jake as fast as she could, while she could. Making a motion to move, though the throng graciously parted ever so slightly, their voices continued.

"Don't go, Jordan."

"Come back soon."

"We love you."

Trembling made her feet unsteady. Fingertip's flicked away the moisture collecting in her eyes before the telltale sign of distress became embarrassingly visible. She was handing her ticket to the flight attendant when the crowd began to clap then became riotous.

"Jake," women screamed.

"Morgan," men shouted.

Having made it to the loading ramp, Jordan solidified.

Despite the security officers surrounding Jake, his faithful followers pressing against the ranks broke through. Needing to touch the man responsible for many broken hearts, they milled around him to permit a closer look at their shamefully good-looking hero.

In route to the airport, Jake decided, this time, he was not going to listen to Margaret. The fact he made it in time was a sign Jordan was his destiny. Instead of waiting for her to make up her silly, female, mind he was going to take charge. If it were the last thing he did, he would convince her to stay. It was not over yet. Without any thought processes in motion as to how he was going to accomplish the formidable task, elbowing his way through the crowd he plucked the microphone from the stunned flight attendants hand.

"Settle down, folks, settle down. Please," Jake commanded.

As though he were a God, the crowd quieted.

Scanning their faces for long moments by the time Jake spoke, his heart found a voice. "Can you believe she is leaving me," he asked pitifully, his face just as forlorn.

"No," the crowd screamed.

"Why," they shouted.

"She does not think I love her enough. Do you, Jordan?"

The melody of her name on his lips stole Jordan's breath, and made her head list slightly. Eyelid's clamoring shut liberated the tears behind them as she shrieked inwardly. "Don't, Jake, don't beg, I couldn't bare it. I cannot stay. I won't."

Refusing to face him, grasping fortitude from the air, her head shaking from side to side, sorrowfully, she managed another step forward.

Fear shifting gears became gravel in his throat. "But, I do, more than life itself. She doesn't know it would take dying for me to get over her," Jake persisted. Words prompting a loud sigh from his captive audience, women's faces gooey with adoration.

"I asked her to marry me, instead she is running away. Can you imagine that?"

Every female, young, and old alike, sighed aloud, "No!"

Microphone in hand, moving to a seated elderly woman, Jake bent down, "If I asked you, would you turn me down?"

"Not on your life," she gushed, as her lips found his cheek.

"How about you and you," Jake inquired moving the microphone to various lips spread wide with smiles of infatuation.

"I'm married, but give me a minute, and I won't be," a middle-aged woman replied.

"You name the day, and time, sweetie, and I'll be there with bells on," another added.

"Why don't you ask her again, Jake? If you don't I will," a man shouted.

"Me too," another man added, and another, and another.

Still maintaining a smidgeon of grit, persevering Jordan refused to face Jake. Though he was a maniac, a stupid, brain-dead fool, for the life of her, she could not stop the twitching smile defying her will. Wringing her hands madly in front of her to keep herself from crumbling, she prayed for the ability to faint. Stiffening she took another step forward. That is when she noticed the pilot, and co-pilot advancing toward her blocking her way.

"It is quite apparent you are the one delaying this flight, Miss. The sooner you agree to marry that idiot behind you, the sooner we can get on our way," the pilot said.

"God, no, the whole damn world is against me," Jordan moaned. At this moment "Idiot" was not a good enough description for Jake, she could easily think of a whole lot better expletives.

A great warm wash of inner smugness made Jake smile. When Jordan began to move again, panic struck another blow. "Jordan, don't you know by now, you are holding on to nothing but the wind, that where ever you go there is bound to be rain that everyone has to make his own happiness, that even joy carries a price. You told me once I was the sunshine on your shoulders, maybe together we can gather enough to hold off the rain. Take my hand. Do not throw away the happiness we can find together. Give us a chance, don't go. Please!"

Clutched fists came to women's breasts tears found every cheek in the crowd. Despite the explosive air, the terminal grew quiet with anticipation. By-standers, withdrawing their video and snap shot cameras began recording a moment in time to play whenever they felt most love were lost forever.

Jake's electric words succeeded in lowering Jordan's guard, more like pulverized it. She was sobbing inwardly, quaking insufferably as she recalled his, dirty cigarettes, drinking, horrible temper, vulgar mouth, one moment, the next the luxury of his arms, his kiss, and his love. The crazy imbecile was wrong when he said she was his once in a million chance of a lifetime. He was her stroke of luck, and she would forever live in darkness if she refused him. Besides, how could she when she heard him say, "Marry me, Jordan Montgomery, I love you, God, how I love you."

Sucking in a gasp of astonishment, lips quivering, heart leaping through her chest, her mind did somersaults. She would collapse from the joy spilling over she just knew she would. Oh, God, Jake knew her last name, surely he investigated her, knew what she was, what she had been. When did he find out, how long did he know, probably longer than she cared to acknowledge? Regardless, he risked his life for her, told her he loved her, proven his love, kept all his promises. The idiot even asked her to marry him. What a fool, what a wonderful, wonderful fool.

Jordan knew now, her past did not matter to him, it never mattered, never would from this day forward she would only see herself through his eyes. Eyes that had lifted her from the gutter, and placed her on a pedestal so high no one could ever hurt her again.

Turning she saw, him on his knees, arms beseeching her, his face, his eloquent tears, heard his heart hammering, and she wondered what she ever did worthy enough for God to grant her such a miracle. The Almighty did not stop at just a part of Jake; he granted her the entire arrogant, self-assured, impossible, egotistical, beautiful man.

Planet Heaven touched down, and was waiting for her to enter its arms. Jordan's smile could have convinced the whole world she was the woman in the moon, and Jake had roped it as she thought, what a revelation it was to see, someone saying I love you to me.

Though she wanted to run to him she was convinced her feet would not move her legs would not support her weight. A crippling weakness she did not give into until he scooped her into arms that spun her around and around arms intending to hold her until they broke.

When their lips met to seal their promise of forever, Margaret bear hugged McMaster's, then kissed him on his mouth, an action making Philip feel a pinch of jealousy too close to his heart. A gush of warmth soared through the normally cold dismal terminal in the form of cheers, roars, and applause.

"Way to go, Jordan!"

"Way to go, Jake!"

People hugged strangers, men slapped five, women plucked tissues, the pilot and co-pilot breathed a sigh of relief, teenagers extended their fisted arms and yelled, "Oaf, oaf, oaf," and bewildered youngsters wondered what in the world was happening.

Chapter 31

Following a hearing at which Jake, and his fellow officers, testified, the judge cleared Billy's mother of all charges. Though ballistic reports proved the bullet retrieved from Scorpios' skull came from her gun, he based the verdict upon her brave attempt to save the lives of DEA officer's, and innocent bystanders.

Billy could not have been prouder of the elegant woman sitting confidently erect staring at him with love drilling his eyes. Forever he would remember her testimony; she returned to claim her son.

During a private inquisition, Jake commended Billy's bravery throughout the raid that wiped out Scorpios' henchmen, and saved his, and Jordan's life. Due to the lack of evidence proving he was in anyway involved with Scorpios' dealings, the judge also exonerated Billy. Reluctantly, McMaster's signed his transfer to the West Coast where he relocated to be near his mother. Later he met, and married a beautiful young attorney. Coming to Chicago often to visit, their relationship with Jake, Jordan, and Margaret became that of family. The couple later became God Parent's to Jake's children.

Thanks to Jake's efforts, the Judge reduced Butch's sentence from twenty-five years to ten, with the possibility of parole in three years. After his arrest, Butch summoned Jake to inform him he replaced the capsule in Marla's purse with a harmless one, and destroyed the pictures, and videos, of Jordan filling the envelope with those of another woman. Unable to inform Marla in time, he would forever blame himself for her death.

Jake and Jordan married. The ceremony a small private one performed by a Judge at City Hall. There was no way, in hell, Jake was going to allow the most intriguing woman in the world to get away again, the reason he handcuffed their wrists together in front of the horror struck Judge. The act combined with the Judges' shocked features causing, uproarious laughter, whistles, and shouts, from spectators managing to cram every inch available. A joke that backfired when reaching between her breasts, Jordan retrieved the key she had swiped from Jake's pocket. Dangling it proudly in front of his nose, her mouth claimed the most colorful expletive known to humankind before tossing the key out the third floor window.

Scooping her into his arms, Jake never released Jordan's lips while carrying her to the elevator, down the concrete steps, and outside to an outrageously decorated patrol car with its flashing lights, and bellowing siren. While fans lining steps, sidewalks, and streets cheered the newlyweds, for one moment in time, all vestiges of cruelty, crime, and death, became irrelevant.

Dull, quiet, far from Jake's life from that day forward, perpetually trying his patience, Jordan kept him on his toes, that is, when they were not beneath the sheets. His life service with the Drug Enforcement Agency nothing compared to the commotion faithfully meeting him at the door each night. Kissing each forehead, he gazed into the tiger-eyes of his two sons, and two daughters' whose eyes matched their mothers, never ceasing from the very instant they collided with his to thrill him to the tips of his hair.

Margaret? While, Philip, and McMaster's took turns wining, and dining her trying to win her affections in the end, McMaster's won to this day his slippers are still beneath her bed.

40707804R00144

Made in the USA
Middletown, DE
20 February 2017